Praise for Elle Croft

'What a clever idea! This kept me reading through the night...' **Jane Corry**

'Excellent writing with intriguing characters and a dark and original premise that kept me turning the pages' **Jenny Quintana**

'Great books pull you into the story, heart and guts from page one. Really great books also leave you staring into space, thinking about them days after. Utterly absorbing and thought-provoking' **Caz Frear**

'I couldn't put this down. Pacy and gripping' **Cass Green**

'*The Guilty Wife* will make you question those closest to you as the plot unfolds at pace, with an ending that pulls the rug from under your feet' **Phoebe Morgan**

'A gripping tale of betrayal, deceit and duplicity. The ending will stay with you long after you've finished the last page' **Jenny Blackhurst**

'What a premise, and packed with suspense – this book has it all!' **Victoria Selman**

'A dark, delicious triumph with all the page-turnability you expect from Elle' **Niki Mackay**

Elle Croft was born in South Africa, grew up in Australia and moved to the UK in 2010 after travelling around the world with her husband. She works as a freelance social media specialist and also blogs about travel, food and life in London.

Follow Elle on Twitter @elle_croft to find out more.

Also by Elle Croft

The Guilty Wife
The Other Sister
Like Mother, Like Daughter

BURIED

ELLE CROFT

ORION

First published in Great Britain in 2021 by Orion Fiction,
an imprint of The Orion Publishing Group Ltd.,
Carmelite House, 50 Victoria Embankment
London EC4Y 0DZ

An Hachette UK company

3 5 7 9 10 8 6 4

A CIP catalogue record for this book
is available from the British Library.

ISBN (Paperback) 978 1 4091 8726 4
ISBN (eBook) 978 1 4091 8728 8

Typeset at The Spartan Press Ltd,
Lymington, Hants

Printed and bound in Great Britain by Clays Ltd,
Elcograf S.p.A.

MIX
Paper from
responsible sources
FSC® C104740

www.orionbooks.co.uk

BURIED

Prologue

The stars wink their complicity as I haul the corpse towards the inky black water.

She doesn't come easily, although there are no sounds of protest from her blue-tinged lips as twigs and stones shred her skin and catch on her remaining limbs. The earth is desperate to claw her back, but I'll win this battle.

My muscles burn as I heave my burden across the dirt. Gripping her cold, rigid forearms, I drag her closer to the water's edge, ignoring the bead of sweat that slides down my face. It's cooled instantly by the frigid night air, an icy finger caressing my skin.

I shudder, but I don't stop. I haven't seen or heard another human since I arrived several hours ago, but there's no way to be absolutely certain that I won't be seen. Assumptions equal sloppiness. And sloppiness will get me caught.

An owl hoots somewhere above my head, startling me. I freeze for an adrenaline-drenched second, then continue the journey that began just a few yards away at my truck, the metal and rubber a gauche addition to an otherwise breathtaking scene. Even my tent seems a monstrosity, man-made and too bright; an eyesore in this setting.

I don't particularly enjoy camping – I get my fill of nature at home, with the added benefits of running water and cold beers – but it's the perfect cover. If I drive to a remote area, the back of my pickup loaded with a tent and tarps and gas bottles and folding chairs, then no one bats an eyelid. If I did the same with nothing but my Muse rolled up in the truck bed, and someone stopped me – asked where I was headed late at night, and by the way, what was that in the back? – well, if I was incompetent enough to do that, I'd be behind bars by now. I'd deserve to be.

And so I camp, my Muse carefully hidden under my gear. I pick the quietest spot I can find by the water, wait till darkness has settled snugly over the landscape, and then I retrieve her from her hiding place and set her free to either become a part of the wilderness, or be discovered. If it's the latter, she'll have the opportunity to be mourned, to be properly buried by those who loved her. But it's not up to me whether or not she gets that kind of send-off. Nature chooses for her.

This particular Muse's fate will be decided by a picture-perfect bay, the surface perpetually glassy, the moon reflecting so brightly that I can almost believe the light source is located in the unseen depths, rather than far above me. With one last tremendous tug I reach the shoreline, which licks gently at my boots as I step in and test my weight.

When I've balanced in the sludge beneath the shallow water, I reach out for my Muse a final time, gloved fingers curling around her narrow wrists. I draw her towards me in a fluid, powerful movement that sends her gliding across the surface. Her glassy eyes stare, unseeing, at the sky above, diamonds strewn across velvet, alluring and completely unattainable. At least for mortals like me.

My Muse, on the other hand, is eternal. It's the gift I've given her, the trade-off for what I've taken. I grip the leg that remains attached to her body, the one I didn't sever above her knee joint, and push her gently away, watching her float like Ophelia, her hair fanning out, a halo glinting in the silvery light.

I wait until she's out of reach, until she's on her final journey, and then I turn back towards my tent, towards my truck. It's time to pack up.

It's time for a brand-new Muse.

Chapter 1

The Seattle Journal

**Latest Coastline Killer Victim? Discovery of body,
believed to be missing local woman Carla Barker
by Marco Reilly
October 4, 2018 | Local News**

The body of a woman, yet to be formally identified but
believed to be missing Bremerton resident Carla Barker,
was found just before 6 a.m. this morning. A local man
named Jerry Mendoza was walking his dog in Potlatch
State Park when he made the gruesome discovery.

'I saw her hair first,' a shaken Mendoza told *The
Seattle Journal*. 'Toby was barking at something, and I
just thought maybe he'd found a skunk. Even when I saw
what had got him so worked up, I still thought it was
some kind of animal. It took me a few seconds to work
out what I was looking at, but then I knew right away
that it was that Carla girl who's been all over the papers.'

Carla Barker, 20, was last seen almost three months
ago, on July 12, 2018, on her way to ballet rehearsal.
Miss Barker was reported missing by her parents when
she didn't return home that evening, and hopes of
finding her alive diminished in the months that followed,

with many fearing that she may have fallen victim to the serial killer dubbed The Coastline Killer.

If the woman found this morning is identified as Miss Barker, she could be the nineteenth known victim of the perpetrator who has been terrorising the Pacific Northwest for at least a decade. Each of the nineteen victims – all female, aged between seventeen and thirty-nine – has had a body part removed before being bludgeoned to death. None of their missing body parts have been recovered.

Each victim has been discovered after washing up along the coast of the Pacific Northwest, from Northern California to British Columbia, Canada.

A local Potlach woman, who does not wish to be identified, was on the scene shortly before police arrived. She claims that what she saw confirms the fact that the woman was murdered by The Coastline Killer.

'She was missing a leg,' the woman said, clearly distressed by what she saw. 'That poor girl was missing a leg. That Coastline Killer is still out there, and the police need to find him. It could be my daughter next.'

Fears such as hers have rippled throughout communities in the Pacific Northwest in recent years, with gun and pepper spray sales skyrocketing after the discovery of each new victim, according to local hardware and sporting goods store owners.

Seattle detective Trey Ryman declined to comment on the case, telling those at the scene that 'The police department is looking into every possibility, and we will release an official statement in due course.'

More on this story: Concerns mount as search for missing woman continues.'

Chapter 2

ALICE

My heart pounds in time with the soft thuds of my feet on the carpet as I pace to the edge of the stage, back to the lectern, and to the other side.

'It's easy to believe that these things will never happen to you,' I say, allowing myself to take a deep breath, and letting it out slowly before I speak again. 'But no one ever believes it'll happen to them, and yet statistics prove that it does happen. Not to everyone, but complacency could be the difference between life and death in the event of an emergency. This isn't about being pessimistic. It's about being prepared.'

I click the button on the remote and glance behind me to check that the screen has changed. My shoulders relax, just a little. This is the penultimate slide, the one before my contact details. I'm almost done, and then I can sit down and take off my damn shoes. When I put them on in my office they gave me a surge of confidence, as they always do. They're the kind of shoes that almost make me believe I'm the expert I claim to be.

It's silly to get assurance from accessories. I know that. But it would be even sillier to get up here without doing what I need to do to look and feel authoritative: curl my hair, wear a brand-new blazer, put on my power heels. It's not about vanity. It's about being professional.

The boost from the shoes was predictably short-lived, though, and the feeling that I was out of my depth returned almost as soon as I introduced myself. And, to add insult to imposter syndrome, the shoes are now practically shredding the skin on my toes.

'Preparedness is key,' I continue, wincing as I put my weight on my left foot. I'm pretty sure my big toe is bleeding into the expensive yellow leather. 'Which is why, during Safety Week, we'll be conducting a series of drills and emergency scenarios for both you and the students to participate in.'

The groan I've been expecting ripples around the room, right on cue. I laugh lightly, undeterred by their lack of enthusiasm.

'I appreciate that this means your lectures will be disrupted, but I can assure you that we're aiming to minimise any inconvenience. At the end of the day, my job is to keep you safe, and if doing so means a few interruptions, that's a consequence I'm willing to live with. And I hope you are, too. In the packs you've been given today, you'll find the schedule, as well as some basic details of each of the drills, and reminders of the procedures and locations we've gone over here today. I'd appreciate it if you'd keep this information to yourselves, and not give the students any warning. Drills are much more effective if they're unexpected. And in the real world, emergencies don't come with a timeline.'

I'd been hoping for some kind of reaction. If not a laugh, then maybe just a sympathetic chuckle. But the room is completely silent. Tough crowd.

'If you have any questions,' I say, changing the topic quickly, 'feel free to get in touch.'

My email address and work phone number appear on the

screen as I press the button on the remote control again. I glance at my watch.

'We still have five minutes. I can take some questions now, if anyone has anything burning?'

I expect the staff will avoid questions in order to claw those five minutes back, but I give them a few seconds, just in case. As I wait, I look around, peering at the faces of the audience members in the rows closest to me. A few are familiar. Many aren't.

My gaze travels back to the furthest rows. Everyone looks bored. One guy at the back might actually be asleep. I can't be sure because his face is hidden by his dark hood, and he's slouched over, showing no signs that he's listening. Or, in fact, living. I sigh. Trying to engage people in safety proced-ures is probably the most challenging – and definitely the least rewarding – part of my job. But it's essential, whether they can see it or not.

I clap my hands together. 'OK,' I say, 'no questions, then. Thank you all for your time, and I look forward to working with you during Safety Week.'

There's a collective shuffling, a gathering of bags, a sweeping up of folders and phones from the tiny tables at each seat, a low drone of chatter.

'My door is always open if you have any safety concerns whatsoever,' I call out, but no one is listening anymore, if they ever were. Carefully, I eject my thumb drive from the auditorium's laptop while the last of my audience files out of the lecture theatre. I replay the presentation in my mind, cringing at the things that went wrong, at the words I faltered over. My cheeks burn as I recall the moment where I said 'risky' instead of 'rescue'. It's mortifying, but I remind myself that I'm the only one who will remember it.

'Miss Dalroy?'

I jump, my heart rate spiking.

'Sorry,' says the deep voice from behind me. I turn, hand clamped to my chest, and come face to face with a man wearing a dark grey suit and a skinny black tie. 'I didn't mean to scare you.'

I nod and let out a nervous, high-pitched laugh. 'It's OK, I just didn't know anyone was still in here.'

'That was a great talk you just gave. Really thorough.'

'Thanks,' I say, tipping my head to the side as I try to place him. 'I'm sorry, but do you work here? I don't think we've met.'

'James Archer.' He holds out his hand, and I shake it firmly. 'I work for the city of Vancouver. Mayor's office.'

'Oh,' I'm not quite sure how to respond. 'Hi, how can I help you?'

'Well, actually,' he says, 'I'm here to offer you a job.'

'Oh,' I repeat, painfully aware that I sound like a complete idiot, but unable to articulate anything more sophisticated.

'We're looking for a disaster planner,' he explains. 'The mayor has promised that we will be prepared for all eventualities, as I'm sure you heard during his campaign.'

I nod. I did hear it, and at the time I wondered how he would deliver on such a bold promise. I'd voted for him all the same. I could get behind a politician who understood the value of being ready for any eventuality.

'We need someone to head up the teams that have been tasked to implement our policies. We have big plans for training, for partnering with emergency services and businesses, for public awareness campaigns. But we need an experienced disaster preparedness manager. And we believe you're that person.'

'Me?' I manage to squeak.

'Yes, you,' he says, smiling warmly. 'You come highly

recommended. And the presentation you just gave was incredibly insightful and engaging. I'm sure you get approached all the time for roles, but I'd love to meet with you to discuss this one, and how I think you can help us.'

I shrug, brushing off his praise. It's an overstatement to say that I'm approached all the time, but I do get calls every so often from recruiters. None have come close to tempting me away from my current job. But then again, none of them have offered me the role of coordinating safety for the whole city.

'Here's my number,' James says, holding a business card out to me. I accept it, too flustered to speak.

'We need someone soon,' he continues. 'So I do hope you'll call. We need to move on this in the next few weeks, and if you're not interested, we'll have to start looking at some alternative candidates. But I want you to know that you're our first choice.'

Heat creeps across my chest, and threatens to climb up my neck. I'm flattered. Of course I am. But I'm also taken aback; too shocked to articulate the jumble of thoughts and questions knotting up my brain.

'I'll think about it,' I manage to say.

'Please do. Just not for too long.'

He smiles, and I tuck the business card into my back pocket. James offers me his hand again.

'Really good to meet you, Alice,' he says as we shake hands. 'I look forward to talking to you soon.'

Before I can respond, he turns and walks away. I watch as he leaves, wishing I could have said something clever, or at least relevant, something that might make him believe I deserve to even be considered for such an enormous role.

My stomach fizzes. I sit heavily on the edge of the stage

and pull my shoes off, massaging my aching feet as I try to make sense of what just happened.

I've just been offered my dream job, I realise as I bend my toes backwards, wincing as the tension is released and sensation returns. My heart thrums with excitement, but it's short lived.

Because as much as I want to run after James and accept his offer here and now, I know that I won't. I can't. And as this disappointing reality settles over me, familiar doubts threaten to strangle the certainty I've worked so hard to reach.

I fight to tamp down the question that resurfaces, reminding myself that I know what I'm doing, that this is what I want. But it rises up regardless, insistent, impossible to ignore.

By going after this one dream, will I be forced to give up all the others?

Chapter 3

THE SCULPTOR

They call me The Sculptor.

It's what they call me because it's what I decided they would call me.

Admittedly, it's not very imaginative. But when I chose my name, when I carefully scraped it into the wax as I moulded the piece that launched my career and irreversibly changed who I am, I knew it was the right choice. Because what the simple label lacks in flair and showmanship, it more than makes up for in accuracy.

I am a sculptor. The work I do has earned me that title. I don't take shortcuts, like so many so-called artists these days. Throwing a pile of tyres onto the shiny floor of a modern art gallery is not a sculpture, and neither is getting a computer to 3D print some strange acrylic shape. No. The people who create such objects are tinkerers; crafters, if you will. Sculptures that are mass-produced, or hurried to completion, are little more than décor.

Beautiful they may be, but sculptures they are not.

What I create is art. Real art, borne of skill and technique and patience. Created by pure sacrifice: sweat, tears and blood. Occasionally, even my own.

I am meticulous, like the old masters. It's absurd to think of Donatello rushing his casting of *David*, or Rodin sculpting the intricate details of *The Gates of Hell* with a deadline looming. My process is no less stringent, which is why each collection takes years to complete.

I have learned, from the art magazines that are delivered quarterly to my PO Box – the one located nowhere near where I live, and registered under a false name – that this scarcity is part of my appeal. That, and my anonymity. Everyone wants to know, in the words of these publications, who The Sculptor is, what his secrets are, who his muse is, where he trained. Some have referred to me as 'fine art's own Banksy', although I haven't quite decided whether to be flattered or appalled by the comparison.

It was never my design to be so deeply scrutinised, or to have my work become so celebrated, but I can't deny that I like it. My sculptures are highly sought after, each one auctioned for increasingly eye-watering prices. One art journal even called them, somewhat hyperbolically, 'modern day masterpieces'.

I can't pretend that I don't enjoy the praise, the accolades. The money. But what I value the most is the privacy my name affords me.

After all, if they knew me – really knew me – their reports might not be so flattering.

Every time The Sculptor makes another headline, a tiny flutter of panic erupts in my chest, and I wonder whether I'm being careful enough. I've never revealed my identity to anyone, relying on layers of anonymity to keep my secret. My dealer speaks only with my lawyer, who speaks only with my agent, who speaks only with my personal assistant. Layers of protection, lies and assumptions. But mostly assumptions. It's people's biases – conscious or not – that really allow me to pull off what I do.

Because the real mystery isn't what my name is. That's

14

not important, in the end. If people knew that, they'd write a few headlines and my five minutes of fame would be over, leaving me as just another person who was interesting for a while. No. What really matters here, what's really at stake, is what's carefully nestled inside each of my sculptures.

If they knew that, they might recognise me by my other name, the one emblazoned across the front pages of altogether different publications. Every newspaper along the coast has mentioned me, multiple times, in the past few years. Only they don't call me The Sculptor.

They call me The Coastline Killer.

Chapter 4

ALICE

'Remind me why I do this,' I moan, stepping aside to let a trail runner pass. I take a sip from my water bottle as I sit carefully on a log, then begin unlacing my sneaker. As I suspected, the heels I wore for my presentation yesterday left my feet raw and bleeding, and this morning's hike is doing them no favours.

'Because you know you'll feel awesome afterwards,' Celia laughs, lunging forward and stretching her calf. 'And because you don't get a view like this at the gym, do you?'

I smile at her in agreement, my lungs burning too much to reply. She's right. The view, just visible through the lush canopy of green provided by the majestic trees surrounding us, is breathtaking. At least, it's part of the reason why I can barely breathe. Mostly it's from hiking up the thousands of steps, officially called the Grouse Grind but often referred to as 'Mother Nature's Stairmaster', which lead from the base of Grouse Mountain to the summit.

The trail is about a mile and a half long, but it basically goes straight up, with hardly anywhere to rest along the way. We've stopped at one of the few points where we won't be holding anyone else up, so I take the rare chance to catch my breath while I rummage at the bottom of my backpack for a Band-Aid to apply to the blister on my toe.

I meant to transfer my portable first aid kit from my old backpack before I left this morning, but I was too distracted, my excitement and nerves drowning out rational thought. I mentally berate myself for being so unprepared. I, of all people, should know better.

'Oh my God,' a voice to my right gasps. I look up just as a woman, red-faced and sweaty, and clad in head-to-toe designer athleisure wear, drops onto the log next to me. Behind her, another woman in a pink headband and matching sneakers slowly ascends the final few steps that lead to the natural landing.

'Are you OK?' I ask, empathising with her pain.

'Please tell me we're nearly at the three-quarter mark,' the woman beside me pleads, and I laugh.

'You're really close,' I assure her. 'And the last quarter doesn't feel as bad as the others, I promise. It's not as steep as this section.'

'Well, it can't possibly be worse,' her companion says dramatically. I find a rogue Band-Aid, crumpled at the bottom of my backpack, and unwrap it, pressing it against my skin, hoping it'll help alleviate the pain. Once I've tied my laces, I stand up to make room on the log for the woman in pink. She throws me a grateful look and sits heavily beside her friend.

'First time?' Celia asks.

'Yeah, we're visiting from Edmonton,' she says. She tips her water bottle up to take a sip, then shakes it hopefully. Nothing comes out. She stares into it mournfully.

'Here,' I say, passing her mine, which is still half full. 'Have some of this.'

'You sure?'

'Yeah, go for it. I remember my first Grind. It's tough.'

'Do you guys do this all the time?'

'Every week, till winter hits,' Celia replies. 'My husband works from home on Fridays, so I can sneak away from my kids for a bit and meet Alice here for an early morning hike.'

'And my PA knows not to put any meetings in my diary before ten on a Friday,' I add. 'So I can get a hike in before work.'

I don't mention that I have the day off today. That'll only invite questions, and I don't want to have to explain myself to strangers.

'Nice,' says the woman in pink. 'So it's true what they say about the Vancouver lifestyle, then?'

'Sure is,' Celia agrees, waving at the view below us. 'It's the best city in the world.'

The woman who took my bottle stands up, and waves her cell phone towards me.

'Would you mind? I'd love a photo of us doing this.'

'I look horrible,' her friend squeals, despite looking anything but. I take a few pictures for them and hand the phone back, and as I reach for my water bottle, perched against the log, I hesitate.

'Actually,' I say, 'would you mind taking one of us, too, please?'

'Good idea!' Celia says. 'We barely have any pictures of us these days.'

I unzip my backpack and pull my phone out, handing it to the stranger. We pose, then wave goodbye to the Albertans, resuming our ascent towards the Peak Chalet, where there's a cafe and a gondola that will take us back down the mountain. As I reach to put my phone back in my bag, a breaking news alert flashes on the screen.

'Oh no,' I breathe.

'What?'

'Another woman's gone missing. From Portland.'

'Shit,' Celia says over her shoulder. 'Do they think it's The Coastline Killer again?'

'I'm not sure,' I pant, out of breath already, 'I just saw the headline. But they only just found that Carla woman, didn't they? I don't understand why they can't catch this guy.'

Celia murmurs her agreement, and then we fall into a mutual silence as our breathing grows heavier and our muscles scream. Eventually, the steps spit us out onto a rocky ledge that leads to the chalet. We take a moment to recover, and then head into the building for refreshments.

'So,' I ask as we sit at a small table by the windows, sipping coconut water, 'how are you?'

'Fine,' she says, flapping her hand dismissively. 'The usual. Diapers. Vomit. Sleeplessness. Endless glamour, you know.'

'Sounds delightful,' I laugh. My tone is playful, but beneath my words there's a familiar twinge of envy. Today, though, it's accompanied by something more fragile, and far more powerful. Today, I'm hopeful.

'Ah, it's all good.' She smiles. 'I love them, even when they're little monsters. And Josh is brilliant. He looks forward to his Friday morning daddy–daughter time, even if they have no clue what's going on.'

For all that Celia's life has been turned upside down – the surprise arrival of twins throwing her career and future plans into disarray – I've never seen her happier. Even on her wedding day, when she was beaming from ear to ear like a cartoon, she didn't have the contentment about her that she has now. Witnessing her evolution – watching her find what makes her happier than she's ever been – gave me the encouragement I needed to pursue what I've always known would make me happy, even if it's not going to look the way I always expected. At thirty-nine, I'd begun to think that my window for happiness was closing. Celia proved to me that it's not too late.

'What about you?' Celia interrupts my thoughts. 'How are you feeling about today?'

I take a gulp of my coconut water, trying to drown the eruption of butterflies in my stomach.

'OK,' I begin. 'Excited. Nervous. Trying not to get my hopes up.'

Celia grabs my hand and gives it a short squeeze.

'You sure you don't want me to come? I can call my mom and she can take the kids—'

'No,' I assure her, 'it's fine, really. I want to do this by myself.'

I glance up at her and catch her eye, the look conveying everything my words aren't sufficient for. My throat starts closing up and emotion threatens to overwhelm me. Sensing this, Celia changes the subject.

'What was your text about yesterday? Something about a job?'

I take a quick sip of my drink, giving me the chance to push down the swell of sentiment, to compose myself.

'It was the craziest thing,' I tell her. 'I was giving a presentation to the faculty, and after I'd finished this guy comes up to me and tells me he works for the mayor and they want me to run disaster planning for the city.'

Saying it out loud makes me wonder if it actually happened. I must have misheard him, misunderstood. But no – he told me that I was their first choice. I didn't imagine that.

'Woah!' Celia says, delighted. 'That's amazing, Alice! That's like, your dream job, right?'

I shrug, not wanting to acknowledge how incredible the opportunity really is. 'I guess.'

There's a pause as Celia assesses me from across the table. She narrows her eyes. I drop my gaze, too ashamed to make eye contact. She knows me well enough to guess what's going through my head. And I know her well enough to know that she won't let this go.

'Alice,' she says gently. 'You are going to take the job, aren't you?'

I make a noncommittal humming noise. She tuts.

'You know, I get that the timing is bad, but you can't just put your life on hold. Change is scary, but you can do this, Al.'

'The gondola's coming,' I say, not bothering with subtlety. 'Let's go.'

I stand up and move towards the gondola station, where the bright red carriage is slowly drifting through the air towards us. Celia shoots me a look, but doesn't press me as we line up, scan our passes and ride down to the car park.

As she drives me back towards my condo, she regales me with tales of the twins' latest diaper explosion, which happened, to her horror, on the Skytrain. I'm in stitches, laughing until my stomach hurts. It's not until we're a couple of blocks from my place that she becomes serious.

'I really don't want you to put all your eggs in one basket,' she says gently. Then she winces. 'So to speak.'

'I'm not,' I lie as I retrieve my keys from my backpack. I'm desperate to shower and get out of my sweaty clothes. I can't be late. 'But, you know, I just don't think it's the right time for such a massive change, when there already could be so much changing so soon. There will always be jobs. Maybe not this one, but other great jobs.'

I sound more confident than I feel. Of course I want to take the job. I've had my finger over the call button on my phone more than once since James walked out of the auditorium, but every time I've swiped back to my home screen in confused frustration. Celia's right; it *is* my dream job. But there are other things I've dreamed of, for far longer, and right now those things might just be within reach. The truth – which I haven't admitted to Celia – is that I don't know if I can do both. If I try, and fail, the consequences could be disastrous.

'You can't control when life decides to throw opportunities your way,' Celia tells me as she pulls the car to the curb beside my building. 'Sometimes it's chaotic. But you just have to grab the chances when they present themselves and work out the rest as you go.'

'I know that,' I reach for the door handle, impatient, 'but I can control some things. And there's nothing wrong with focusing on one part of my life for a while and letting the rest coast along. Besides, I have a perfectly good job. It's not like I'm failing in my career.'

'Of course you're not failing, Al, you're brilliant, and you're killing it! All I'm saying is that you deserve it all. And you deserve more than just perfectly good.'

'Thanks.' I open the door, signalling that I'm done with the conversation. I have too much on my mind to be debating my career choices. It can wait, at least until I know the outcome of today. 'Thanks for this morning.'

Celia flares her nostrils in frustration, but then she breaks into a smile and grabs my hand, pulling me across the console for a hug.

'Thank you, Al,' she says, and I lean into her, grinning as well. It's impossible to be upset with Celia. 'Good luck today. I'll call you later to find out how it went, but if you need anything at all, you call me, OK? Oh, and don't forget to send that photo of us over to me.'

'I'll do it now,' I promise her, shouldering my backpack as I get out of the car. 'Wish me luck.'

She has already, but I need as much of it as I can get.

'Fingers and toes crossed for you.'

I'm typing a message to her, complete with the photo of us on the trail, as I approach my front door. I'm distracted. Too busy scrutinising my red, sweaty face in the photo. I don't see it coming.

My vision bounces. It's just for a split second, but the lock on my door jolts unnaturally before my eyes. My brain scrambles to make sense of it, confusion descending over me in the moment before the pain arrives. But there it is, splitting my skull. For the tiniest fragment of time, my mind explodes in fear.

And then my world disappears into darkness.

Chapter 5

THE SCULPTOR

I never meant to become The Coastline Killer. Hand to my heart, it wasn't part of my plan. It was never something I aspired to, or fantasised about.

I'm only interested in the art. You don't have to believe me, but that's the truth.

Another truth you might not believe, but which is no less true, regardless: I am not a violent person. I have committed violent acts, I will admit, but that's not who I am.

Who I am is ambitious. Talented. Dedicated to my craft.

And that's why I pluck my Muses right out of their day-to-day lives and bake them into exquisite sculptures. For the sake of the art.

It all happened by accident. That first time – the moment that catapulted my career and launched me into a strange kind of fame – was, I have come to realise, a gift. From above, or below, I'm not yet certain.

At that point in my life I was the stereotypical impoverished artist. I created because I had to create, because the need to bring into existence what was inside of me was greater than the need to live somewhere trendy, or have a retirement plan, or dress in designer clothes. My soul told me to create, and so to do anything else would have been a betrayal of myself.

I've always had talent. I knew that my abilities weren't my issue. What I was lacking was a voice, something to say. I couldn't see it at the time, but now I understand that I was focusing too much on the object I was crafting, and not on its purpose. Its story.

I'd been sculpting in bronze for a while by then, obsessed with Rodin as I am. I knew that my pieces were proficient and beautiful. If not incredible, at least sellable, I'd figured. I created miniature animals, mostly, and was meticulous about making them as life-like as possible, spending weeks on the tiniest of details. And yet I couldn't get anyone to buy them. I was told by dealers that they weren't unique enough, that I needed to have something to say with my art if I could expect to succeed.

I didn't understand what they meant.

Until my very first Muse stumbled into my life, lost and afraid, and I took her in. I only wanted to help. But as I watched her – a hiker, with lean, muscular legs – I was struck by a bolt of inspiration. I had to recreate her perfect leg in bronze. Not because I believed it would be a commercially astute decision, but because I had to, because I was being called to. Because, much like creating art instead of going into a more stable career, I would die if I didn't.

So I'd tried to convince her to stay, to pose, to allow me the privilege of immortalising her body in burnished, shining bronze.

I don't think I came on too strong. I didn't mean anything by it; at least nothing physical. I wasn't interested in her in that way. All I wanted was for her to be my Muse. I needed to recreate the beauty – the life – that she exuded.

But she refused. I should have known she wouldn't trust me. Just like the beautiful girls in high school, who never gave me so much as a second glance, who never acknowledged my existence. I should have known she'd be the same. I should have guessed that she would try to leave.

I don't know what came over me; I really don't. I'd never done anything like it before. But when she tried to get away, tried to take the one thrill of pure inspiration I'd ever felt, something inside me snapped. I struck her over the head, intending only to immobilise her, to keep her still so that I could study her skin, and the way her muscles rippled underneath it.

The blow must have been harder than I thought.

She was dead.

At first, I'd panicked. But then I realised that to waste my Muse's sacrifice, to fail to bring meaning to what had become of her, would be a terrible tragedy. And I understood that, despite things not going to plan, I had what I wanted: I had my model. And so I created a perfect leg from clay, taking all the time I needed to study her. When I had what I needed, and my place was starting to smell too suspicious for me to easily explain it away, I knew I needed to do something.

Thankfully, I have a kiln. And a saw. It was horrifying, dividing my Muse into pieces small enough to fit into the blazing heat that melts wax and bronze and, it turns out, human parts. I threw them in, one by one, until all that was left was the leg I'd recreated, the perfection that had started everything.

And it came to me in a moment of absolute, brilliant clarity. The thing that would set my work apart wasn't the fact that this piece was better than anything I'd made before, or that it was so realistic it almost looked as though I'd cast it by moulding my clay around her flesh. It was both of those things, but they weren't enough. No. The thing that would set me apart would be what lay at the core of my work.

To my delight – but not really my surprise, as I knew how special this piece was – it sold, and quickly. I used a new name – The Sculptor – and made certain to conceal my identity with multiple layers of deception. Suddenly the art world was talking about this mysterious newcomer with so much potential.

I tried to recreate the magic without a Muse after that, I really did.

But the pieces I tried to sell – an arm, a hand, a foot, all sculpted by closely observing sitting models, paid to pose in studios, all very much alive and free – went nowhere. The dealer told me, via my hastily arranged but convoluted system of communication, that she needed to see more like that exquisite leg I'd made, and I knew. I knew that I had opened Pandora's Box and, now that I had peeked inside and understood its contents, I couldn't live without them, consequences be damned.

And I knew that I had to find another Muse. It was the only way I was going to recreate the magic of my very first successful piece.

Every sculpture I've created with the help of a Muse has been a roaring success. The few I've tried without one have failed, spectacularly so.

I never meant to become The Coastline Killer. And really, I'm not a murderer. Not like the ones you read about in the papers who kill for sport, for the bloodlust of it. That's not me.

It's not my fault. As I've already explained: I am only interested in the art.

Chapter 6

ALICE

Even before I'm fully awake, I'm aware that something isn't right.

My eyes still closed, I strain to hear anything other than my own breath, which is loud and rasping. There's the beating of my heart, too, which sounds like a drumline in my ears, but otherwise there's nothing. Silence. No traffic noises, no voices or footsteps or general buzz of life.

I force myself to count in my head, slowly and purposefully, while taking deep, controlled breaths. I reach ten, and then I flutter my eyes open, preparing for everything to fall into place, anticipating the flood of relief when my situation makes sense.

But nothing is familiar. I'm in a dimly lit room. There's a lightbulb hanging from the ceiling a little to my right, but it's switched off. The light source is coming from my left. I turn my head slowly to find it, inhaling sharply as pain slices through my skull.

Instinctively, I try to probe my head for blood, for bruising, for any clue as to what's happening. But my arm won't move. A flame of panic licks at my insides, but I try to extinguish it. I try once again to lift my hand. It's stuck. I switch to the other hand. That one won't move, either. The fear has escalated. It's no longer a flickering flame, but a

28

roaring fire, raging through my chest and filling my head and searing my veins.

I wriggle my fingers and my panic eases, just for a moment, when they move. I focus on the sensations in my hands, my wrists, my arms, on the cool, smooth surface under my fingertips. Slowly, gently, I attempt to roll my right wrist, but something is stopping me. I wriggle it around. Something rough and firm rubs against my skin, restraining me. I try the other hand, but it's the same. I kick my feet and realise that they're immobilised, too.

Dread builds, snowballing into something enormous and unstoppable.

I lift my head a little, ignoring the pain that's screaming at me to stop. Peering down the length of my body, I discover that I'm on some sort of metal table, a few feet off the ground, although it's too dim to gauge my height for certain.

I have no idea where I am, or how I got here. My head is in excruciating pain and I am utterly alone. My throat starts to tighten, but I close my eyes and force air into my lungs, focus on breathing deeply and smoothly. I have to figure out what's going on. I can freak out later, once I'm safe.

I try to retrace my steps, to piece together what the hell is happening. My face scrunches up involuntarily, the concentration so intense it's physical. I hiked the Grouse Grind with Celia. We met those women from Alberta. We had a photo taken together just before the three-quarter mark. I strain, but that's all I remember. Did I have an accident on the way up? Did I fall?

No. Celia gave me a ride home. She dropped me off at my condo. I remember getting to my front door. And then there's just a blank, where the answers I need should be.

My appointment! I remember with sudden, awful clarity that I'm supposed to be somewhere, that I can't be late. Did

I make it to the clinic? Was I sedated? They said I wouldn't need to be, this time. Instinctively, I try to sit up again, but again, I'm held back. I need to understand what's going on.

'Hello!' I shout as I lose my fight against the restraints. 'Hello? Can anyone hear me?'

I wait for a reply, but there's no answer, just my own voice echoing and returning to me in fragments.

Thinkthinkthinkthinkthink, I tell myself, clenching my eyes and fists closed, willing the memories to appear. I'm desperate to squeeze them from my subconscious. But no matter how hard I try, the void can't be filled. It's frightening, the idea that anything could have happened to me, and I don't remember it. Did something go wrong during my appointment? On the way home? Everything in me wants to lift my hand, to lower it protectively, but I know I can't.

I have to stop speculating. I can't force my memories to come back. I have to accept that fact – for now, at least – and work with what I know instead, what I'm certain of. I open my eyes and lift my head again.

Beyond my feet, there's a wall that looks like it was probably white once, but with the paint now grubby and peeling it's turned a sort of mustard yellow. Just to the left of my feet is a thick, brick column. I let my eyes drift up its surface to the ceiling, which is made up of wooden beams, the gaps between them stuffed with yellow, fluffy insulation batts. My gaze keeps moving, to the black, industrial-looking lamp that's been strung from the wooden beams above. It's facing me, shining directly into my eyes. I squint against it, and try to look around again, to gather as much information as I possibly can, but there's almost nothing to work with.

There are no windows, no personal touches in this room to glean any information from. It looks like an old, abandoned basement, but I don't have any concept of where it is in relation to my home, or who might have brought me here, or why.

I try to focus, despite the bubble of panic that's expanding inside me, and the pounding at the back of my skull. Was I attacked? Hit over the head with something? My mouth goes dry as I consider the possibility. I shake my head, regretting it instantly as the pain wraps around my temple.

There has to be another explanation. I'm just cata-strophising. Of course I wasn't attacked, kidnapped, brought to a basement and tied up. That's impossible... isn't it?

Except... I am tied to a table, in a dark, unfamiliar room. I have no recollection of what happened after I left my condo. I want there to be another explanation... I just can't think of a single one.

I strain my neck to see if there are any signs that I've been injured. I don't feel any pain, aside from the pounding in my head, but I need to see with my own eyes that I'm OK, that I'm still intact. To my relief, there's no blood in sight, and I'm still fully clothed. Apart from that, I don't know anything.

The pace of my heartbeat has increased, gradually at first, until now it's thrumming, one pump indistinguishable from the next. I need to sit up, clear my head so I can stop focus-ing on the terror and start thinking about how to get out of here. I'm trying to breathe, but all I can do is desperately gulp at the air around me. I'm spiralling.

I close my eyes, and I begin counting to one hundred, just to stay calm, to keep my mind off the horrifying scenarios that keep appearing, unsolicited, in my imagination.

And then, when I reach sixty-two, the footsteps begin.

Chapter 7

ALICE

I have the same nightmare every once in a while.

I'm in danger – mortal, real, horrifying danger – and I'm trying to scream. I know, even without really understanding what the danger is, that screaming at full volume is the only way I'll be able to escape the formless, faceless threat that's coming for me while I sleep. I open my mouth, fill my lungs and let out a bloodcurdling cry... except nothing comes out. I scream, and scream again, my whole body desperate to make a sound, but it's just air, no noise, and I know that I'm going to die, and I keep screaming until I wake up, panting, wanting to shout into the darkness of my bedroom just so I know that I can.

This is just like that nightmare.

Someone is walking towards me, and I know I should say something – do something – to keep myself safe from harm. Maybe I should yell out for help, or beg for mercy, or try to charm whoever it is into letting me go, or thank them for coming to rescue me. Whatever it is, I know that I should do something.

And yet, just like in the dream, when I'm faced with danger, I do exactly nothing. I keep my eyes closed, my whole body completely frozen, paralysed by fear. My mind is petrified, stopped in time, overwhelmed by the idea that

I'm about to come face to face with whoever is holding me captive.

The moments between hearing that first footstep and the tap of the person's shoes stopping beside me are both infinite and instant. I thought I'd felt fear before, but this is like nothing else I've ever known. My mind and body refuse to cooperate. With each other, with me.

'Alice.'

The deep whisper sends terror ripping up from my tailbone to the base of my skull. I keep my eyes squeezed tightly closed. Those two syllables, so familiar and yet, from his lips, somehow raw and needling at my nerves, tell me everything I need to know.

I am going to die.

My body is awake and alive in a way I've never known before, every cell alert, every thought sharp and clear and booming. I know that I am about to be killed. This man, whose whisper felt like thousands of tiny knives slicing my skin, is going to end my life.

And then my fear gives way to anger – I have somewhere to be that's too important to be derailed by a psychopath – and I'm suddenly emboldened by my rage. My eyes fly open. I turn my head to the right to face my captor, and when my gaze settles on him, I gasp.

He's wearing a mask. It's plastic; white and shiny, and completely devoid of any real features. It's flimsy, like it was bought at a dollar store in a pack of ten, and it doesn't quite cover his ears, which stick out at the sides, little pink peaks that would look ridiculous in any other context, but which somehow manage to look menacing here. There are lips moulded into the plastic, slightly parted and completely neutral. A triangular nose, inhuman and cartoon-like, and

33

ridges for eyebrows above the dark, blank eye holes. He has brown hair, the colour my mom would describe as 'mousy'.

I tear my eyes from his ghoulish mask and they fall to the apron he's wearing over a black, long-sleeved top, then to the white latex gloves that cover his hands. The apron, I realise with a shudder, is not the kind to cook in. It's the type that butchers wear.

And then hope flares inside me, bright and strong. He's wearing a mask. He doesn't want me to see his face, which means he's going to let me go. Relief flows through my veins, and the terror fades a little. It doesn't leave – death isn't the only thing that scares me – but at least, whatever happens next, I can cling to the fact that he'll let me go at the end of it. I want to cry, to break down and weep. But I also want to survive, and something tells me that keeping my composure will help.

The man in the mask is walking around the table. I follow his steps as he passes my feet and moves around the pillar to stand under the light. He bends down, and there's a rustling sound, like plastic bags being moved around.

I turn my head, gritting my teeth through the pain in my skull, and face him again. When my eyes land on what he's holding, my insides liquefy. It's a hypodermic needle; the kind used to administer drugs to patients. Or poison to victims.

He's holding it awkwardly, his hand curled around the plastic barrel, rather than the way I would hold it – the way I've held similar needles so many times over the past few months – balanced between my forefinger and middle finger, my thumb resting on the plunger. My mouth goes dry as he turns his wrist and the metallic needle winks in the light, the sharp bevel aimed straight for me.

'Wait! What are you doing?'

Whatever the answer is, I won't want to hear it. And yet, I have to know. I have to understand what's coming so that I can try to stop it, or at least, mentally prepare for it.

'Shut up,' he snaps. 'I just need to . . .'

'Ow!'

I'm shocked when he jabs the needle into my arm without warning. The sharp point has been plunged deep into the soft skin on the inside of my left elbow, the tip of it hitting bone. I cry out again, and the man tuts as though I'm a small child disobeying orders.

'Stop squirming.'

'What are you doing?' I demand again, desperate to understand, yet terrified to know. What if he's injecting something dangerous into my veins? What if it causes permanent damage? My stomach lurches at the thought.

'Taking your blood.'

His words send a ripple of fear across my skin. What could he possibly need my blood for?

'No.' I try to pull my arm away, but of course, I'm strapped down, and can't move out of reach. I struggle against the restraints, but it's no use.

'Stop it. Keep still,' he growls, pressing on my upper arm with his free hand so that I can't do anything but let him poke at me. He struggles to find a vein, hitting what must be tendons and nerves instead, then trying to pull the plunger back, which sends fresh pain shooting from my fingertips to my shoulder.

I moan, but I do my best to remain still. Not because he told me to, but because I know that finding a vein will be much more difficult – and even more painful – if I'm offering a moving target. He pokes around a bit, and I feel each movement deep inside my arm, metal pressing against bone, tendon, nerve. I try to focus on anything other than the gruesome sensations in my limb, but it's impossible.

'Aha,' he says, exultant. I lift my head to see red liquid oozing into the barrel of the syringe. As disgusted and scared as I am, I'm also overwhelmingly relieved that he'll stop his jabbing. And that my body is poison free. I let my head fall again, and wait for my blood to fill up the syringe. When he pulls the needle out, I'm left with an ache in my arm and a growing sense of fear in my belly.

There's more rustling down on the floor to my left, and then the mask appears over me again, and the panic rushes back like a tidal wave.

He's holding a hand saw, old and rusted, like it's been used to make tables and desks and benches over the years. Jagged teeth run along the edge of it, which is roughly the length of my forearm. My eyes flit to his face, but the mask holds no clues, gives me no indication of his intentions.

'What are you going to do to me?' I whisper. I don't know why I ask, but the words spill out of me before I can stop them. I mentally will him to tell me that he's sawing through my restraints, setting me free. But of course, that's delusional.

'This isn't about you, Alice,' he says. He sounds distracted, like my question is an inconvenience to him.

He gently runs his gloved fingers down my arm, from my elbow to my wrist. I swallow down a scream. When he lifts his hand, my skin tingles where he touched me. I feel sick.

'Such a lovely arm,' he whispers. 'But it has to go.'

My stomach lurches.

'No,' I groan.

'Yes,' he says, almost wistfully, 'but don't worry. Just your arm. The rest of you, I'll let go.'

Bile burns my throat. My terror mingles with the tiniest

spark of relief. He's going to let me go when he's done with me. When he's taken my arm.

'I'm thinking perhaps a lake,' he says, and my head spins. He's not making sense.

'The ocean's too wild,' he continues. 'I don't want to risk you washing up too soon.'

The realisation washes over me, icy and stark.

'You're The Coastline Killer.' My voice is strangled. It doesn't sound like me. The reality of my situation is crushing, a physical weight pressing down on my ribs, my guts. I picture my body, missing an arm, floating face down in the ocean, and despite my best intentions to remain composed, a sob leaps from my chest. This can't be happening.

'Shhhhh,' the man in the mask coos. 'That's really not going to help.'

But I can't stop, now that the tears have started. I don't want to die. Not when I was so close. And I don't want to go through what I know is going to happen. I can't handle pain like that. The blood, the fear, the horror of it. I let out a wail. I'm not strong enough for this.

'Please,' I beg through my sobs. 'Please don't do this. I can't do this. Please.'

He lets out a noise, a sort of sigh, a puff of air against the plastic of his mask. There's a hissing sound, as though he's whispering under his breath, words that only he can hear, the sound reverberating against the brittle white plastic. I strain to catch what he's saying, and as I focus on this one thing, the sobs subside and I'm left panting on the cold metal table, trying to hear the words of the man who is about to kill me.

He lifts the saw, and I know it's over. I close my eyes so I don't have to see my body being torn apart. I beg my mind to give up, to pass out, to shut down so that I don't have to

37

feel the pain, so that I can just stop existing without being aware of what's being done to me. If I'm going to die, I don't want to know about it.

The saw, cold and sharp, touches the inside of my elbow. A whimper escapes my lips.

Metal teeth bite into my skin.

My shriek bounces off the walls and returns to me, split into a thousand screams.

Chapter 8

THE SCULPTOR

In order to fully appreciate what I do, you need to understand the process I follow to create my bronze masterpieces.

It's an ancient technique – modified only by the use of a few modern materials – known as the lost wax method.

You can't carve bronze like you do marble, with a hammer and chisel, so to begin with I create the sculpture in clay. I make it intricate and detailed, with ridges of skin, fine, feather-light hair, blemishes and folds ... whatever minutia I want to be visible on the finished sculpture.

I observe my live model for days, weeks, or – occasionally – months, while I'm working with the clay; my Muse will move and dance and jump and writhe as I instruct her, and as I watch, I catch the movements of her muscles and the ridges of her skin, and I replicate these in my clay, intricate detail by intricate detail. I edit. I perfect.

Then I cover the clay model with liquid rubber to create a cast, an inverted version of the clay original. The rubber captures all of the details; the bumps in the skin, the pores, the creases, the cuticles. Everything that appears on the clay will also be part of the rubber cast, including my fingerprints. Which is why I always, always wear gloves when I'm working.

The cast is removed from the clay, and here's the part

where my sculptures gain their souls: instead of filling the rubber cast with pure cement like most sculptors do, I add a little something extra to the core. A little bit of my Muse. A talisman, of sorts.

It's at this point that my Muse and I part company. I've kept what I need – a femur, a radius, phalanges, a spine, depending on the specifics of the collection – and the rest, I release to the wild.

You might wonder why I don't just use my kiln, the way I did with my very first Muse, and that's a fair enough question, but I do have my reasons. The first is that I absolutely hate sawing my Muses apart. It turns my stomach. An arm here, a leg there, I can just about tolerate. One torso per collection is doable, after a few big gulps of whisky. But I can't bear to completely dismantle my Muses every single time, which would be necessary, because I can't fit a complete adult human inside my kiln.

The other reason is a matter of respect. These Muses give their lives for me. Returning them to nature, where they can be found and mourned by the people who loved them while they were trapped on earth, is the least I can do. It's my parting gift. Or a kind of clutching at redemption. I'm not really sure, yet. I just know that it's the right thing to do.

Once my Muse is gone, there are only a few more steps until my work is completed. After the cement core has hardened, I scrape away a thin layer of it, leaving a small gap between the core and the rubber cast, where hot wax is then poured.

This wax layer, another perfect replica of the original clay piece, is my last chance to make changes and, of course, to scrape my signature into the piece, before covering it with a heatproof ceramic layer.

The whole lot goes into my kiln, where the wax melts and

drains away, leaving a space where the bronze can be poured inside. When that's cooled, the ceramic layer is broken away to reveal the finished work – its magical core hidden safely from the world – ready for final touch-ups and polishing and the application of a patina to give it depth and colour and shine.

You'd never guess the secrets that a piece by The Sculptor conceals.

All the art critics see is my talent. My skill. They see the mysterious persona that they've created for me.

But honestly, I wouldn't be The Sculptor without the women whose remains were found washed up along the coast, from Kyuquot on Vancouver Island to Eureka in Northern California. Those women are the life and soul of my work, their limbs forming my inspiration and driving my hands to create, to replicate.

Their bodies might be decomposing in their watery graves – or, in the cases of those who have been found, literal graves – but my Muses live forever, encased in bronze, one piece at a time.

Chapter 9

ALICE

At first I assume it's just the roaring in my brain getting louder and more insistent, my mind's way of drowning out the pain of the saw's rusted teeth dragging through my skin, slowly, purposefully, the sensation of it eliminating rational thought. But after a few seconds the sound is all around, not just in my head, and it's accompanied by a rumbling, like there's an enormous truck driving right beside me.

Vibrations ring through the table I'm lying on, gently at first, then with more force, an increasing shudder that reverberates through my skull. It's too much for my brain to process, and so instead of attempting to understand, I lie frozen, my mind blank, my bones rattling against one another.

The saw is lifted from my skin. The absence of pressure, of cold metal and searing pain, returns my senses to me, starting with a relief so palpable I'm certain my lungs inhale it. But it's short-lived. There's no time to celebrate.

A gruff whisper of 'Oh my God', barely audible above the groaning, creaking, grumbling that fills the room. Only, that's not right. What did he say? There's no time to register his words as the rumbling intensifies and my eyes fly open, because I know. I know because I've spent years studying this, preparing for it.

It's an earthquake.

My brain – inexplicably attempting to be optimistic, even in the midst of this – considers the possibility that it's just a tremor, nothing to worry about, just a small shift in the Cascadia Subduction Zone.

But my eyes overrule this hopeful theory. The walls are rolling as though they're made of fabric rather than brick; gauzy curtains being moved by a breeze. The overhead light is swaying wildly, the single yellow beam of the lamp swinging from left to right, up and down, dizzying and disorienting. The man in the mask has disappeared, ducking for safety or knocked off his feet, I don't care which, as long as he's nowhere near me. I struggle against my restraints, knowing that the safest place to be is on the ground, under the table I'm strapped to, which is bucking violently as the earth flows like waves.

Over the rumbling – a kind of runaway freight train noise – there are other, more frightening, sounds. Crumbling, cracking, booming, like the world is collapsing and I'm about to be crushed under the weight of it. Wild screaming reaches my ears, and I can't be sure if it's coming from me, or the man in the mask, or the building crying out under the earth's assault.

Another crack, this one sharper, louder and much, much closer, is followed by the explosion of heavy objects landing nearby.

Exposed like this, I'm in the worst position I possibly could be during an earthquake. My hands instinctively move to cover the soft flesh of my belly, but the ties around my wrists are tight, and no amount of straining against them is loosening their grip. I can't hear beyond the all-encompassing noises the quake is throwing at me. It's impossible to think with clarity. The room is filling with dust; clouds of it billow through the swinging yellow light, so thick that I begin to choke.

I squeeze my eyes closed and press my nose and mouth against my shoulder, hoping that the fabric of my top will provide some kind of protection, because if falling pieces of building don't kill me, the dust will. I might not be able to move, or get to safety, but I can do my best not to suffocate. The table tilts dangerously to one side, balancing on two legs, hovering for a horror-filled moment, long enough for me to imagine falling to the ground and smashing my skull, and then, just as suddenly, it tips back, right side up.

There's no time to feel relieved. Another chunk of concrete or brick or metal glances off the edge of the table beside my ear, the noise so loud that I'm certain my skull will shatter. I fling my head to the other side just in time to avoid the debris, but I'm showered with pieces of shrapnel that feel like bullets as they strike my body.

I can't see anything coming, so I don't have time to think, or move, or understand before something large and heavy slams into my chest and bounces away, knocking the wind from my lungs and filling my body with a blinding pain that radiates from my torso and fills every nerve and vein and cell.

My reaction is to scream, but I can't breathe, and as my lips part, a cloud of dust rushes into my mouth and lungs, coating everything in a thick, gritty film. I cough, and the agony drowns me in blackness.

The oblivion I'd wanted just moments ago is coming for me, sucking me into its gaping jaws as the world around me crumbles.

Chapter 10

THE SCULPTOR

The rumble comes first.

It's slow, distant, not dissimilar to wild waves crashing in a storm. It's there, but it's little more than a background hum, something I'm dimly aware of, not quite enough to distract me from my task.

And so I continue, pressing on with the plan I've spent months perfecting. I've accounted for every possible scenario. Nothing is unexpected.

Well, almost nothing.

It doesn't take long before the rumbling becomes a thundering, constant roar, and the slight vibrations I'd felt in the soles of my shoes become tremors that make my teeth chatter against one another.

As I clamp my mouth closed to stop my teeth from knocking each other out, I understand what's happening. It takes me a moment to recognise the word that's hovering at the edge of my consciousness. When it arrives – earthquake – I feel it, reverberating inside my ribs, jolting me out of my daze.

My Muse temporarily forgotten, I wonder how best to respond, everything I've ever learned about earthquakes suddenly absent from my clamouring mind. Should I stand in a doorway? But no, I remember reading somewhere a few years ago that door frames aren't safe, even though that's what I was told as a kid. A bathtub, then? But there isn't one nearby, and I'm pretty sure that's for fires.

These thoughts flash through my mind in a panicked, confused microsecond, and then I'm left with no choice as I'm thrown from my feet by the bucking, roiling earth. I land heavily, and roll onto my stomach, covering my head with my arms, peeking out from beneath my elbow. All I can focus on is survival as I watch objects flying in different directions and solid structures behaving like they're liquid. I no longer know which way is up.

Something comes crashing down beside me. I wince, but I'm too frightened to move, in case I pick the wrong direction.

My mouth opens automatically, a scream unfurling without my permission, and is filled with dust and grit that makes me cough and gag. I curl into a ball, hugging my knees to my chest, dipping my chin down in an attempt to cover my airways. I'm helpless as the room bucks and shudders, and I wonder whether I'll be buried alive, whether the building is structurally sound.

I doubt it. Nothing could be strong enough to withstand an assault like this, surely?

The part that surprises me the most is the noise.

It's a symphony of destruction. The earth is violently crashing against itself, groaning and crunching like monstrous machinery deep in the earth. Added to that is the crumbling of man-made things; things we're so proud of, things that we believe to be permanent. In the end, they're no match for the immense power of nature.

I imagine it all being torn apart above me, around me. That road, tarred and compressed and designed to last hundreds of years? Opened up with no more difficulty than a can of tuna. Those buildings, claiming to be earthquake-proof, built to sway in a tremor? Tumbling like they're made of Jenga blocks. I can't see them, but the screams of metal bending to breaking point, and the booming of tons of offices and apartments and hotels collapsing fill my head.

My whole body is bucked with no more difficulty than if I were on a trampoline playing Crack the Egg, like I used to with my brother when I was eight or nine. I'm flung upwards, then sideways. My limbs flail in the air before I hit the ground with a force that shakes my bones.

My Muse's face pops into my head, but I rupture the thought before it forms. She is no longer my main concern. But before I can begin to think of a plan, a piece of rubble the size of a fist comes flying at me, straight towards me. I try to move my hands, to protect my face, but I'm too slow.

The chunk of debris collides with my skull.

Chapter 11

BBC News Online

BREAKING: Magnitude 9.1 earthquake hits Vancouver, Canada
12 October, 2018
7 minutes ago

Seismologists at the Southern California Earthquake Data Center at Caltech in California reported a magnitude 9.1 seismic event, which took place just off the coast of Vancouver Island, Canada, just moments ago. The quake originated in the Cascadia Subduction Zone, a 620 mile-long fault located parallel to the western coast of North America. Tremors were felt as far south as Sacramento, California, but scientists have confirmed that the epicentre of this seismic activity is in southern British Columbia, where the city of Vancouver is located.

Experts have already speculated that this could be 'The Big One', an until-now hypothetical magnitude 9 earthquake that seismologists have predicted for a number of years. The last major earthquake to hit the area was in the year 1700, and with major quakes occurring every 400–600 years, another similar quake has been, according to scientists, 'inevitable'.

Although the city of Vancouver has spent years

preparing for such an event, estimates suggest that an earthquake of this magnitude could kill upwards of 10,000 people, with tens of thousands more injured.

No official reports have yet emerged from the city, which was hit by the quake only minutes ago, at 10:19 a.m. local time. Residents in communities along the west coast of Vancouver Island will likely be evacuating ahead of expected tsunamis, with the metropolitan area of Vancouver following, if conditions allow.

Follow this story live for updates as we receive them.

Chapter 12

ALICE

The silence that presses against me once the earth has finished rearranging itself might actually be more frightening than the earthquake itself.

It's an awful, sickening absence of noise, like the whole world has ended and I'm the lone witness to its funeral. I'm too scared to move. The room I'm in feels like a house of cards, like all it will take is a puff of air to bring the whole thing down. But it isn't long before my lungs demand oxygen, so I take a tentative, shaky breath, wincing for the collapse I'm sure is coming.

To my relief, nothing caves in.

The space around me is heavy with fragments of the building I'm lying in; the air I inhale is bitter and solid. The pain is excruciating – my ribs are on fire, and grit scratches against my organs – but I force myself to swallow the sob that races up my throat. It'd be a waste. My body would instantly demand more air, and all it would get is more dust and debris. So I concentrate on pressing my mouth into my shoulder, and I moan into the fabric of my top.

The thin material, and the awkward angle I'm forced to hold, can only do so much to stop the clouds of cement and brick and paint and insulation and I-have-no-idea-what-else from rushing down my windpipe and into my lungs. It takes all of the strength I still have to keep breathing, to fight against the urge to cough and yelp and gasp.

One of the first tactics I teach any student of mine to help them survive after an earthquake is to cover their nose and mouth. I've said it more times than I could possibly count. I even have a stash of dust masks in every room of my condo for this very reason. I never thought I'd be incapable of completing the most basic step required to stay safe and alive.

I try to gauge how badly I'm hurt. The headache I had when I first woke up in this room now feels insignificant, sidelined by more pressing injuries. My lungs and throat feel like they've been scoured with sandpaper, but that's nothing compared with my chest, where the chunk of rubble slammed into me, from a direction I couldn't pinpoint if I tried.

Judging by the near-blackout pain that comes every time I take a breath, I'm pretty certain that I've broken at least one rib. Probably a few. But it isn't my bones I'm really worried about, it's what's underneath them. At least the rubble hit my chest, and not a few inches lower. I try not to think about what could have happened, then. What that would have meant.

I wriggle my fingers. Then my toes. I breathe out as gently as I can, a small sigh of relief. I haven't lost sensation in my limbs. And, mercifully, I didn't lose my arm to that rusty saw.

With a flash of clarity, I realise that I don't know where the man in the mask is, which means he could be hovering just out of my line of sight, ready to pounce and continue his attack.

Trying not to cry, because that would only add to my pain, I wheeze in a lungful of air, ignoring the ache that follows, and move my head from my shoulder, my eyes searching wildly for any sign of him. Dust burns my eyes but I blink the tears back and force myself to look, to locate the man who brought me here, to understand exactly what my situation now is.

To my relief, he's not behind me, or to either side. I squirm, pushing against the restraints to look around, but he's not here. At least, not right next to me.

I crane my neck, but I can't lift my head high enough to see the ground below, to check if he collapsed where he was standing, while sawing away at my arm. The bits of floor that I can see are covered in unidentifiable shapes, all the same dirty grey colour that makes it impossible to tell if what I'm looking at is a body – dead, or unconscious – or just a pile of brick.

Staring at a shape beside me, roughly where he might have fallen, I try to make out any kind of movement. I stare until my lungs are shrieking and my neck muscles are trembling from the effort, but I still can't tell whether it's a body or debris.

I let myself rest, closing my eyes and straining to hear any noise that might indicate that the man who took me is alive, that he's breathing, that he survived. The building creaks and groans as it shifts into its new position, and there's the occasional distant crash as something falls, as well as my own rasping breaths. But there's no sign of another person.

Maybe he's dead. I hope he is, but I can't rely on that being the case. If he's unconscious, he'll wake up soon. Which means I need to make a plan, or at least spot an escape so that, if the opportunity arises, I can make a run for it.

I try not to think about the other, much more pressing concern, because there's absolutely nothing I can do about it. I know that aftershocks are coming, and that they could be just as bad – possibly worse, if what just happened was actually a foreshock – as the quake that almost buried me alive.

In any case, I don't have much time.

I take another breath, filtered through my top, then continue my limited visual search. The room has been transformed. It's like a renovation in reverse, with shapeless piles of rubble where structure and right angles once were. I try to remember what I saw before the earthquake, but I'd been too focused on surviving the man in the mask.

To my left, the pillar is still intact, thank goodness. If that had come down, it would have brought the whole ceiling with it, burying me. Beyond it, I can't make out any distinguishing features beyond more rubble, dust and destruction.

It's clearer to my right, although the dim, still-swaying lamp above me doesn't allow me to see too far across the room. There's no natural light, which isn't a good sign. But if the man is gone, if he's managed to find his way out already, then there must be a clear exit. I contort my neck to try to see behind me, gritting my teeth through the agony.

There are piles of broken brick, or wall, or concrete, as far as I can see. But no exit, no door. Through the haze I can make out the shadows of a few more pillars. I don't know much about engineering but it's obvious, even to me, that they're the reason I'm not crushed under the remains of a building.

I lift my head again to see over my toes. There's nothing but a partially collapsed wall, veiled by clouds of dust, with pieces of metal that jut out of gaping holes like teeth in some vicious creature's jaws. The holes in the wall reveal another solid layer of brick, but no escape.

I can't see a way out, but I also can't see anyone else. Maybe the man in the mask is already far away from here.

The relief that flares up in me is short-lived.

If he's gone, then I'm no longer in danger of being murdered, which is obviously a good thing. But it doesn't change the fact that I'm trapped here – wherever here is – strapped down and injured.

No one knows where I am. No one even knows I'm gone.

I'm completely alone.

Chapter 13

ALICE

My mind whirrs with the improbable knowledge that an earthquake just saved my life. I close my eyes, say a little prayer of thanks to the earth for her timing, and then bring my attention back to the present. I didn't survive an attempted murder and an earthquake only to die strapped to a table in a basement.

It wasn't just any earthquake I lived through, either. What happened wasn't merely a tremor. I've felt small seismic movements before, and have studied them for enough time to understand that this was a big one. Possibly even The Big One, the one I've been preparing myself and others for almost every day of my adult life.

A little ironic laugh bursts from me involuntarily, and I wince as my ribs scream their disapproval. I've never counted how many hours I've spent trying to get ready for this exact moment. It must be thousands, possibly more. But none of my training, none of the courses I attended or experts I spoke to or seminars I delivered have prepared me for what I'm facing.

I knew I could end up trapped. Just not like this. I'm not pinned down by a piece of shrapnel or a boulder, or crushed by my car. I'm imprisoned. And, unlike in any of my preparedness scenarios, I have no idea where I am, how far I am from help, or if help will ever actually come along at all.

Depending on what time the earthquake struck, my friends and family would expect me to be at my appointment, or possibly still at home. Even if they're able to reach those places to search, and if they can't find me, they'll have no clue where to look next. I'll be lost, swallowed up in the chaotic aftermath of a natural disaster.

I can't rely on anyone coming for me. I have to get out, or let someone – anyone – know that I'm trapped.

I close my eyes and try to push through the fog of my panic. I'm trained for this. If anyone can work out how to get out of a situation like this one, it's me. When I speak to students and the faculty at the university about earthquake survival, I tell them that, if they're ever trapped, they should bash on pipes using something solid to get attention. The sound will travel as far as the pipes go – often this reaches to the outside of the building. It's an effective way to attract attention with minimal effort and resource.

There's no pipe, though. Or at least, no way for me to look for one, or anything to smack against it. I need to get off this table.

I struggle with as much force as I can manage to loosen my restraints, but they're just as impossible to get out of as they were before. Exhausted, I let my body go limp, burying my face in my shoulder again.

A piece of dust gets caught in my throat and I cough, the movement making me cry out in pain. Frustrated, I lift my head just a little and smack it back down again, forgetting my original injury. The pain is fierce, and as the metallic clang echoes in my head I curse my stupidity. Stars pop and flash in my vision. I blink furiously. If I'm going to make it out of here alive, I'll have to start thinking clearly. I have to be smarter.

As I wait for the pain in my skull to subside, my heart beats faster, realisation settling over me. There might be a way to call for help without a pipe. My fingertips brush against a layer of dust and grit that coats the metal table. I move slowly, carefully, not wanting to disrupt anything, probing the small area of the table my hands are able to reach. My range of movement is limited – maybe an inch to the left and right, and if I wriggle my shoulders, an extra inch or two down towards my toes. I try my left hand first. Something is wedged under my thigh, large enough to pinch between my thumb and forefinger. As I grip it, it crumbles. My heart plummets as I brush it to the floor.

I try again with my right hand.

Inch by inch, I explore the tiny area of table under and around my fingers. Every movement, no matter how tiny, is agony. My index finger runs along the smooth surface, and then hits something. I stop, scared that I'll accidentally sweep whatever it is off the table. I lift my finger, shift it, and slowly lower it back onto the object, pressing down firmly. It's solid. My stomach flutters with hope. This just might work.

I pinch the piece of debris gently between my thumb and forefinger. It's about an inch long. I squeeze. No give. Gripping it as tightly as I can without risking it pinging out of my grasp and skittering across the floor, I rap it tentatively against the table.

And suddenly I'm grinning like an idiot into my shoulder, the tinny tap echoing in my ears. It isn't loud, the sound muffled by my body resting on the table, but it's something. I hit it against the metal again, more forcefully this time.

The noise rings out, distinct and clear, although at a much lower volume than I'd hoped for.

It's not going to be as effective as smacking a pipe, but it's the only chance I have of someone out there knowing that I'm in here, and that I'm alive.

I begin my rhythmic tap, tap, tap, sometimes switching to Morse code, drumming out three short raps, three longer ones, three short ones again for SOS, sometimes just beating stone against metal in a slow, constant rhythm.

My wrist grows tired, so I take a break, breathing into my shoulder as much as I can, trying not to think about how unlikely it is that anyone will hear my pathetic drumming. But I know that, if trapped, I shouldn't shout – that's too risky with all the dust in the air – and I shouldn't try to move things around. I have to trust the process. The process I taught so confidently, without any clue what it was really like to be in this situation.

My body tenses as something in the air shifts again. I squeeze my eyes closed and try to prepare for an aftershock. It's inevitable, and it will, in all likelihood, be the thing that kills me.

But it isn't an aftershock. It's something falling, a piece of the room caving in, collapsing to my right. I wince, bracing for the pain of something heavy and solid falling on me again, but nothing comes, just a rush of air and dust as the room once again moves and morphs and takes on new dimensions.

It stops.

And then I hear it: the smallest groan, a puff of air. And then a cough.

My captor is still here. And he's alive.

Chapter 14

THE SCULPTOR

My consciousness arrives gradually, like I'm being woken after knocking back a couple of incredibly strong sleeping pills; a sensation I became intimately familiar with in the months that followed my first Muse lying motionless on my kitchen floor.

The world comes slowly into focus again. My mind strains to piece together the facts, to understand what's happening.

I'm alive. This realisation comes as a bit of a surprise after the force of destruction that's just been hurled at me.

The next piece of information that my brain processes is that, when the earthquake hit, my next Muse was within reach.

And then the earth shook and I was thrown off my feet and onto the ground, and pieces of building started landing on me, a hailstorm of shrapnel. I must have been knocked out. I must have missed the end of it. Because now the world is silent, apart from a persistent knocking that's making the pounding in my head intensify.

I groan, and open my eyes. For a terrifying moment I persuade myself that I've been blinded, that my eyes have been so badly injured in the earthquake that I've lost my sight. Panic swells inside me – how can I sculpt without vision? – but then I turn my head and there's a faint light above me, filtering through a thick, dark cloud of smoke.

No, not smoke. Dust.

I sigh in relief, but when I inhale, it's particles that reach my lungs instead of oxygen, and I cough them back out. I concentrate on taking small, shallow breaths rather than drawing in deep lungfuls of dust. Slowly, I bring my breathing back to a steady rhythm, willing my body not to cough again.

The incessant pounding in my head drowns out almost all other sensation. I can tell that I'm injured, but I don't know how badly. I squeeze my eyes closed, and wait for a surge of nausea to pass.

When it does, I lift my head and look around. My eyes have adjusted slightly to the hazy darkness, so I can just make out the shadowy silhouettes of pillars and stairs, and a table next to me. But where there was a door, there's now just a mess of rubble. My chest seems to shrink a little as the idea of being trapped settles over me.

I need to get out.

I need to protect my secrets... before it's too late.

Chapter 15

ALICE

For a terrifying split second, I'm convinced that my heart has stopped beating. When it starts again, it's thunderous, and I'm certain the drumbeat against my tender ribs is echoing through the room.

How did he survive? I barely did. The odds of both of us making it have to be low. And yet . . .

I strain to detect another sound, a sign that he's definitely still here, that my imagination isn't conjuring a worst-case scenario to torture me with. I swallow. My hand is frozen, poised above the metal table, the piece of debris wedged between my fingers. Slowly, carefully, bit by bit, I lower it, my arm trembling. I don't let go of it altogether, though. It's all I have. It's my only chance of being rescued.

Something moves beside me. My body goes limp, my fear so utterly consuming that nothing else can function.

I wait for my brain to adjust to the new, horrifying information that he's still alive. I'd convinced myself that he was dead, or that he'd fled. I'd told myself that survival was just a matter of attracting the attention of a rescuer.

But now, with one small groan, and a tiny clatter of rubble, I understand that I'd only believed what I so desperately wanted to be true. He was never gone, and now I have to survive him before I can even think about how to get out of here. Earthquake or not, there's no reason to believe that he won't finish what he started.

He coughs; the sound is weak and pained.

My hope flickers back to life. Maybe he's dying. He was, after all, unconscious for some time. He's clearly injured, probably concussed. These could be the last breaths of a man who's finally getting what he deserves. I swallow a sob, overwhelmed by the unknown, wondering how long it will be before my fate is clear, before the suspense is over and I can just deal with what's coming next.

The noises are coming faster now. And louder. It sounds as though he's pinned down, like he's struggling to heave something heavy from his body. Pieces of the room fall and crash and slam into one another. He groans again. A tear squeezes out from under one of my closed eyelids. If he manages to free himself, then he'll come for me. I picture whatever's holding him down – something huge, and completely immovable, ideally – and I will it, with all of the inner strength I can summon, to stay there. As the tear slides slowly down my cheek, I silently beg him to give up, to bleed or suffocate to death, so that I can resume my tapping and be rescued.

He ignores my mental pleas. Scraping and scratching and rustling replaces the groans. And then, with a strained scream, something falls to the floor with an almighty crash that reverberates in the metal table and up my spine. I stay completely still, too scared to make any movements, no matter how small. I decide – a split-second calculation – that my best strategy is to pretend that I didn't survive the earthquake.

My heart fights against my ribcage, thrashing like it wants to break free. The room falls silent once again.

There's a pause, and I almost begin to wonder – again – if he's dead.

A violent retching sound answers my question, along with more coughing, more moaning. Another silence.

It seems to go on forever; this cycle of him moving clumsily around, groaning, vomiting, and falling, with stretches of silence between.

'Fuck.'

His voice is raspy, his throat no doubt coated with dust, like mine. I try to picture his movements in time with the sounds he's making, the shifting and falling of the space around him being disturbed, the clatter of objects I can't identify. I visualise him brushing himself off. Then he staggers; one, two steps. Then he falls. Swears again. Slowly, carefully, he gets up once more.

The table I'm lying on jerks suddenly. I choke down the yelp of surprise that threatens to burst out of me, and force myself to remain perfectly still, my breath as shallow and controlled as I can manage. I'm not getting enough air, but my chest can't move conspicuously or he'll know I'm alive. Judging by the rasping breaths coming from the end of the table, he's standing over me, leaning on the table for support.

As long as he doesn't try to touch me, to take my pulse, then I can do it. I can convince him that the earthquake killed me; that he doesn't need to. Then he can find a way out. And I can focus on doing the same.

His breathing, laboured and rattling, is close, at the end of the table. But he's not moving around anymore. I concentrate on sipping the air, not gulping it. I need more. My body is screaming for a decent lungful, and I know it's only a matter of seconds before I have to take a proper breath.

If he's looking, if he's inspecting me for signs of life, he'll know. And then it'll be over.

My head is fuzzy. My entire body aches. Something clatters; there's another fumbling noise, and I take the chance, hoping it's a window of opportunity, hoping that he's distracted. I lift my lips just a fraction from my shirt and heave a great, aching breath. The pain in my chest feels like I'm being stabbed, but I lie as still as I can, trying to control my urge to wail, and play dead.

The tickle begins slowly.

My lungs are filled with air that wasn't filtered through fabric. It's the biggest breath I've taken since the earthquake ended, and every inch of the room is still clotted with dust. The fire in my ribs distracts me for a few seconds, but when I notice the itch in the back of my throat, it's all I can think about. I'm horrified at my body's betrayal.

Now that I need to cough, though, it's an inevitability. I press my mouth harder into my shoulder, and swallow as firmly as I can. The tickle is still there, growing more insistent, impossible to ignore.

The cough rises up like a living creature refusing to stay chained down, starting deep in my chest and crawling up my throat. I fight it, a mental battle as much as a physical one. Silently, I scream at my brain to tell my body to shut it down. Doesn't it know that this is life or death? I constrict my throat, hoping that it will somehow scratch the itch, but it's useless. The cough is barrelling up my airway, and I'm helpless to stop it.

It bursts out of me all at once, one huge, heaving, traitorous cough, and then another, and another. I think I might choke on my own gasps or die from the pain that's blooming across my chest, but then, finally, the fit is over, and the room is terrifyingly quiet.

I open my eyes. There's no point playing dead any more. The light is dim in the thick cloud of particles, so I can't see much, but what I do see tells me everything I need to know.

The mask is still hiding the identity of the man who's standing at the end of the table, although it's tilted to the side, so he looks like some kind of awful nightmarish puppet. His bottom lip is exposed, his chin and chest covered with the contents of his stomach. A thick layer of grey dust has settled over him, so I can't tell apron from arm from neck from head. He's one giant, grotesque ghost. Only he isn't a ghost. He's very much alive, his only visible injury a thick smudge of blood on his head, flowing down the side of his mask.

He's looking directly at me.

Chapter 16

ALICE

'So,' he says quietly, the mask inching closer to my face. 'You're alive.'

The smell of the vomit covering his chin and shirt makes my stomach turn, but I don't react. I don't move. I couldn't, even if I wanted to.

He emits a kind of low growling noise, close to my ear. My heart flutters furiously, the palpitation making me dizzy.

It's too much for my brain to process. I survived, but I'm trapped. I lived through a natural disaster, but will probably be murdered. I try to breathe slowly, to keep my inhalations shallow, but my body's taking over and deciding for me.

My lungs aren't getting enough air. I'm trying to slow my breathing, but it's not helping. And every breath, no matter how gently I try to suck the air into my lungs, sends a screaming pain across my chest, the agony so intense I wonder how many times I can repeat it. There's a whimpering sound, and I realise that it must be coming from me. It gets louder, more strangled.

'Hey,' the man says, the mask hovering in front of me. 'Hey. Stop that!'

His voice is strangely echoey, like it's coming from far away, at the end of a narrow, long tunnel. I try to focus on his words, on his voice, but it's like trying to clutch the details of a dream. The tighter I try to cling on, the more it turns to vapour.

He snaps his fingers in front of my face, like he's an illusionist and I can be made to magically do his bidding. I can smell the latex of his gloves, but I can't control what's happening in my body.

'Hey!' he shouts, still clicking madly. 'Tell me how to get out.'

My heart is pounding now, a drum-beat on my already-battered ribs, and my chest seems to shrink, like my body is attempting to suffocate me, my skin wrapping itself tighter and tighter around my torso.

I recognise what's happening to me, even though the sensations aren't familiar. I've heard Celia describing the panic attacks she used to suffer from enough times to know, objectively, that this is what this is.

But knowing that I'm having a panic attack isn't enough to combat the certainty, cemented in my scrambling brain, that I'm dying. The wave of terror this knowledge brings hits me with as much power as the earthquake I just survived. As I press my face into my shoulder I take shallow, intentional breaths, the pain still present, but less urgent than the feeling of imminent death that's descended on me.

I close my eyes and mentally remove myself from the room I'm in, going instead to where I desperately wish I was: Celia's house, complete with two perfectly chubby babies and piles of laundry scattered across the floor. I imagine sitting on her blue sofa, once pristine, now dotted with unidentifiable stains, and holding one of the twins; its wriggly, warm body making my arm – and my heart – ache. I think of Celia laughing, throwing her head back, her joy infectious.

And then, when the tiniest sliver of calm breaks through

the cracks of my terror, I remind myself that what's happening will pass, that I have everything I need to recover.

Slowly – so, so slowly – my muscles begin to unwind, and my breaths become more controlled, more fluid. I lie to myself, repeating phrases in my mind, things like *I'm safe*, and *I'm OK* and, *I'm going to get through this*.

I don't know any of that to be true, of course. But I need to trick my body into relaxing. And if that means believing my own lies, then that's what I have to do. It's emergency DoubleThink. And it works.

I take another deep, shaking breath, and allow myself to come back to the basement.

Gradually, as though I'm travelling through a thick fog, emerging into the clear air, sounds begin to filter through my fear. There's shouting.

'Alice!'

My eyes fly open. The mask is close – too close – and he's yelling my name. His fist looms above me. I close my eyes, screwing my face up in anticipation of the pain I know is coming. There's an explosion of sound next to my ear, and the table shakes beneath me. I crack one eye open, just a sliver.

His fist has connected with the table. He's leaning over me, blood and sick mingling under his chin, and his breath, escaping from the bottom of the mask, blows on my face as he howls with pain.

My stomach turns to liquid as he grapples with this new injury. He's a wounded animal, dangerous and unpredictable. He missed my face this time, but what about the next? Or the time after that?

He's out of control. He's violent. And I'm completely at his mercy.

Chapter 17

ALICE

'Are you done?'

The mask is still hovering in the space above me, the threat of violence hanging in the dusty air between us. Tears trickle silently down my cheeks, but I don't react. I have no idea how I'm supposed to behave. Should I be vulnerable; subservient? Or should I be strong and stubborn, refusing to be cowed by him? If I knew what would give me the greatest chance of survival, I'd put on the performance of a lifetime.

But I don't know anything.

'I'm OK,' I whisper, deciding that all I can be is myself. And it's the truth – I'm broken and scared and in pain, and my heart is quivering, but I'm alive. That has to be enough, at least for now.

'I didn't ask if you were OK. I asked if you're done with your tantrum, because you need to start thinking about how to make yourself useful. I shouldn't have to remind you what I'll do if I don't need you. Do you understand?'

I nod miserably.

'Good. OK. Now, the door, which was the only way out of here, has disappeared. But I know what you do for a living. I know you can help.'

Fear threatens to overwhelm me again. How does he know what I do? Has he been watching me? What else does he know? With difficulty, I force these questions, and the dread they bring, back down again. I have to focus.

'I can't help while I'm tied down like this.'

'Oh, sure. You want me to release you so, what, you can attack me? I'm not stupid, Alice.'

My skin crawls every time he speaks my name.

'Please,' I whisper. 'I won't attack you. I'm too weak. I can barely breathe, I just need to be safe. If an aftershock comes, and it will, then I'll die.'

He shrugs. 'I think we've established that I'm not too worried about that.'

I look up at his masked, blank face, glowing eerily white under the single dim light. I press my lips together defiantly.

'If you're not worried about me dying, then you can't be too worried about your own survival. You said it yourself, you know what I do for a living. If I'm dead, I can't help.'

'Well, you're alive for now,' he says calmly. 'And yes, I do know what you do. I saw you give that talk at the university, so I know that you don't need to move to teach me how to survive.'

My stomach churns with horror and confusion. That was a presentation for faculty members. It wasn't open to the public. How would he have seen it? My scalp tingles as I think about the man I noticed at the very back of the lecture theatre, hood up, slouched over. Was The Coastline Killer watching me? What else did he observe?

'Not until you let me go,' I reply, my voice shaking with fear. I'm calling his bluff, and gambling with my life, and he must know that I'm terrified.

His fist seems to come from nowhere, and the knuckles of his uninjured hand connect with my face. My nose explodes. For just a second, this pain overtakes the fire that's blazing through the rest of my body. Consciousness begins to slip away. I fight back against oblivion, my brain struggling against my body's instinct to protect me from pain. I need to feel it to remain conscious. And, more importantly, I need him to believe that I'm useful.

He cradles his left hand. 'You'll tell me how to get out of here or I will kill you.'

His tone is matter-of-fact. Whether I live or die is not important to him.

He's won. It's not worth holding on to my knowledge if it'll die with me. I don't have any choice but to help him escape. Perhaps, if he can get out, there will be a way out for me, too.

'OK,' I gasp. 'I'll tell you. I'll tell you what you need to know.'

'I thought you might,' he says smugly. He sways a little, then seems to lose his balance for a second, tipping to his left. He rights himself, but grips the edge of the table for support. Maybe what he said was true – maybe I could attack him if I was free.

'There will be an aftershock, and probably soon,' I croak. 'When it hits, you need to drop, cover, and hold.'

My lip hurts when I speak, and now that my nose is filled with what must be blood, I can only breathe through my mouth, which is covered in a glue-like layer of saliva-moistened dust. I'm so thirsty. 'You need to get as low as you can, stay under something solid, like a table ... I can't see around the room properly to tell you the best place to go—'

'Under the gurney you're lying on, probably,' he cuts in. So that's what it is. My eyebrows draw together as I try to work out why a hospital gurney would be inside an abandoned basement, but I dismiss the question and concentrate on making myself essential to this man's survival.

'That'll work,' I reply thickly, my head still ringing from

71

the impact of his punch. 'So then once you're under, hold on tight so you stay under it with one hand. With the other, cover the back of your head. The gurney should protect you from getting crushed.'

I try not to think about the words I'm not saying: My body will be crushed instead of yours.

'Is that it?' he asks scornfully. 'I mean, for someone who's an expert, that's kind of just common sense.'

'No, that's not it,' I say, desperate to assure him that I'm of use. 'We need to cover our mouths and noses.'

I don't point out that I'm not an earthquake expert. I'm an emergency preparedness expert, which includes knowing what to do in case of an earthquake, but it mostly means being prepared for one, so that people aren't stuck in situations like the one I've found myself in. He doesn't need to know that. I need him to believe I can get him out of this. I need to believe it, too.

'I guess you're OK, that mask is probably protecting your airways pretty well. But I could really do with something over my mouth. Do you think you could . . . ?'

I let my words trail off. He's clearly not impressed with my knowledge so far. I haven't given him everything he needs to survive, but maybe it's enough for him to give me something – even just a way to breathe freely – in return.

'You're not in a position to negotiate, Alice.'

I clench my jaw. I hate to admit it, but I know he's right. The only way I'm going to get anything from him is if I can make myself indispensable.

Guilt nags at my conscience as I offer meagre scraps of information to this man, but I don't have time to think about the ethics of my own survival. Because, in the end, this isn't about keeping him alive at all. It's about finding a way to get out of here, and to make sure he ends up behind bars, where he belongs. Helping him is the only chance I have to do those things.

I try to look around. I can't see the whole room. I can't assess our situation properly. But I'll have to try.

'You said there's no exit?' I ask.

'There was only one to begin with, but that doorway has collapsed. We're in a basement, so I guess there's been some kind of collapse above us. The staircase is just rubble now. I tried to shift some of the debris when I woke up, but there's too much, and it's too heavy. I don't think I can dig my way out, and in the state you're in...' He trails off as his neck swivels, his eyes doing a visual sweep of my body. 'I think I'm stuck.'

I cringe at his use of the word 'I'. Like I don't exist. Like this is all about making sure he's all right.

'OK.' I nod, resigned to the fact that I'm assisting a killer to save my own skin, even while knowing that I might die anyway. I can't see an alternative. 'No one knows we're here, which means no one will know to look for us in the building. It looks abandoned, is that right?'

The mask bobs up and down, a nod, then disappears from view.

'Hello?'

'Just... I just need a second,' he says, breathing heavily. There's a long, agonising silence, and then there's a pained heaving sound. The vomiting comes in waves. I lie still, waiting for it to pass, or for him to die. But his breathing doesn't end – it's so loud there's no doubt he's still alive.

'I didn't tell you to stop,' he groans. 'Keep going.'

'Are we near the city? Or is this a remote area?'

'It's—' He hesitates, as if weighing up whether or not I can be trusted with our location. 'It's really none of your business, Alice.'

Balling my fists in frustration, I consider pressing him for more information, but decide it isn't important enough to risk upsetting him again. He might be on the ground now, but his anger when he punched me seemed to come from nowhere. I don't need any more injuries.

'Fine. Is it safe to say, though, that there won't be lots of people walking around outside or, say, needing rescue nearby?'

'Well... it's not impossible, but they're not exactly going to be searching for anyone in here.'

'Great,' I groan. 'So... in a normal disaster situation, with emergency services stretched to capacity, we could expect rescue in around seventy-two hours. But without them knowing where we are or looking for people generally in the area, it could take much longer. Which means we'll probably die of dehydration before they even have a chance of finding us.'

The mask appears beside me again. I can't see his expression, but if I could guess, I'd say there's horror concealed under that white plastic. He looks around the room, as though seeing it for the first time.

'Where am I going to get water from?'

'That's what I'm going to help you with,' I say quickly, reminding him that I'm the one with the information, that he needs me alive. 'Is my backpack here? Did you bring it?'

'What?'

'My backpack, I had it with me when... well... before. It has a full water bottle in it. That'll keep us going until we can find another water source. Did you bring it here with me?'

I silently thank Celia for always insisting that we refill our bottles at the top of the Grind. 'You need to keep hydrating, even if you're not feeling thirsty,' she always tells me, and I always roll my eyes. When I get out of here, I'll have to tell her that she was right.

My mind tries to flit away, to thoughts of whether my friend survived, whether the twins are OK, whether my family is still alive, but I can't let myself go there. I can't bear to consider any scenario in which we don't all make it through this. I need all the hope I can muster right now, so I need to stay positive, and believe the best.

'Uh . . . yeah,' the man mutters, 'it was around here somewhere.'

He's looking down, as though somehow my backpack might magically appear at his feet.

'If you untie me—'

'I've already told you, I'm not letting you go,' he snaps. 'I'll find your goddamn bag. Just give me a minute.'

He stumbles out of view, his movements so jerky and erratic that if I didn't know better, I'd think he was drunk. He mumbles to himself as he picks his way through the ruins, tripping and swearing along the way. The revelation about how long we might have to wait for rescue, as well as the bombshell about our water situation, seems to have shocked him into action. Which is a good thing, because it means that I've told him something he didn't know. And that means maybe – just maybe – he'll see the value of keeping me alive.

But I still have almost no leverage. Either I keep as many survival tips to myself as I can, drip-feeding him as he does things for me, or I give him more information now to make him see that I really am an expert, and therefore too valuable to kill.

For now, I'll try to play it somewhere in the middle. I'll give him enough information to make him see that I really can help us survive. But I won't give him everything. And, if I sense that I'm in danger, if I think he might try again to kill me, I'll remind him that I still know more.

It's risky. But I can't see another way.

'While you're looking,' I call out into the darkness, 'there are a few other things you should know.'

He makes a sort of hmm sound, although it sounds more pained than interested.

'If there's a gas leak, we could be in serious trouble,' I tell him. 'So keep an ear out for a hissing sound. And obviously, if you smell gas, we'll have to find a way to plug it. Fires could also be a problem, but I don't see any starting in here, unless there's some kind of electrical issue. Which reminds me, there could be live electrical wires around, so be careful. We can't access the mains, so we really just have to hope that there are no problems there.'

'The power's off,' he says. I shrug, although he doesn't see it.

'Still,' I say. 'Stay alert.'

There's another lull. Minutes go by, accompanied by the sounds of pieces of debris being picked through, moved aside, stumbled over, punctuated by the occasional curse. From what I can see of the room, it's almost impossible to move through. It's slow going.

After what feels like hours, there's a triumphant 'Aha!'

I crane my neck to try to see what he's found. He's crouched down across the room, his back turned to me. My neck screams with the effort.

'Did you find it?'

'Yes. But – oh, shit.'

'What?'

He holds up my water bottle in one hand, and something else in the other. I struggle to make out the details, but even from a few feet away, in the flickering darkness, I can see that the water bottle is empty. In his other hand is the lid, shredded like a threadbare rag. It's heartbreaking.

'We have to find a water source, then. It's that, or we both die.'

I use the word we, wanting to reinforce to him that he's not in this by himself. That there's more than just his own life at stake. Chances are, he doesn't care. But I have to try. He looks at me, those blank, hollow holes that hide his eyes pointed towards me for several agonising seconds, and then he tips his head slightly, as though just remembering something.

'That's impossible,' he tells me. 'I've tested the faucets, the whole building's shut off.'

'There may be a way,' I say as he begins the laborious process of working his way back towards me, holding the useless bottle.

My mind races through everything I've ever learned, every piece of information that might be relevant, or useful.

'Did you remember seeing a water heater?' I ask when he's back by my side. 'Because if you did, then we might—'

I don't get to finish my sentence, because the room tips violently, and the shaking, roaring, rolling nightmare envelops us once again.

There's a strangled cry, and I see a flash of movement as my captor dives under the gurney, protecting himself from the force of the aftershock.

Chapter 18

ALICE

The worst day of my life was a crisp, sunny Tuesday in March. I was seventeen, and my best friend Mel had just turned eighteen. We were excited; bursting with all of the possibilities that lay ahead of us.

We were going camping that weekend. Mel's parents were letting her borrow their car, and we were planning to drive to Tsawwassen, where we'd catch the ferry to Duke Point and drive to whatever remote beach we could find, somewhere we could drink and smoke in peace, without any adults telling us we shouldn't.

It should have been me.

I was going to pick up a tent from an ex-colleague of my brother's. He didn't need it anymore and he told us, through Craig, that we could have it if we collected it before Wednesday, when he'd otherwise be throwing it in the trash. I was chasing a deadline on an English essay, so Mel offered to go and meet this kind stranger instead of me. She was in his apartment building when the fire broke out, seven floors below.

The fire system in the building had been neglected by the landlord for years, so no alarm went off when the elderly woman's toaster went up in flames. By the time Mel smelled the smoke, there was no way out. She was too high to jump, trapped by an inferno that was altogether preventable.

It should never have happened. No one should have died. But still. If someone had to have died, it should have been me.

There have been times over the years when I've thought my parents might be right. Perhaps I have spent my life indirectly trying to save Mel, the noble but ultimately impossible mission of a grieving teen who didn't realise that life could be so randomly cruel, that accidents could – and did – happen. I obsessed over the fact that it could have so easily been prevented. It haunted me.

After Mel's funeral, I'd called the university I'd been provisionally accepted by, and I told them that I no longer wanted to study History. I wanted to be enrolled in their Emergency Management programme.

That tragic, sunny Tuesday propelled me into a career focused solely on making sure things like that didn't happen to other people's best friend, sister, daughter.

That Tuesday was the worst day of my life.

Until today.

Terror floods me as the room bucks and shakes and rolls. I fling my head to the left, an attempt to cover my airways with my hair – anything to keep breathing. A few strands fall across my cheek, but not enough to act as a mask. I tuck my chin into my collarbone and press my face into my shoulder like before, straining to manoeuvre my neck into the awkward position I need to be in to cover my nose. The muscles in my neck and shoulders cramp violently, but at least I'm getting some oxygen, rather than clouds of toxic dust.

Fragments of rubble fall on me like lethal rain. Each time something makes contact, my already-bruised flesh screams in protest, and when a solid chunk of debris hits my leg I cry out, a primal noise that I feel in my bones.

The only thing I can control is keeping my breathing as shallow as possible to make sure my airways are clear, so that's what I focus all of my attention on. Anything to avoid thinking about what's actually happening, how close I am to death.

I mentally chant *twenty-eight, twenty-nine, thirty, thirty-one,* and then the sounds begin to change.

The rumbling softens. The trembling slows. There's a long, painful tearing sound, as though the walls are being ripped apart. And then, as suddenly as it began, the aftershock stops.

I pant into my top, but otherwise I remain totally still. The room is still precarious. Things I can't see fall and crumble, some close, some distant, coming from outside. Perhaps from other rooms in this building, maybe other buildings altogether. My senses are all off, and the sounds are coming from every direction.

But after a few minutes silence descends on me again, stretching wide, reminding me that I can do nothing but wait. To be rescued, or to die with the man in the mask. That's when the one thing I've been desperately trying not to think about looms too large to ignore.

Today was meant to be the day. Instead of being here, I should be at the surgery. Instead of being buried alive with someone who wants me dead, I should be on the brink of my dreams coming true.

Today's the day I should be getting pregnant.

Chapter 19

ALICE

I've always wanted to be a mom.

As a kid, whenever I imagined my life as an adult I saw myself surrounded by a whole brood of children. I pictured a busy, noisy household with constant movement and laughter and shouts. I'd be married, of course, in this imagined future. My husband and I would have a nice house, a big yard, and in winter he would hose down the street so the kids could play hockey with the neighbours.

But life had other plans for me.

I've never worked out exactly how I ended up so far off course, but I think it was incremental, rather than a dramatic veering in a new direction. Mel's death changed my career path, perhaps made me nervous of getting close to new people, but I know the blame doesn't lie entirely with that single event. A few of my friends found their partners when they were young, but many didn't. Like me, they were having too much fun to worry about anything so permanent. I dated. I had boyfriends, although none serious enough to consider marrying, or having babies with. Those things lay somewhere down the road, far ahead of me, inevitable but as yet out of sight. They were tomorrow's problem.

Only tomorrow never arrived, and suddenly I was in my mid-thirties, and most of my friends were married and having babies, or trying to, and I was still single. I panicked, then. Not my proudest moment, but I tried a slew of dating apps and blind dates in a frantic attempt to course-correct, dating a few men I'd never normally spend time with, because I worried that they were my only chance to have the thing I'd always wanted: a family of my own.

I'd hold friend's babies and feel that pull inside me, the inexplicable need to hold my own, and when I got back to my lovely and quiet and completely empty condo I'd long for nothing more than milk stains and cries and sleepless nights – all the things my friends told me I should be grateful not to have to worry about.

At a routine check-up earlier this year, I confided with my doctor that I wanted children but was worried that, as my mom had often warned me, my biological clock was ticking. She'd sent me for a fertility test, which revealed that I only had a few viable eggs remaining. They recommended extracting them, freezing them. They pressed brochures into my hand. I went home dazed, hollow.

A few days later, I read the brochures. The disaster planner in me went into solution-finding mode, and soon I was booking an appointment to extract and freeze my eggs, and providing my bank details for the exorbitant fee. It was a first step, but it wasn't the full solution. My eggs would be safe, but I still wanted to have children, preferably before I was fifty, and if I waited around for the right guy, that might never happen. I wasn't going to settle for some guy who happened to be single and interested, just to get pregnant. But, as the brochures explained, there were other ways.

It was shocking to me that I'd never considered it before, never even entertained the idea of parenting alone. I knew I could do it, knew I'd be a great mom, fully capable, fully involved. I had my parents, Celia, a supportive workplace. I knew married women who had far less support than I would have. And suddenly it didn't just seem like *an* option; I knew it was *the* option.

Since then I've been waiting for today, counting down to the moment when I might finally, after all this time, become a mom.

But instead of lying on a comfy, clean clinic bed, my stomach in excited knots, I'm tied to a cold metal gurney, my stomach filled with dread as I recover from an aftershock.

This is not how today was supposed to go.

Rage pulses through me as the man in the mask crawls out from his hiding place slowly, tentatively, coughing and snivelling. He steadies himself against the gurney, his hands right next to me, and looks me up and down, assessing my frame.

'Where's the water?' he croaks.

'I'm not telling you, you asshole,' I wheeze. If I had the energy, and if my mouth wasn't so clogged with blood and dust, I'd have spat at him. 'You're going to let me die while you survive? Forget it. If I die, you're dying with me.'

'Tell me how to find water!' he roars in my face, the mask close enough for me to feel a puff of air against my cheek.

'No,' I say defiantly, setting my jaw. I don't want to die, but I'm not sure I have a choice anymore. I'm injured. I don't know how badly, but I know that I've been unbelievably lucky so far; nothing has crushed me to death. But there will be more aftershocks, and the next one, or maybe the one after that, will kill me if I'm still strapped down.

If he punches me again, it's his loss. I know how to find water . . . he doesn't.

I turn my head to the side to protect my nose and mouth against the impact I know is coming, but it never arrives. After a few seconds of waiting, I face him. He seems to have come to the same realisation as I have. His arms hang limply by his side, and his head is heavy against his chest. The wound on his forehead glistens with dark, fresh blood.

'Please,' he says, his voice quiet and trembling. Then he sobs, a great, loud, self-pitying cry. Despite the dire situation I'm in, I have to resist the urge to laugh at him, at his pathetic reaction.

'Please,' he whispers again between sobs. 'I'll untie you. I'll do it now. Here.'

My heart stutters hopefully as he begins working at the restraint on my right wrist, his fingers trembling so violently that I can feel the shaking through the fabric that's holding me down. He struggles to grip the webbing, his gloved hands fumbling at the buckle, loosening it until I can wriggle my hand free. With a surge of triumph, I flex my fingers and roll my wrist, blood flowing back to my hands. It's blissful.

He moves around the table, untying me bit by bit until I'm able to move my arms and legs freely. I want to sit up, but I'm terrified. I don't know if big movements will cause me to lose consciousness, or do some kind of irreversible internal damage.

Instead, I use my hands to probe my body for signs of injury. I'm bruised everywhere, but the worst pain is in my chest, where I can't even brush the fabric of my top without crying out in agony. There's a strange lump, just above my left breast, and when I press it softly with a fingertip, the pain makes me gasp. My abdomen is tender, but no more so than anywhere else. I wonder whether I'll be able to get pregnant after all of this, if I survive, or whether all of those months of hormones and hope will have been for nothing.

'I've only untied you so that you'll find the water,' he mumbles, sitting heavily on the ground. 'So you'd better deliver.'

I shift my head so I can look at him, but he's hugging his legs to his chest, his face planted on his knees. All I can see is the top of his head, his brown hair matted with blood, and covered in the ashes of the dying building.

'Did you see a water heater?' I pant, knowing that I need to get on with finding water, not just because I'm thirsty, but because then I can plan what to do next. 'Before the earthquake?'

The mask tilts to one side reminding me, absurdly, of a mime deep in thought. His head wound is still bleeding quite badly, and blood dribbles a gruesome trail down the white plastic.

'There might have been one, but I can't remember. I came here before, to . . . well, to make sure everything was perfect.'

My mind slides over the horror of what he's saying, over the word perfect. I can't let myself dwell on what might have been, on what still might be to come.

'I looked around, back when the plan was just—' He pauses, laughs. 'I planned so well. I planned for everything – well, I thought I had.'

I resist the urge to confess that I can relate. Planning is my life, my career, my passion. And yet, here I am. Here we both are, our plans in tatters. I wonder briefly what my colleagues would think if they knew I, the professional disaster planner, found myself without a plan. But there's no time to dwell on my job. I have work to do.

The man in the mask doesn't offer any further information, and I decide that I'll just have to search the room myself, see if I can find the water heater he may or may not have seen.

Gingerly, I slide my legs over to the right-hand side of the gurney until they're dangling off the edge. Then I use my elbows to sit up, whimpering with every tiny movement.

Eventually, though, I'm sitting, my legs over the edge of the metal table, my body upright. The effort is so exhausting that I consider lying right back down again. But I need to move. Moving means surviving.

Glancing down to make sure I'm not being watched, I grip the bottom hem of my top. It hurts to twist my body, but I clench my jaw and pull it over my head, stifling a scream. Once it's completely off, I use my teeth to create a small tear in the bottom hem. It takes a bit of gnawing, but eventually the fabric breaks, just a fraction. I pull at either side of it and watch the shirt splitting up the middle. When the tear is long enough, I take one piece of it and pull parallel to the hem, until a whole whole strip has separated from the bottom.

I reach up gently and wrap the strip of Lycra around my head so the cleaner side, the part that was touching my stomach, is pressed against my bloodied nose and mouth. Immediately, breathing is easier, although my ribs are still on fire.

Part of me doesn't want to see how much damage has been done to my body, but I can't avoid looking. I'm horrified to see that my stomach is slick and red, although when I gently wipe it – smudging dust into the blood and making a dark, gritty mud – I can only see a couple of small cuts.

I pull my top back on, confident that there's nothing I can do to mend my own broken body. I need medical attention, but it will have to wait.

I didn't need to worry about being exposed. The man in the mask is still moaning into his lap, still completely absorbed with his own discomfort, and I'm relieved that he didn't see anything. For a moment, I wonder if I should attack him – take him out while he's vulnerable, knock him unconscious. But I'm too weak. If I hit him, it has to be hard enough to render him harmless. Otherwise he'll just kill me. I can't take a risk like that; not yet. Before I can even think about fighting, I need to regain some of my strength. Which means I need water.

I manage – slowly, wincing with every movement – to slide off the gurney until I'm half standing, half leaning on the metallic table. I look around as much as I can without moving my torso, desperately trying not to pass out from the pain.

When I try to stand, pain shoots up my right leg. I don't think it's broken, perhaps just badly bruised, but I can't put my full weight on it without it buckling. My left leg isn't much better, either; every time I try to balance on it, my hip protests violently. I tell myself that I can do this, that I have no choice. Because the alternative is giving up, and that's not an option.

I remind myself of the people I've read about who have survived incredible pain. There was the guy who had to cut his own arm off to escape a canyon. The people who almost froze to death on Everest, but who lived to tell the tale. There must be countless stories like that, where people pushed through their suffering in order to survive. I have to channel whatever strength it was they tapped into.

'Where did you see the heater?' I ask.

'I think it's over there, under the stairs. Well, where the stairs used to be.' A shaking finger points to a corner of the room I haven't seen yet. It was out of my line of sight when I was strapped down.

He's far less injured than I am, far more capable of movement – even with his concussed stagger – and yet he's sitting there expectantly, his finger stretched towards the dark unknown.

I wonder if I should just refuse to help him, accept that

I'm going to die, and make sure he dies with me; one final, selfless act. I probably should. But something – survival instinct, I suppose – tells me that I have to do what it takes to stay alive while there's still a chance of getting out, no matter how slim. I clench my fists. For now, I have to do what he says.

Because he's still capable of killing me.

He still might want to.

Chapter 20

The Edmonton Press

**Magnitude 9.1 quake devastates Pacific Northwest
by Mitchell Walters
12 October, 2018**

A magnitude 9.1 earthquake shook the city of
Vancouver, B.C., along with several major cities along the
Pacific Northwest at 10:19 a.m. today, with widespread
damage reported already. Experts suggest the death toll
could reach tens of thousands.

Just twenty minutes after the quake, the west coast
of Vancouver Island was hit by multiple tsunamis, with
waves as high as fifty feet. Warning sirens, triggered by
the earthquake, gave residents an opportunity to escape
to shelters and designated safe zones further inland, but
for many, escape was simply not possible.

The city of Vancouver suffered extensive damage,
with many buildings in the downtown area collapsing
in the initial quake and the 7.3 magnitude aftershock
that followed soon after. Tremors were reportedly felt
as far south as Sacramento, California, and as far east as
Lethbridge, although the damage outside of these main
metropolitan areas has been minimal.

Troops are reportedly preparing to be deployed from

across the country to Vancouver, where there are an estimated ten thousand residents stranded and in need of assistance. Many hospitals in the area were severely damaged, so helicopters are being sent to Vancouver to transport those in need of urgent care to facilities in other parts of British Columbia, as well as Alberta, Washington State and even Oregon.

Emergency services coordinator Ed McBride asked Canadians to stay calm, and to make the work of the first responders as easy as possible.

'We understand that people are worried about their loved ones in the Vancouver area,' he said during this morning's press conference. 'But right now, phone services are limited and we need the lines to be kept clear for emergencies. We ask that you refrain from making phone calls to anyone in the Vancouver area for the time being. We will issue more information as we're able, but please be assured that we are doing everything we can to get as many people on the ground for the rescue operation as possible.'

An emergency fund has been set up, and those wishing to donate can do so on this page.

More on this story here.

Chapter 21

ALICE

I scan the room, trying to make out shapes and objects in the dim light of the lamp that's still hanging from a beam, hunting greedily for any way of escape. But all the walls look solid, and there's no sign of a door.

There's a washing machine and tumble dryer in the corner closest to me. The appliances have survived, although after the violence of the quake, the door of the washer is holding on by what seems like a tiny piece of plastic. Next to the dryer is a small metal cupboard, still closed, and above it, a sink.

That's where I'll start my search. It's closer than the corner I've been instructed to check, and if there's a working water source, we won't need to try the water heater route.

'I'll try here first,' I say, not waiting for his permission before I turn my body around as gently as I can.

'I told you already, the water's off.'

'I know,' I say. 'But just in case.'

He's probably right. But I'm not going to take his word for it. I'm not going to be foolish enough to trust him. The only thing he's said that I believe is that there's no exit. If there was a way out, he'd have escaped already, leaving me strapped to the gurney to die.

I take a tentative step on my left leg, which protests, but

I know this pain is nothing compared with what I'll feel when I put weight on my right leg. Gritting my teeth, I step forward. I choke back a scream, almost crumpling to the floor, but I manage to stay upright, and I force myself to carry on.

As I take my next step on my left leg, there's a crack from behind me. My heart hammers against my crushed ribcage. Is he moving around? Suddenly I realise: I don't know where his saw is, the one he was going to hack my arm off with before the quake hit. What if he's finding it among the rubble now, so he can continue with his original mission? My mouth goes dry, but I tell myself that I'm imagining things, that he won't kill me. Not yet, anyway. Not until I find water.

I take another step on my right leg, and stifle the scream that races up my chest. If I cry out, I won't hear whatever noises he's making. I won't hear him sneaking up on me, raising his saw up, bringing it down on my neck—

Spiralling into a state of pure panic, I half hop, half stumble the last few steps over to the sink, yelping as my leg catches on a pile of fallen bricks. I grip the edge of the sink with all my weight, preparing for it to collapse, taking me with it.

Miraculously, it holds. I look over my shoulder, expecting him to be looming behind me, saw in his hand, his eyes gleaming manically. But he's still huddled over by the gurney, watching, motionless.

My mouth is dry with the stress of it. I slide onto the floor, panting from the exertion of my journey.

When I make it back to the gurney, I need to find his saw, and keep it out of his reach. If it's still intact, I can use it. I can gain the upper hand. I'll have a weapon.

'What are you doing?' his deep voice rings out across the shadowy room.

I shake my head and lift my hand, unable to catch my breath. When my lungs find a kind of rhythm and I'm able to speak again, I call out: 'I need a break. This isn't going to be quick.'

'Well, just – don't do anything stupid.'

I'm not sure if it's a tip, or a warning.

Gathering my strength, I remind myself that I have no choice but to keep going. I move like a sloth, the only way of making sure I don't pass out. I feel like I'm decades older than I am as I push myself onto my hands and knees, then with a burst of movement I grab the sink to heave myself onto my feet again. My muscles sing their complaints, but I ignore them as I turn to one side, knowing that no matter what I do, I'll be in pain.

I can't let him out of my sight. I can't stand not knowing. Shifting so he's visible out of the corner of my right eye, I lean over and twist the tap. Nothing happens. My heart drops, but I'm not surprised. My guess is that, if this building has been abandoned, the water supply was switched off ages ago. I try the other one, just in case, but the faucet remains dry.

'You should have listened to me,' his tone is low. It sounds less like gloating, and more like a threat. 'I told you there was no water.'

'I know. You did,' I say quickly, wanting to placate him, my face still aching from the impact of his fist. I can't tell him that I simply don't trust anything he says. 'I wanted to check, just in case the earthquake loosened something up, got water flowing through the pipes.'

I hope it sounds plausible. I don't know if an earthquake

could do that. Probably not. He doesn't reply, so I turn to face the opposite corner of the room.

As I move, I spot a piece of dull red plastic on the floor next to me, which might once have been a mop handle, now broken in two. I reach over and pick up the longer of the pieces, sizing it up. I hold the smooth end of it in my right hand, and dig the jagged end firmly into the ground. Then I test it, putting my weight on the makeshift walking stick instead of on my leg. It works. It's not going to get me around the room gracefully, and it won't dull the pain, but it might save me from further injury.

I glance over at the man in the mask again. He's watching me hobble, watching me watch him as I go, across the debris towards the corner he pointed at. He said the heater might be under the stairs, but I can't see any stairs. That whole area of the room has been decimated, with rubble piled upon rubble, as though the entire side of the building has collapsed. He's right – we can't dig our way out of here.

While I'm picking my way across the room, I try to size up the man hunched on the floor by the gurney. He's not particularly tall; at a guess, I'd say a few inches short of six feet. Decidedly average. Nor is he bulky. His arms aren't threatening to burst through the seams of his shirt, and he doesn't have bulging veins in his neck. He's not the bodybuilding type, but he's solid. Strong.

I knew that already, thanks to the punch he delivered with his, presumably, non-dominant hand. I'd hate to know the state I'd be in if he'd used his full strength. Apart from the gash on his head, he doesn't seem badly hurt. There's no blood on his body, his arms, his legs. It seems he got off pretty lightly, with little more than concussion.

In any case, he's stronger than me, and in much better condition. There's no way I could overpower him, not with my injuries. I'm not going to get out of this with force. I have to be smart.

I don't have to cover a great distance to reach my destination – it's probably only twenty feet or so, from one corner to the other – but it feels insurmountable. Bits of concrete and brick and wood and insulation and other random items: a plastic chair here, a bucket there, are piled up, obstacles that wouldn't be difficult to navigate if I was uninjured. Wounds aside, I have no choice but to move slowly and carefully. Any movement could cause an avalanche that could kill me.

I step cautiously, using the mop handle as a probe, as well as for support, to hobble across the room, stopping every couple of steps to catch my breath, to check what he's doing, and to look around for signs of daylight, cracks in the building big enough to squeeze through. There's nothing, though. Just solid walls, rubble and dust.

Eventually, I reach the far side of the room, panting as though I've just reached the summit of the Grind. Squinting, I peer into the gloomy corner I've arrived at, and can just make out the shape of what was once a staircase. A few steps remain, but the entire middle section has collapsed, leaving just a few stairs at the top, almost entirely hidden by chunks of concrete and wood, and a couple at the very bottom, leading nowhere.

And there's a door. It's directly beneath the upper portion of the staircase, still intact, the handle attached. For a second, hope is kindled inside me. This could be a way out. Perhaps this door is my escape, and I'll open it and be in the outside world. Even as I think it, I know it's just a desperate wish. But I am desperate.

Pausing to make sure I'm balanced, I reach my hand out to touch the handle of the cupboard door. Slowly, cautiously – because I have no idea what's on the other side, what could have flown around in the quake and could come hurling out at me – I pull. The door widens just a couple of inches until it smacks against a brick at my feet and stops short.

Using the mop handle, I push the brick aside to clear a path for the door and I try again, this time with a little more force. The movement of pulling the door sends knives of pain slicing through the muscles along my right side, but I close my eyes and command my brain to ignore it.

When I open them again, I manage a small, weak smile of triumph. There's a water heater inside.

Maybe I can survive being trapped, after all.

I just need to work out how to survive the man I'm trapped with.

Chapter 22

BILL

It isn't Bill's shift today.

He's at home with Chris and the kids, enjoying a lazy breakfast and planning a trip to Stanley Park to cycle the Seawall, when the earthquake starts.

They've done drills before, the four of them, diving under tables and holding on. The kids thought it was fun, then. They don't when the house is shuddering and their belongings are flung from shelves and cupboards by an invisible hand, and a crack appears in the wall opposite their dining table, where they're all huddled together for shelter.

But it's over now. At least, the main quake is over. There will be aftershocks, Bill knows.

He quickly clears the dining room, making sure there's nothing left to fly around and cause injury. He instructs the kids to stay where they are while he fetches their bike helmets, and Chris rummages in the supply cupboard for the box of food and candles and blankets. They're all set up, as safe as they can be, when Bill gets on to the radio he keeps in the kitchen for this very purpose.

He knows he'll be needed today. And he also knows that his family will be OK. They've prepared for this. There are even some games in that big plastic box, so Chris will be all right for a day or so. They've talked this through. They're a team.

The radio crackles and snaps, and then his chief's voice fills the air around him.

'Caruthers, that you?'

'Yes, sir. How can I help?'

'Your family's OK?'

'Yes, sir. They're set for a few days at least, if necessary.'

'Good, good. Roads are chaos. How long do you think it'll take you by foot?'

Bill knows the answer to this. He's run to work plenty of times before.

'Twenty minutes, maybe longer if there are obstructions.'

'OK, just get here as quickly as you can, but be safe. Helmet and boots. And a respirator. The dust is bad.'

'Roger that,' Bill says. 'See you soon.'

He hangs up the phone and gets himself ready, clutching a water bottle and pocketing a few protein bars, just in case. He kisses Chris, Tanner and Amelia, his heart swelling as he takes a moment to be grateful that they're all unharmed. He knows how lucky he was to be home when the earthquake began. Many of the guys he'll work alongside today won't have the luxury of knowing their loved ones are safe.

'I love you,' he says, peering under the table.

'I love you too,' three voices reply.

Bill puts on the helmet and respirator the captain ordered him to wear and steps out of his front door.

He sucks in a breath, adrenaline beginning to course through him as he considers what he'll be dealing with.

Power lines are strewn across the road, cars are parked at strange angles, and a huge crack, at least a foot wide, has appeared in the sidewalk outside Bill's home. He looks up, in the direction of the city, and his heart plummets as he sees a cloud of brown dust, thick as smoke, ascending into the otherwise clear blue sky.

This is worse than he imagined.

He begins running, pushing himself harder than usual, because he knows that every second is crucial. It's going to be a long, long day.

Chapter 23

THE SCULPTOR

Logically, I'm aware that I have more pressing matters to worry about – my throbbing head, for example, or how the hell I'm going to get out of here – but the only thing I can think about, the single thought that's running through my mind, over and over again, is how deeply unfair this is.

This isn't what I wanted. This isn't what I asked for.

My work, my art . . . it was mandated by a higher power. Exactly what – or who – the supply of this power is, I'm yet to find out.

I don't think it's God, at least not the one I learned about the few times I was dragged to Sunday School by my Aunt Jocelyn, a severe woman we saw rarely, which was still far too often. The God I was introduced to there appeared to be fairly clear about his stance on murder. A God that was so against killing others seemed an unlikely candidate for encouraging me to dispose of women, no matter how divinely beautiful the resultant art would be.

Other gods, I learned after researching, frantically seeking the source of my vision, felt the same way about taking another's life. So religion wasn't going to help me get to the bottom of my mystery.

In the end, unable to pinpoint the entity that created The Sculptor, I settled on my own name for it: divine energy.

My point is, where the hell is this supposed divine energy, now that I really, really need it? Because, honestly, if there's a higher power on my side, as I've been assuming for all these years, since that hiker came my way, now would be a great time for it to show up.

And if this same energy could reach down into my soul and bestow upon me the gift of inspiration, why can't it get me out of here? Or, perhaps a better question: why did it lead me here, to this Muse, today?

That's the thing that's so unfair about all of this. I didn't ask to be the facilitator of this whole thing. All I wanted was to create beautiful art, to create something that mattered, to leave a legacy. It's not like I begged the universe to send a solution that involved women sacrificing their lives.

But now I am begging.

I'm asking for something in return for my servitude, my unflinching commitment to creating works of art so beautiful they're worthy of the process they demand. I'm asking for a way out.

Not just because I'm scared for my own life.

Not just because I'm trapped, buried under brick and steel and concrete and glass, with the Muse whose arm lured me here, who has seen far too much. But because she's not the only one I need to worry about.

There's the other Muse. The one in the white room. She was there when the earthquake hit.

But now – well, now she could be anywhere.

Which means she could be the end of me.

Chapter 24

LUCY

Fourteen Hours Ago

The black and white photograph – already artistically blurred – became even more indecipherable as Lucy squinted to make sense of it.

'Is it . . . is it like, a sandwich?' she whispered to Stephen.

'Uhhm—' He considered her theory. 'You might be right. I've been staring at it for a solid five minutes, and I'd convinced myself it was a stack of mattresses.'

'Well, damn. I thought it was a centipede,' Jackie snorted.

Lucy laughed along with them, but she managed to quickly rearrange her expression as Maria, striking in a sparkling, multi-coloured dress, sidled up beside them.

'Well?' she asked.

'You're incredible,' Lucy said enthusiastically. 'Congrats again, I can't believe you have your own show!'

Maria laughed, delighted, and held out a long-stemmed flute, filled with champagne, for her friends to clink their own glasses against. They acquiesced, and for a few moments the four of them sipped in silence, all staring at the giant print on the wall before them.

'So . . .' Maria pressed. 'What do you think?'

'It's—' Lucy paused, unsure whether to be honest, at the risk of offending her oldest friend. After a few seconds, she exhaled dramatically and confessed, 'We've been debating whether this one's a sandwich, a centipede or some mattresses, so we really need you to step in and let us know what we're looking at here.'

Maria threw her head back and cackled. A few people turned to see the source of the disturbance, but they quickly went back to mingling and eating tiny, pointless canapés.

'Well, which is it?' Stephen asked.

'A magician doesn't reveal her secrets,' Maria said with a wink, laughing again and drifting away to a small group of guests who were gathering around a photo of what could conceivably be either a cat's tail or a household duster.

'We're never going to know, are we?' Jackie lamented, and then, taking a deep gulp of her champagne, hissed, 'Drinks alert. Quick, finish up, the next tray is here.'

All three of them swigged the fizz from their glasses and waved the server over, swapping their empty glasses for full ones.

'God,' Stephen said. 'I don't know how she deals with these people.'

Lucy nodded as she took a generous sip of her champagne. The bubbles seemed to travel instantly to her head, making the world around her just a little bit softer, the edges less sharp.

'Ugh,' she said. 'I know what you mean.'

She glanced around the room at the other guests – men in bow ties with carefully-groomed beards, and women in stylishly oversized jackets and designer glasses – but her eyes seemed to slide off everyone without absorbing the details.

'I think I'm tipsy,' she announced, to no one in particular.

'That's because these canapés are so damn tiny that eating them makes you more hungry,' Jackie said.

Lucy's stomach growled in response.

'Shall we get burritos?' Stephen asked.

'Definitely,' Jackie said. 'I'm in. Luce?'

'Absolutely. Let's go!'

She drained her glass and put it on a passing server's tray. She closed her eyes for a moment to clear her head. She definitely needed something to eat.

'Do you think Maria will be OK if we leave now?' Stephen asked.

'She'll be fine,' Lucy waved away his concern. 'We came, we showed support. She's with her art people now, anyway. Let's go say goodbye.'

They pulled their friend away from her conversation to announce their departure.

'Thanks so much for coming,' Maria said to them. 'It means a lot to have you here. Let's go for drinks soon?'

They all responded enthusiastically, and took turns hugging their friend. As Lucy wrapped her arms around Maria, she whispered in her ear, 'It's a sandwich, isn't it?'

Maria chuckled and pulled away. 'It's whatever you want it to be.'

Lucy rolled her eyes, smiling, then turned to follow the others.

'Oh, before you go,' Maria said, touching her friend lightly on the shoulder. 'You see that woman over there, in the pink blazer?'

Lucy span around and followed her finger, spotting the woman in question. She was impossibly stylish, with blunt, dark bangs and sharp, angular cheekbones. 'Yeah. What about her?'

'She owns this gallery, and she's looking for a PR. I can set up a meeting?'

Lucy inspected the black leather of her boots, heat

rushing to her cheeks. 'Oh! Uh . . . I don't know if that's a good idea . . .' She trailed off, embarrassed.

'Why not? Come on, Lucy. I know it didn't exactly work out before, but this would be an amazing opportunity. You should at least meet with her.'

'I'm not ready. I still don't have—'

'Bullshit,' Maria said, stopping Lucy mid-sentence. 'That's bullshit, Luce,' she said, not unkindly. 'I know how badly you want this. And you deserve it. Don't just give up, OK?'

Lucy bristled. 'I'm not giving up. You make it sound like it's so simple.'

Maria held her hands up in surrender. 'I know it's not, Luce. I just don't want you to give up on your dreams because it's all just too hard.'

'Whatever,' Lucy said, angry now. 'I have to go.'

'Love you,' Maria said, one eyebrow raised, an infuriating smile on her face. Lucy scowled and walked away, fuming. What did Maria know? She didn't have any idea what kind of work it would take to set up a business, how risky it could be. Maria lived in the world of artists, who seemed to thrive on uncertainty, or at least were accustomed to it. Lucy wasn't a quitter. She was just – cautious.

She stalked outside and found the others huddled under the entrance, shielding themselves from the pouring rain.

'Shall we get an Uber, or make a dash for it?'

'I'm actually just going to head home,' Lucy said. Her enthusiasm for a burrito had evaporated, along with her good mood. She just wanted to curl up into Rhys's side as he watched the Seahawks game, and not have to explain herself, or her reaction to Maria's innocent, and very generous, offer to connect her to a potential client.

'Something we said?' Jackie teased, mocking offence.

'No.' Lucy forced a smile. 'I just remembered Rhys is making lasagne and I told him I'd be home for dinner.'

Jackie shrugged. 'OK, your loss though.'

Lucy pulled up the Uber app on her phone, selecting her home address and tapping Confirm UberX.

'I can drop you?' she offered. 'My ride's – uh – three minutes away.'

'It's OK,' Jackie yelled, stepping out and pulling the hood of her jacket over her hair, 'it's literally one block over. We'll be there before your car arrives. C'mon, Stephen! Bye, Luce!'

The two figures ran into the night and were quickly swallowed by the torrential downpour. Lucy swiped out of the ride-sharing app and into her messages, where she sent a quick *On my way home x* to Rhys.

'Lucy?'

A black Prius appeared in front of her, the driver squinting to see through the downpour.

'Yeah, that's me,' she shouted, dashing across the sidewalk to get in, her hair getting soaked in the process. Safely inside, she sighed, relieved to be out of the deluge. She hadn't been lying about Rhys's lasagne, just the part about promising to be home, and now her stomach grumbled again in anticipation.

'There's a charger in the middle there,' the driver said, steering away from the gallery and swinging the car into a U-turn. 'And some bottled water in the seat pocket.'

Lucy leaned forward and gratefully plucked the bottle of water from the seat pocket. The movement of the car, combined with the buzz from the champagne, was making her feel queasy.

'Thanks,' she said, taking a swig and watching the lights of the neighbourhood speed by in a watery blur. She closed her eyes and tried to forget the feeling that had overtaken her when Maria had mentioned the potential client.

Instead, she tried to sink into the drowsiness of the champagne, reminding herself that she'd be home soon, that she wasn't a quitter, she was just tired.

And she was – suddenly, alarmingly – so very, very tired.

Chapter 25

LUCY

Nine and a Half Hours Ago

It look Lucy longer than it should have done to work out that something was terribly, horribly wrong.

She emerged from unconsciousness reluctantly, kicking lazily towards awareness, sleep pulling her down like seaweed in a dark, freezing lake. But she kept fighting the draw of the deep, sluggishly at first, and then with more determination until she surfaced, panting and confused, on a polished concrete floor under bright white fluorescent lights.

Blinking, she tried to sit up. Her head throbbed in revolt against the movement. She let her body go limp and lay completely still for a few seconds, trying to work out where she was, what was happening. She wasn't at home. She wasn't anywhere she recognised. How had she ended up in a strange, silent room? She tried to work backwards, to piece together what she knew.

She had been at Maria's photography exhibition. That was the last thing she could remember. Her stomach churned and her head pounded, as if reminding her of the extra glass of champagne she'd downed before she left. The few minutes that followed came into focus, then, too. Her awkward conversation with Maria. The pelting rain. Her friends running off into the darkness, laughing, squealing, in search of Mexican food. The Uber driver. The bottle of water. The drowsiness.

Then . . . nothing.

Lucy's spine crawled with dread, her fear now in full bloom. Where was she? And how had she got there?

She sat up as gently as she could, wishing she had a painkiller handy. Her mouth was dry, and she felt sick. But before she could nurse her sorry head and rest her tender body, she had to work out where the hell she was.

Standing, she turned a slow, deliberate circle, taking in the room, horror mounting with each new inch of wall she saw. She spun again, willing her brain to see something different on the second turn.

But the reality remained: the room had no doors, no windows. No way out. Lucy looked up and down, and turned a third time, but there was no escape. Panic welled up inside her. A scream clawed its way up her throat. Bile threatened to follow. She was dizzy. Her head hurt. And she was trapped in a white box.

She forced herself to breathe, to think. She couldn't see a way out, but there had to be one. She was brought here by someone, had been left here, alone and confused and frightened. If there was a way in, there had to be a way to get out. She just hadn't found it yet. She took in the room once again, inspecting every detail this time.

The space was maybe fifteen feet long, and the same width and height, a perfect cube with polished concrete floors and shiny white walls and ceiling, made from what looked like plastic, or maybe a kind of coated metal. Something hard and clinical. And, it occurred to Lucy with a shiver of alarm, easy to clean.

Just above her eyeline was a shelf. It was about halfway up the wall directly in front of her, almost out of reach, but not quite. It looked like one of the shelves she and Rhys had considered buying when they were in IKEA just a few weeks previously, the white lacquered ones that seemed to float against the wall.

Lined up on the shiny white shelf that matched the shiny white wall were a dozen or so water bottles. Lucy rushed forward, her dry mouth desperate for relief, but as she reached up to curl her fingers around the plastic, she stopped.

The Uber. The water. The last thing she remembered. Had her water been spiked? That would explain how she had no memory of anything that followed. She lowered her hand again. She needed to stay hydrated, but she also needed to stay conscious. And, preferably, alive.

Stepping back, she continued her appraisal of the space. On the wall to the right of the one with the shelf, a huge clock was hung high up, a sleek-looking thing that was probably four feet in diameter, its glossy white face punctuated by two impossibly thin black hands, the smaller one hovering just past where Lucy imagined the number two would be, the longer hand just beyond that. So it was a quarter past two. But she couldn't tell whether it was early Friday morning, or later that day. Or, in fact, another day entirely. She suspected, judging by the still-ropey state of her stomach and head, that it had only been a few hours since she'd left the gallery.

Opposite the clock, against the wall to her left, was a metal toilet with no lid and, beside it, a tiny metal sink. On the floor in the corner, to the left of the sink, was a drain, covered by a latticed metal grate. She rushed over and, lowering herself onto her hands and knees, tried to pull the covering away, digging her fingers into the tiny gaps in the metal, tugging with all of her strength. It didn't budge.

She moved closer, her face just inches from the opening, and shouted.

'Help! Help me! Is anyone there? Hello? Can anyone hear me? Hello? Hello! I need help! I'm trapped. Help me!'

She waited, her words echoing back and bouncing around the cold, hard walls. She screamed her pleas again. And again. She screamed until her voice was hoarse and her throat felt like it was being clawed by invisible hands. And then she stopped.

Lucy rested her head groggily against the cool, shiny white of the fourth wall, the only one that was completely bare, a blank canvas. She closed her eyes. She tried not to think about what the drain was for, what would be washed down there. Her stomach seethed.

She found herself regretting that last glass of champagne, quaffed on an empty stomach, and it occurred to her – as she considered that Rhys would be looking for her, that the police would be searching, if not yet, then soon, and that the media might even get involved – that they would almost definitely report on the fact that she'd been drinking.

Fury rose up in her at the very idea. Yes, she'd had a few glasses of bubbles. But that had nothing to do with the fact that she had woken up in a doorless box. They'd probably ask what she was wearing, too, and she wondered if the answer – jeans and a leather jacket over a high-necked blue top – would make their search more thorough, their coverage more sympathetic, than if she'd been wearing a dress or, God forbid, a V-neck.

Her hands clenched into fists as she thought about it. And she decided that there was no way she was going to let her outfit, or those few glasses of celebratory bubbles, be the story they told about her. She was getting out of the room that had no escape. She was going home.

Just as soon as she could come up with a way out.

'Come on, come on, come on,' she whispered to herself. 'Facts. Start with the facts.'

It's what Rhys was always telling her, whenever she jumped to conclusions about someone's behaviour; usually his. He always reminded her that without facts, her assumptions were fiction. He'd make her list the things she knew to be certain until she understood that anything else was just conjecture. He was a researcher; it was easy for him. Her job, on the other hand, basically required her to live in the blurry space between fact and fiction, and it was hard not to let that overflow into other areas of her life.

Trying to swallow down the fear that was crawling up her chest, threatening to choke her, she concentrated on the things she knew. She whispered them aloud, her own voice making her feel a little less alone.

'I'm trapped.'

She tried to think of another truth – of any other truth – but her brain would only cling to that one, solid, immovable fact.

Because there was nothing. Only that she'd been taken. Kidnapped. And now she was being held in a white box with no doors and no way out.

Chapter 26

THE SCULPTOR

I had a plan.

When I left home this morning, it was stretching out ahead of me like an open road, beckoning, promising adventure. I was single-minded in my approach, as I always have been. As I have to be. Because if I ever allowed myself time to contemplate what I really, truly do, I'm not sure I'd ever do it.

The trick is to do. To plan, yes, but not to the point when action becomes terrifying.

This particular plan was ambitious. Dangerous. But it's been simmering under my consciousness for so long, an artistic itch I haven't been able to scratch, an urge that I always knew, one day, would become a compulsion.

I've been creating my collections for years. I know what I'm doing. I have a process. It's taken some time, but it's been perfected, the chances of me getting caught so slim because I am incredibly meticulous about every detail of my work.

The plan, from the very beginning, after my first Muse-inspired piece sold and I finally understood my voice, was to create nine collections, one for every ancient Muse, each one a goddess of an art or science. My vision for each has been crystal clear, but none have been so perfectly formed in my mind than the collection representing Erato, the Muse of love poetry.

For this collection I envisage two bodies intertwined, the poetry of intimacy portrayed in the meeting of skin, two people so close that you cannot tell one from the other. Apart, they'd be beautiful sculptures, finely crafted but emotionally unremarkable. Together, they'll be electric.

I know it will work. I've seen it, have marvelled at it when I've studied pictures of *The Cathedral* and *The Abduction*, two of Rodin's most moving pieces, both exquisite for their marriage of two separate figures who, only in their union, achieve absolute perfection.

A sculpture formed by two oversized right hands meeting to form a steeple, *The Cathedral*'s negative space is as important as the hands that meet gently, tenderly, at the top of the arch. By contrast, *The Abduction* is an intimate embrace, a moment of utter abandon and passion between *The Crouching Woman* and *The Falling Man*, two separate sculptures that, when combined as they are, so close that they become one, form a piece so arresting that it's impossible not to have a visceral reaction at the sight of it.

That's the kind of work I want to create – the kind where the artist's soul is visible, where the viewer can't help but feel, and feel deeply – with my Erato collection.

Which means that I need two Muses.

I've thought of nothing else for months, even as I was putting the final touches on my last collection.

I've considered all of the alternatives, toying with the idea of studying the Muses individually, then creating the pieces of them together, so that I don't need to have two with me at the same time. But I know – I just know, the way I first knew that adding a piece of my Muse to that initial sculpture would make it special – that I need them together. I know because when I sculpted from observing models who sat voluntarily for me, there was no magic in the resultant pieces.

I need to see how one Muse's muscles will look when they're pressed against the muscles of another. I need to understand the way their skin moves, the way their limbs are woven together.

I need two Muses.

I've tried to fight it, tried to tell myself that each Muse will be my last, that I don't need to complete all nine collections, that I've made enough money to live multiple lifetimes in comfort, but it never works.

My Muses whisper to me in the night, desperate to be immortalised in my art, begging me to find them, to bring them to me. I'm powerless.

And finally, after months of planning, this morning I was ready.

The first step, as it always is, was to find my Muses. My last collection, Terpsichore Divided, was my most ambitious to date. Terpsichore was the Muse of dance, and so all of the Muses I selected, as well as all being roughly the same size and shape, had to be athletic, too. Their component parts, when shaped and preserved and recreated and encased in bronze, had to look like one coherent body. A dancer, with well-defined calves, muscular thighs, graceful arms ... a goddess, but in pieces.

Once I'd found the potential candidates, I watched them. Slowly. Carefully. I got to know their lives, their habits, their weaknesses. Their vulnerabilities. And then I narrowed it down, selected the ones who could go missing without causing too much initial alarm. It might sound simple enough, but that was the most difficult part of the project – it always is – especially as I'd required athletically talented young women. It was challenging.

But not impossible.

Nothing is impossible when you're smart. And able to blend in to any situation. Patient, too. Biding my time is key. From the time I selected my first Muse until the collection was complete – five Muses locked inside, their perfection frozen in time to be admired forevermore – over two years had passed.

And in the end, it was no different to any of the others. Not really. Yes, the poses I'd created were more powerful than usual. The limbs were lithe, the muscles practically rippling across the immovable bronze. I'd outdone myself, technically.

But I'm capable of more. Which is why I knew the time was right for my depiction of Erato to begin.

The first of my two Muses for this piece was easy enough to find. I wasn't looking for any specific physical attributes, aside from the usual. Same size, same shape. But she didn't have to be in peak condition, or possess any unusual traits. I just needed women, soft and supple and beautiful, and alive. For now, anyway.

Last night, I brought her to the white room. She came without a fight, as they always do. She made it easy, gulping down the water I left for her without question. If she hadn't, my task would have been a little more challenging, but I had a backup plan. And a backup in case my backup plan failed, too. That's how I operate, how my plans succeed.

Before I left this morning I kept an eye on her from a distance. I observed her arms, her legs, her torso. Deciding which part of her I would keep. In the end, I settled on her left hand, which of course meant her companion would be offering her left hand, too.

It had been difficult to tear my eyes off her, to leave, even though I knew that it would be worth it.

At least, I thought it would be worth it.

Because I'd planned for everything. Except, of course, this.

Chapter 27

ALICE

'Is there water?' the man in the mask calls out from across the room.

'There's a heater,' I reply, unable to hide the triumph from my voice. 'I don't know if there's water inside. I'm going to need a hand to check.'

He doesn't argue, doesn't tell me to do it myself. I let myself feel a tiny flicker of hope that he's willing to work together, after all.

But I tamp down my optimism with a reminder that he's not interested in teamwork. I grip the mop handle tightly as he picks his way towards me. The end that's pressed against the floor is jagged and broken, and I think I could use it as a weapon if I had to. I imagine lifting it and plunging it into the killer's belly. Could I do it with enough force to make sure he's unable to retaliate? Could I do it at all? My stomach churns at the idea. I know he deserves worse, that it would be a form of self-defence . . . and yet, I'm pretty sure I couldn't just attack him.

But if he does try anything – well, if it's a choice between him and me, I hope I'll be able to do what I need to do. As he approaches, I squeeze the handle tighter and tighter, as though I might lose it, and therefore any chance I have of fighting my way out of here. My fingers begin cramping.

My breathing is laboured and raspy by the time he gets to my side, but if he notices, he doesn't seem to care. He stands at the door. I take a step back. He peers in.

'It looks intact,' he says casually. Like we're discussing a dropped plate at a dinner party.

I nod. All I can think about is what will happen after we discover water. I find myself hoping, just for a moment, that we don't, just so I can stay alive a little longer. But I know, even as the thought flies through my head, that I'm not being rational. I can worry about my next steps once we're hydrated.

'So,' he looks at me, 'where's the water?'

'It'll be inside, but we can't just start pouring it out. We need to check if it's gas or electric first,' I tell him. 'Does it say anything?'

In the dim light, we both lean forward to try to read the small, black print on the side of the large, white cylinder. My head is still pounding, and reading is a challenge. The words all blur together.

'Gas,' he announces. 'It says here.'

He points, and I peer closer, squinting. There's a small sticker on the side of the heater, slapped on at an angle, that reads 'GAS SAFETY INSPECTION', with a date some four years gone. It isn't safe, but it might just save our lives.

'We have to turn it off first,' I tell him. 'If we try to get water from it while it's still turned on it could be dangerous. There should be a switch here somewhere... there!'

Locating the dial on the front of the heater, I reach over and turn it off, holding my breath. The heater remains silent. I breathe out.

'OK, now we need to turn off the main water supply. There's isn't a supply, as such, but it needs to be off. Um, I can't reach. Can you see a faucet or valve at the top?'

The man in the mask looks into the darkness, peering through two small holes in the plastic. He stretches up onto his toes and uses the frame of the cupboard to lean further in.

'This could come in handy,' he says, sliding something off the top of the heater and holding it out for me to see. A roll of duct tape. I nod.

'OK, yeah. But is there a valve up there?'

He slides the roll of tape onto his wrist and leans into the cupboard again.

'Yep, here. Which way should I turn – oh, there it is. OK. I think it's off.'

'Right. Relief valve, now.'

As I slip into familiar territory, a sense of calm washes over me. I've demonstrated this in my training sessions plenty of times before, on countless different models of heater. I know how to do this, it's my comfort zone, and this is the first time since I first woke up in this room that I've felt even vaguely in control.

I reach up to the pipe that leads into the heater along the side and flip the relief valve so it's sticking straight up.

'We need something to put the water in,' I say, turning around and seeing only a blank plastic face. 'It'll come out here.'

I point to the small faucet on the side of the boiler. 'But I don't know how much is inside. I don't know how long this building's been abandoned for, and whether the water – if there even is water – is safe to drink. But we can't afford to waste any, so we need a container.'

'Your water bottle,' he says, already staggering back towards the gurney to collect it.

'Oh, yeah. Good idea,' I reply encouragingly, forgetting for a moment who I'm talking to. Since I found the heater, I realise, he has been less threatening. I can't get complacent, but maybe, if I keep being useful, he'll see that he doesn't have to hurt me, or restrain me.

I sit on a large pile of bricks and watch as he stumbles and sways across the room, pausing to catch his breath, or regain his balance. At one point he sinks to his knees, clutching his stomach, and leans over to vomit, lifting the mask as he does so, then placing it back over his face. My nose wrinkles in disgust. I lean against the door frame, watching him struggling over the short distance, wondering if I'd even need the mop handle to take him down.

After an extended break at the gurney, and what appears to be a challenging journey back across the room, he returns, holding the clear plastic bottle. I force myself to stand again, my body objecting after the brief respite. He places the bottle under the faucet, and I notice that his hand is shaking slightly. He needs this as much as I do.

'Turn it to the left. But slowly!'

He does as I instruct, and I hold my breath as he moves the lever steadily to open the faucet. If there's no water inside, or if the water is stale, we'll be out of options. Unless we can escape from here, which seems unlikely.

The lever moves all the way across. Nothing happens.

My heart plunges into my stomach. But then, as despair seems to press in around me, there's a gurgling sound from the heater. A split second later, a trickle of water emerges.

I let out a whoop of triumph. The man beside me does the same.

At the sound of his glee, the smile slides off my face. I try to shake away the unsettling guilt I feel for daring to celebrate with this man, for wanting the same thing he did, for being happy when we achieved it together. Should I have scowled, despite the relief and joy I felt at finding water?

121

The faucet offers a steady stream for a few seconds.

'Quick, turn it off, we need to make sure it's drinkable!' I cry, my voice still animated with excitement. I shrug my confusion away. There are far more important things to worry about right now than if it's wrong to share a moment of elation with a murderer.

He flicks the lever back across to the right and the water stops flowing. My mouth seems to dry out in anticipation as I look at the small puddle of liquid at the bottom of the water bottle. I grin under the strip of Lycra that's covering my face.

'Is it fresh?'

'You try it,' he says, holding it out to me. I grit my teeth. Of course I'm the tester, the one who will get sick if the water's stagnant, or tainted. I swipe the bottle from his hand and pull the fabric from my face, flaring my nostrils at him defiantly.

I hold the bottle up to my nose and sniff. It smells slightly metallic, although that could just be the blood clogging my nostrils. I can't detect anything noxious, which is a good sign. I lower the bottle to my bottom lip and hold it there, willing it to be fresh; clean. Then I tip it and take a tiny sip of the cool liquid, my heart pounding in my throat.

I let the water sit on my tongue for a moment, waiting for a terrible taste to hit. It never comes. I try to swallow, but my mouth feels like it's coated in glue. The dust has mixed with the water and it's like dough lining my tongue, my teeth. I cough, then cry out as my beaten ribs are aggravated.

'What?'

I shake my head, take another sip and swirl it around in my mouth, gargling the metallic water, then spitting it on the ground beside me.

'Is it bad?'

'It's fine, I think. I just need to get rid of this dust.'

I tip the bottle up and drain most of it into my mouth, swishing and spitting again. My tongue is still coated in grit, but at least I'm not worried it'll choke me. I finish the last few drops, swallowing this time.

'I think it's OK,' I tell him eventually. 'It's a bit old, but it should be drinkable.'

'All right!' he says, genuine joy in his voice. He takes the bottle from me, and I replace the covering on my nose and mouth. He holds the water bottle under the faucet again, filling it to the brim.

In one sudden, swift movement, he pulls the mask from his face. My stomach twists as I look into the eyes of The Coastline Killer.

Chapter 28

BILL

By the time Bill arrives at the station, he's already exhausted.

It's taken him far longer than he anticipated to get here, thanks to all the stops he had to make along the way. It felt like there was someone who needed help every few yards. The sheer scale of it makes his chest feel tight, like his ribs could crush him. But he knows there's no time for perspective. He just has to do the next thing he can. And then the next.

First along his route had been the woman whose car was crushed by a lamp post. Miraculously, she was unharmed, but she was trapped inside her vehicle, and too scared to move in case her luck ran out. Bill had pried open the back door and helped her to manoeuvre out into safety. The task would have been so much easier if he'd had his usual equipment to hand, but the road ahead of the woman's car was traversed by a gaping crack. No one was getting to him with equipment, even if there was anyone available to help.

Just a little further down the road, an old lady had waved at Bill from her doorway.

'Young man,' she'd called to him. 'I can smell gas. Can you help?'

He'd turned off her gas supply at the mains, and instructed her to keep her doors and windows open for a few hours, and not to light candles or have any kind of open flame in her home. He'd also rummaged in her pantry for bottled water and tinned food, which he'd carried to her dining room, where she could take cover if another aftershock struck. He couldn't leave her without making sure she had the best chance of survival. He couldn't risk it.

A little way along, there was a kid running towards him, must have been fifteen or sixteen, with blood running down his face. He'd been standing next to a window when the quake had hit, and he'd been showered with shards of glass. Some of them had pierced his cheek and, as Bill quickly discovered, his torso, arm and leg on the side that had been closest to the window.

Bill had taken the boy to a nearby house, and had asked the owners, a middle-aged couple with a kid of their own, to patch him up and make sure he stayed safe and let his family know where he was as soon as they could. When the aftershock rumbled through the house, Bill had huddled with the four strangers under their dining table, the boy whimpering in his ear, thoughts of his own family filling his chest.

When the shock was over, he'd left them with an ache behind his ribs, wishing he could say something to take away the fear in their eyes. He'd rounded a corner not far from their home, and had found an ambulance crew trying to free a woman trapped beneath a collapsed garage.

He didn't think to ask, but as he runs the final few hundred feet to the station, he wonders if the people who are lucky enough to be offered help will be able to get anything beyond the basic level of first aid. The roads are a mess. The power seems to be off in most of the areas he's run through, with just a couple of blocks here and there still getting a supply. The woman with the gas leak, and the couple who took in the cut-up teen, all told him that their cell phones had no signal.

He tries not to think about the others he saw on his way here, the ones he tried to help, but couldn't. He has to focus on the ones he can save, the people who still have a chance.

He has no idea how this day is going to go. All he knows is that he's never seen an earthquake of this magnitude before, and that what he's already seen is just the beginning.

Chapter 29

LUCY

Six Hours and Forty-Five Minutes Ago

Lucy lay panting on the cold concrete floor.

She was exhausted, freezing, terrified and now tender and bruised.

For hours, she'd alternated between bashing her fists against different sections of the white, cold walls, and screaming through the metal grate into the drain. Her throat felt like it had been scoured, and the edges of her hands were pained and swollen.

She reached for a bottle of water and took a long, deep drink. She hadn't trusted the water that had been left for her, but she had felt herself becoming more dehydrated, and she knew she had to drink something to keep her energy up. To stay conscious.

She'd run the faucet in the small metal sink, and had inspected the flow of water for signs of contamination. She'd sniffed the clear stream that poured into the sink and gushed down the drain, and decided that she had no idea if it was safe or not, but that if she didn't drink something soon, the dehydration could be more dangerous than whatever might be poisoning the water supply.

So she'd reached up and grabbed a water bottle from the shelf. She discovered some protein bars wedged behind the bottles, which she'd laid aside to inspect later, if she was desperate. She was hungry, but not enough to risk being poisoned. Not yet, anyway.

Twisting the lid off the bottle, she'd dumped the contents into the sink and had refilled it, lifting the full bottle to inspect the water against the stark white wall. It had looked clear. She'd taken a swig, and had flashed back to the night before, or whenever it was that she'd been taken.

She'd been sipping from the water bottle that had been offered to her by her Uber driver, and she'd spilled it down her shirt as she'd tried to call out a warning that they were going the wrong way. Her surprise had turned into the tiniest bud of apprehension. There was nothing after that, no memory, good or bad. Nothing to tell her how she'd ended up in a stark, empty room, alone.

Had they – Rhys, her family, the police – worked out that she'd gone missing after getting into the Uber? She'd racked her brain, trying desperately to scrape new details from her memories, but no matter how hard she concentrated, she couldn't recall anything beyond the driver taking a wrong turn.

She'd texted Rhys just before she got into the car. She'd even offered to drop Stephen and Jackie at the restaurant on the way. She wondered how different things would be now if they'd accepted. Or if she'd just gone with them, as she'd originally planned, before Maria accused her of giving up.

Her stomach twisted at the memory, but she forced herself to focus. Now wasn't the time to be nursing her bruised feelings.

The point was, people knew where she'd been going, what she was doing. When she didn't arrive home, Rhys would have been worried. He'd have contacted the police – if not immediately, then definitely after calling her friends, and then her family – and they'd have looked at her Uber account and tracked her driver and they would have found her by now ... wouldn't they?

So why hadn't they found her?

Lucy's brow creased as she considered the possibility that the driver was behind her kidnapping, and that perhaps it hadn't been an Uber she'd slid into after all. The black car had been in front of the gallery as she'd stepped outside, and the driver had called out her name. It was raining, and she'd just wanted to be warm and dry and at home with Rhys, so she hadn't double-checked the licence plate or the driver's name, like she usually did.

But how else would someone have known her name and location, if the app hadn't provided it?

The blood in Lucy's veins chilled as she considered the possibility that she'd been watched; stalked. She shuddered.

If she'd been taken by a driver who wasn't registered with the app, then no one would be able to track her. Rhys could see where her phone was, using the Find My app, but the fact that the police hadn't rescued her yet made her suspect that maybe her phone hadn't come with her to – wherever it was that she'd been taken.

Her shoulders dropped as she considered, for the first time, the possibility that they might not be able to find her. She slumped back down on the concrete floor, defeated.

Maria's words from the gallery opening echoed in Lucy's head. *Don't just give up.*

The same anger she'd felt then bubbled up inside her again. She wasn't giving up. But there wasn't any other choice – was there? This was out of her hands.

She'd already tried everything.

There was no way out.

Chapter 30

ALICE

I don't know what I imagined lay beneath that shiny white plastic. Maybe a man who's so angry with the world that his face has absorbed some of his twisted rage. I suppose I expected some kind of physical manifestation of his intentions, a signal for anyone who so much as glanced at him to understand that he's dangerous, that they should run, that they should never engage.

I'd imagined a monster.

But the man standing next to me is nothing short of normal. Somehow, that's worse than if he was grotesque, if he was disfigured by his inner distortion.

With huge, noisy glugs, this average-looking stranger drains the water bottle in just a few seconds. As he reaches down to fill the bottle again, his sleeve inches down his wrist and the digital display tells me that it's twenty past one in the afternoon.

'Woah, easy,' I say, concerned. I lower myself onto a chunk of rubble to rest my legs. 'You'll make yourself sick if you keep downing it like that. Besides, we don't know how much is in there. We should probably pace ourselves.'

He sits facing me and holds out the now-full bottle.

'Go ahead,' he mocks. 'Pace yourself.'

But I can't. Within seconds, I've emptied it, just like he

did. Energy flows through my veins again, every cell in my body seeming to exhale in relief all at once. I lick my lips, and hand the empty bottle back.

We take turns, passing the bottle between us slowly, drinking in silence. There's no hurry – the urgency of finding water has passed – we have nothing to strive for but rescue, now. After a while, our desperate gulps subside to smaller, more dignified sips, and the time between each one stretches out. Eventually, we're sitting, both of us slouched over, occasionally reaching for the bottle, or shifting to get more comfortable. Between each drink, I pull the makeshift mask back over my nose and mouth, desperate to protect my lungs.

As my captor sips, I steal glances at his face. I've already seen the light brown hair sticking out from the top of his mask. I've already tried to ignore this incongruently normal feature, but now I'm faced with more strikingly human details: dark brows, brown eyes, a slightly off-kilter nose that might have been broken at some point. He has a square jaw, thin lips, and crow's feet around his eyes.

He could be my colleague, a passenger who gives up his seat on the bus for me, a driver who waves to signal that I can have the parking space we both arrived at simultaneously. He's the kind of man I would trust, whom I would smile back at. My spine prickles with this knowledge.

I wonder, if I passed him in the grocery store, or sat opposite him on the Skytrain, whether I'd have given him a second glance. If I'd have looked into his eyes and thought they were cruel. Or if I'd have let my gaze travel, immediately forgetting him.

And then I'm struck by a thought that's so much worse: if I'd seen his description in one of the hundreds of potential donor profiles I've leafed through in recent months – dark

131

hair and eyes, strong build, average height – would I have considered him? After all, the donor I selected has similar features, aside from his height. Would this man have made it onto my short list? The idea fills me with a kind of cold dread I've never felt before, and I'm suddenly overwhelmed with relief that I couldn't make my appointment – the appointment I should be walking out of right about now – because now I have a chance to reconsider my choice. I need to know more about him. I need assurance that the father of my child isn't just healthy and fit and strong, but a good person, too. I need to know that he's not a monster.

Perhaps it's just the water renewing my strength, and not the idea of my precious few eggs being wasted on a donor I'm no longer certain I can trust, but whatever the reason, I'm suddenly filled with a new sense of determination to get out of here, to outsmart my captor and find my way home. To get to that paperwork and read it much, much more thoroughly.

I stare at him, trying to work out my next move. Now that his plastic mask is gone, he should be protecting his lungs from the dust and debris that's still hovering in the stale air around us. I debate whether I should stay quiet, let him choke to death, or whether, unprompted, I should tell him what he needs to know, to prove to him that he still needs me around.

It feels like gambling, like trying to calculate odds on a game of pure chance. If I stay quiet, he might die, and then I'll be safe. But if he lives, and he thinks my usefulness has expired . . .

'You should cover your face,' I say eventually. 'This air is full of really dangerous toxins. And given the age of this building, there could be lead and asbestos particles in the air. They could cause some pretty serious damage.'

He stares at me for a moment, as though trying to work out whether I'm manipulating him somehow, then quickly unties his apron. He tugs on the left cuff of his top, then pulls his arm out. I look at my feet, not wanting to see any more of him than I have to. There's a tearing sound, and when I look back, one sleeve is missing from his shirt. He's wrapping it around his face, presumably turned inside out, as it's black rather than the dirty grey colour that's covering everything else.

Blood oozes from the gash on his head, dripping onto the clean piece of fabric that's now acting as a mask.

'That's a pretty nasty wound you've got there.' I nod towards his forehead as he refills the bottle once more. He touches a hand to his head, then draws it away and looks at his fingers. They're glistening.

'Why am I still wearing these?' he murmurs, rubbing his fingers together. He still has his gloves on, the ones he wore, presumably, to keep any trace of his identity off his victim, off me. They're torn in multiple places, although the dust means his skin and the gloves are all one dull grey colour. His DNA is all over the room now. There's no hiding who he is, gloves or not. He might as well add his fingerprints to the mix.

He peels them off, the left first, and then the right. Then he touches his forehead again, wincing. When he pulls his fingers away, they're red.

'Is it bleeding badly?' he asks.

I glance up, but I know the answer already: 'Yeah.'

He swears lightly under his breath.

'I need to stop the bleeding.'

I don't reply. We don't have anything we can use to dress our wounds.

'First aid kit. We need a first aid kit,' he groans as he stands up.

'Right,' I say without thinking. 'I'm sure there are plenty of those lying around in this dungeon.'

He stares at me, his face completely blank.

I shiver suddenly. The temperature seems to have dropped.

'I think it's best if you at least try to help, don't you?'

'Or what?' I stand to face him, my jaw set, my nostrils flaring.

'You know what,' he says. His voice is low, a warning. I should be scared. I am scared. But I'm also in complete disbelief that he's still threatening me after everything.

'Because you're so strong?' I ask sarcastically. I'm appalled at the words that are tumbling out of my mouth – reckless, dangerous words. But I can't seem to be able to stop them. 'I could take you out, you know.'

I think I mean it, too. I am in no shape to be in combat – no matter how badly injured my opponent is – but given how much he's swaying, and how slowly he's moving, I might just have a chance.

He laughs, mocking me. 'Go ahead. Take your best shot.'

I pause, willing myself to rise to the challenge, to take him out, to show him what I'm made of. Perhaps I could do it, could kill him, right here and now, and my chances of survival would increase exponentially.

He sways a little to the left. My eyes travel up to his forehead, to the gash where blood is oozing, marking a trail down his jawline, pooling on his neck. He's weak. I just don't know how weak.

Gripping the mop handle even more tightly, I tense every muscle in my body, ignoring the pain, preparing to take him out. I hesitate. I'm not certain I'll win this fight, and if I lose,

I'll die. Despite his weakness, he still has the upper hand. Because he's willing to kill, and I'm not sure I am.

Without warning, he jumps, his hands flying out towards my face.

'Boo!' he shouts. I scream and, in my fright, drop the mop handle.

He bursts out laughing, a demented cackle, a cartoon villain. My blood turns to ice, and I realise that I never really had a chance against him. He knows that I won't hurt him, even if I'm physically in better shape. Even if he gives me permission. Because I'm not like him. And that means he'll win.

Blinking back hot tears of shame and fury, his mocking laugh ringing in my ears, I reach down for the mop handle, which I understand now is useless for anything except propping me up.

'So,' he says, still laughing to himself. 'Let's find a way to patch me up, then, shall we?'

I nod miserably.

Chapter 31

LUCY

Three Hours and Three Minutes Ago

Lucy's heart beat an excited little frenzy when the rumbling first began.

Someone had arrived! She was certain that the sound she was hearing, the quivering of the room she was in, came from a car or truck outside. It had to be extremely close.

'HELP!' she screamed, using the full force of her lungs. 'HELP ME! I'M IN HERE!'

She slammed her palms against the wall closest to her, then balled her hands into fists and continued pounding as she screamed at full volume.

Then she froze.

What if the vehicle outside didn't belong to her rescuer? What if it was her captor?

She fell silent for a moment, her brain scrambling to come up with a plan.

If it was her kidnapper, should she stay as quiet and still as possible? Or keep making a noise? She wasn't sure which way to play it, but then again, she wasn't really sure of anything. Frustration burned inside Lucy's chest. She needed information, and the only way she was going to get it was to face the person who was keeping her there, to find out exactly what she was up against, and what the hell they wanted from her. Without knowing any of that, she couldn't make a plan to get out.

And she really, really needed to get out.

She resumed her assault on the wall, and let her shouts for help reverberate around the room.

It was a few seconds before she realised that the grumbling and creaking noises had intensified to the point where the sound was drowning out her yells, and that the shaking had escalated. Something moved behind her. Lucy whirled around, frantically trying to work out what was happening, her mind grasping for an explanation.

She watched, fear expanding inside her as the water bottles rattled and jostled for space on the shelf, then, one by one, like synchronised swimmers plunging into a pool, toppled to the ground below. They rebounded off the concrete, then rolled and hopped across the floor in every direction. As they did, a word popped into Lucy's mind, and everything clicked terrifyingly into place.

Earthquake.

Chapter 32

LUCY

One Hour and Fifty-Four Minutes Ago

Lucy had always believed herself to be brave. But when the earthquake had struck, she wasn't proud of the way she'd reacted.

As the earth had roared and shuddered and exerted its power, she'd stayed huddled on the floor, her arms over her head, her chest heaving with sobs of self-pity and of fear.

She was by no means an expert, but if the violent shaking was anything to go by, Lucy figured that what was happening wasn't just any earthquake. Scientists had been talking about 'The Big One' for years. Decades, even. It was expected. It was planned for. Lucy had even made plans of her own after attending a mandatory workplace safety event.

Normally, she didn't pay much attention to meetings like that. They were boring, and she figured that they were mostly just box-ticking exercises that her company had to deliver to prove that they cared about their employees.

But the trainer had caught Lucy's attention. It had been her outfit that first made Lucy sit up and take notice: perfectly tailored black suit, white shirt that she suspected was silk, and the most gorgeous yellow leather heels she'd ever seen. Lucy, in her standard uniform of black jeans, black boots and a polyester top selected on the criteria that it looked vaguely professional and required no ironing, was awe-struck. And then the woman had opened her mouth, and Lucy had hung on to her every word. Everyone had.

For a topic as boring as safety, this woman managed to keep the team's attention for a full hour. She'd been passionate and authoritative, explaining in great detail what could happen in an earthquake, and how they could stay safe. The fact that had most shocked Lucy was that, if she was standing downtown during an earthquake, the shower of glass that would rain down from the office buildings, apartments and hotels, would be a few feet deep. She had shuddered at the idea, and had sat up straighter and started scribbling notes.

Her company, she learned, was ready. There was a metal cabinet on each level of the office, which housed enough supplies for everyone on that floor to survive for seventy-two hours after a natural disaster. Her home, by contrast, was woefully underprepared.

When she'd got back to her apartment that evening, she'd gone straight to her computer to find those perfect yellow heels. It took her ages, but she'd found the exact same ones, discovering with profound sadness that they cost more than her monthly rent. What she could afford, however, was supplies.

She'd added water purification tablets, a first aid kit, a wind-up radio and flashlight to her shopping cart. Then, after a bit of googling, she'd thrown in a gigantic box of candles, along with lighters and a few extra blankets, in case the quake happened in winter and she was stuck without heating. The next weekend, she'd driven to Costco and had stocked up on non-perishable food; at least a week's worth. It wasn't just oats and rice and long-life coconut milk and tinned chickpeas she'd bought, though. She'd figured that if she was going to be trapped – possibly alone, for up to a week – after something as traumatic as an earthquake, she'd want a little bit of comfort food.

So she'd added dark chocolate to her basket, along with some of her favourite cookies and salt and vinegar chips. And on the way home, she'd stopped at the liquor store and picked up a couple of bottles of champagne. Not cava; the good stuff. She figured if shit really hit the fan, at least she'd go out in style, too drunk to really know what was happening to her.

Now, though, she was terrifyingly sober. And achingly aware of what was going on.

As Lucy lay on the cold concrete floor of her stark prison cube, she wondered whether she was anywhere near home, and whether the quake had hit Portland. She wondered where Rhys was, if he was OK, and if he would remember the stash she'd so carefully stockpiled, the supply that she'd planned to maintain every few months, just like the trainer had advised.

'Luce?' he'd called out to her from the hallway, the day he'd moved in. They'd only been dating for a year, but it had felt so easy between them. Just so – and she really hated the cliché of it, but in this case it was true – so right. He'd been the one to suggest finding a place to rent together, but she'd been the one to invite him to move into her much-loved – and rent-controlled – apartment, the one she'd moved into a few years before she met Rhys at that ridiculous Halloween party her colleague had dragged her to.

'Yeah?'

'Can I clear out this cupboard?'

She'd walked out of her bedroom – their bedroom, officially, but she wasn't used to that just yet – and had raised her eyebrows when she'd seen which cupboard he was standing in front of.

140

'Why do you need that cupboard?'

He'd waved a helmet in her direction. 'My ice hockey gear.'

Lucy had put her hands on her hips. 'There's a locker down in the garage. You can store it there.'

'Why can't I just put it in here? This is just some food and crap. Can't that go in the kitchen?'

She'd taken a deep breath. 'It's not just some food. Those are my earthquake supplies.'

'Earthquake supplies?' he'd laughed. 'Oh, God. You're not one of those doomsday preppers, are you?'

Her face had flamed. 'No!'

'You are! You're a prepper!' He could barely squeeze the words out through his laughter. 'Do you have, like, a zombie-proof shelter out the back, too?'

'Don't be a dick,' she'd huffed. 'It's just some stuff that the government recommends you to keep in case there's an earthquake and you can't leave your house for a few days. Besides, if something does happen, you'll be glad I was prepared.'

He'd stopped laughing.

'Sorry,' he'd said, coming over to give her a hug. 'I shouldn't have laughed, I just wasn't expecting that. And you're right, being prepared is smart. I see you've got booze in there, so I guess if the zombies do come for us, at least we can go out with a bang, right?'

She'd swatted at him playfully, and he'd gathered up his hockey gear to put in the locker downstairs.

Now, alone and unsure just how bad the earthquake was, or how far it had reached, she hoped that Rhys would remember those supplies. And she hoped the food was still edible. It had been about two years since she'd frantically bought everything she thought she'd need, but she hadn't really bothered to restock anything since then. Every so often she'd remember the contents of the cupboard and wonder if she should pull anything out that was no longer edible and replace it with fresh supplies. But the urgency she'd felt on the day of her training had faded, and it just didn't feel so important anymore. She had some supplies. She'd planned.

But not for this. This scenario, the one where she'd been kidnapped and held against her will in a white box, without any escape, hadn't been part of the training that day. No one had explained what to do if an earthquake hit after you'd been taken to an unidentified location. There was no procedure to follow, no plan to go over with your family ahead of time.

And so she lay, curled up with her arms wrapped around her head and a bottle of water wedged behind her knee, long after the earthquake had ended and the floor had stopped trembling.

Without a clear plan of her own, Lucy pictured Rhys tucking into her supplies and grinning when he got to the champagne. She hoped he popped it, that he was getting good and tipsy like she wished she was.

She was still lying in a foetal position, dreaming about being teased by her boyfriend, when the aftershock came. And so she curled up even tighter, and wondered if anyone would ever find her huddled, lonely body.

Chapter 33

ALICE

I once watched a documentary about a fish called a bluestreak cleaner wrasse, and this little reef-dweller somehow stuck in my memory. I remember thinking that it must be the most cunning fish in the sea.

In an environment where small fish like the bluestreak are prey for plenty of predators, this one has developed a skill to stay alive: it offers other fish a cleaning service, eating parasites off their slippery bodies. In return, clients don't eat their cleaners. I vividly remember one snippet of this documentary, showing a bluestreak cleaner wrasse inside the mouth of a devilish-looking moray eel. One snap of its jaw and the fish would have been a tasty sashimi snack for old Flotsam or Jetsam. But it swam boldly out of its enemy's mouth unharmed, its stomach full.

The powerful, vicious eel and a tiny, vulnerable fish need each other.

So do the killer and I. I'm in his jaws. And I have to trust that, if I do a good enough job of cleaning him up, he'll let me go, unharmed and able to live another day.

'I suggest you start looking for a first aid kit,' he says, his tone cold. Sinister. He makes a waving motion with his hand, like I'm a pet that's not following instructions.

I don't have any bargaining power, other than the fact

that I am able to tend to his wounds. So, like it or not, that's what I'm going to have to do. And I'll have to do it so well that he can't possibly risk not having me around.

I glance once more at the gash on his forehead. It's still oozing blood. I shiver, from the dropping temperature as much as my revulsion. He's right – it needs to be dressed.

'OK, but first can we get back to the gurney? I don't like being out in the open like this. If another aftershock hits...'

His eyes widen at the thought and he nods, snatching the water bottle from me and staggering back towards our little base. Before I begin the painstaking journey back, I take one last look inside the cupboard in case there's anything useful – a first aid kit, a magic button I can press to get out... but it's empty. Adjusting the strip of Lycra so it's fully covering my nose and mouth, I limp weakly across the room with my makeshift crutch.

Eventually I reach the gurney. My captor is slouched on the ground, the water bottle propped up against one of the legs of the metal table, held in place by a couple of broken bricks.

'Give me a sec,' I wheeze, sitting heavily next to him and panting until I can speak again.

'Do you have any other medical supplies?' I ask after a moment.

He looks at me like I'm the unhinged one.

'The syringe?' I prompt. 'You took my blood, remember?'

'Oh,' he says, so casually that I want to scream. 'That.'

'Yeah,' I reply through gritted teeth. 'That. So... do you have a whole bag of supplies with you, or what?'

'No, I... no, no supplies. Just the needle. Batteries. And a bunch of plastic sheeting.'

I know I shouldn't ask. Even as the words spill out of me, I want to take them back, to just forget it and move on.

'So what was with the needle? What were you taking my blood for?'

He mutters something I can't make out.

'What?'

'It's none of your business, OK? Forget it.'

Sure. No problem. So easy to forget that a lunatic, who doesn't even know first aid, drew some of my blood before attempting to kill me.

I stare at him, incredulous. But he just stares right back, his dark eyes boring into mine. I can't stand it, the intimacy of looking at him, of seeing him.

Using the mop handle to help me up, I stand again, wincing as I put weight on my leg. It buckles and I collapse onto the rubble, my hands flying out just in time to save my face. I stay where I am, slumped across the dusty bricks and stone and wood and plastic sheeting, my palms throbbing from the impact.

'I . . . I don't think I can walk,' I say, defeated.

I need him to believe that we're working towards the same goal, need him to know that I'm doing my best. But I've failed. He takes a long, hard look at me, his face stony. Eventually, he sighs.

'Fine. I'll look. But you need to tell me what to look for. If there's no first aid kit, there's got to be something that'll work.'

I nod and heave myself back up so I'm sitting, my back against one leg of the gurney.

'Start with the cupboard under the sink over there,' I suggest, pointing towards the washer and dryer.

The thing about those bluestreak cleaner wrasses is that they're cunning little fish. They lull their clients into a false sense of security by giving them a thorough clean in one session, a little massage the next . . . and just when the poor unsuspecting fish or eel relaxes, they take a sneaky chomp of their flesh.

I need him to trust me. And then, when we're safe and out of here, I'll strike. I will find a way – I haven't worked out how yet, but I know there will be a way – to get to the police and tell them everything I can about The Coastline Killer.

I know a few things about him already. I know what he looks like. Before he covered it with a piece of his shirt, I made sure to notice – to really take in the details of – his face. I memorised his features, the things that make him recognisable: the slight distortion of his nose, the way his lips turn down ever so slightly at the corners, his hooded brown eyes.

And I know that he's from out of town. He has to be. If he lived anywhere along the coast, he'd know about earthquake safety. Most companies give annual training to their employees, and councils encourage their residents to prepare, offering information and strategies.

If he was from somewhere prone to quakes, he'd have a plan in place, he'd probably have been able to access the water from the heater without my help, and he'd have known that we might have to be self-sufficient for days before rescuers arrive.

He hadn't known any of those things, which means he isn't from around here. His victims may have all been found along the Pacific Northwest, but he's from somewhere else. It's not much, but it's a start.

As he staggers and sways across the uneven floor, I keep my eyes trained on him, watching his every move. He picks his way over to the cupboard next to the dryer, then kneels in the debris and rattles the door. It squeals as he pries it open. I cross my fingers that it's not empty. There's nowhere else in this room where any supplies could be hiding, although I'm not hopeful there's anything there, either. An abandoned house is unlikely to have a first aid kit lying around. Or much else, for that matter.

There's a scraping echo as he drags something from the metallic shelf.

'Have you found something?' I call out.

'Uh – laundry supplies,' he replies. His voice sounds thick. Drowsy. 'Hang on. There's a bunch of stuff in here.'

'Anything useful?'

'No . . . not yet. A box of pegs,' he says, frustration audible in his reply.

There's more rustling, scraping, clanging. And then a sigh.

'There's no first aid kit,' he calls out over his shoulder. 'But maybe we can use some of this stuff.'

He finds his way back, his arms laden with items I can't identify in the dim light. I'm amazed that we have any light at all, but thankfully the lamp that's still hanging from one of the ceiling beams is glowing yellow. It must be battery powered.

The meagre findings are dropped at my feet, like a cat bringing its owner a bleeding mouse. The man sits heavily beside me. I pick up a bottle, the plastic gone brittle. It's stain remover, the same brand my mom uses.

My stomach clenches at the thought of my parents. I try to picture them, squeezing my eyes closed to imagine where they would have been when the quake hit. They should have been home, unless something happened that messed with their usual routine. And if they were home, they'd know what to do. I've trained them, and I've set them up with everything they need to survive, for weeks if necessary.

They'll be safe, but I also know that they'll be worrying about me. The plan has always been that if something like this happens, I'll call my Aunt Meg in Montreal to tell her I'm OK, and they'll do the same. In an emergency, long-distance calls are often more reliable, as the local phone lines quickly get jammed. Meg would act as our messenger, so that we could communicate with one another, at least to reassure one another that we're alive.

They are, no doubt, listening for the phone to ring, wondering where their daughter is, panicking that I've been caught in the collapse of a downtown apartment block, or crushed by falling glass. Never in their wildest imagination would they guess what's really happened to me.

I force myself to take a few deep breaths. I need to focus on what's happening right here in this basement. My parents will be OK. I have to believe they're fine. Because right now, I need all of my energy. And all of my concentration. I set the bottle aside and reach into the pile of random goods to see if anything can be used.

The next item is a pack of dryer sheets. Then a pair of dirty rubber gloves, an ancient-looking bottle of hydrogen peroxide, and a couple of filthy rags.

'OK,' I say, my mind scrambling for solutions. 'It's not great, but I might be able to work with some of this. Could you please hand me my backpack?'

I can see it behind him. All he has to do is reach out and grab it, then pass it over. But instead, he wrinkles his brow, suspicious.

'What for?'

I'm too tired to be snippy.

'Tampons,' I say wearily. 'To stop the bleeding.'

'Oh,' he says awkwardly, reaching behind him, swaying as he does so. He stops, holds his hand to his head, then passes the bag to me.

'Here.'

I take it, and reach inside, feeling for the small metal tin I keep an emergency stash of tampons in. For the second time in a day, I berate myself for not having my first aid kit with me. I can picture it, in the side pocket of my old, hole-ridden backpack, the one I just replaced. It's full of Band-Aids and sterile wipes and cotton buds and absorbent pads, mundane items that seem almost mythical to me now. But I'd been too distracted this morning, too excited about my appointment to think logically. To prepare for any eventuality, like I usually do.

My fingers brush my wallet, the empty wrapper of a protein bar, my deodorant. For a moment, I wonder stupidly if my phone is in there, too. But it was in my hand when I was taken. It's probably on the ground outside the door to my condo. Disappointed, but not surprised, I pull the tampon tin out, dropping my otherwise useless backpack at my feet.

As it falls, dust billows around the blue nylon, and something smooth and dark peeks out from under the powdery coat of debris that's covering every surface in the room. I lean in to get a closer look, and my heart pounds against my ribs. It's the saw that was being used to remove my arm when the earthquake hit. The skin on the inside of my elbow stings in recognition.

I steal a glance at the saw's owner to see if he's spotted it, too, but his eyes are closed. I push my backpack with my foot so that it covers the tool, my mouth dry with nerves. I failed at my mop handle attack, so there's no telling if I'd be able to accomplish anything with a rusty saw, but I'll be damned if I let him get his hands on it again.

Certain that the weapon is completely covered by my bag, I open the container in my hand. There are three tampons inside.

'OK,' I say. 'Here we go.'

Trying to touch them as little as possible, I turn the gloves inside out. The yellow rubber is filthy, but my own hands are worse, my nails caked in dust and grime and blood. The white powdery insides of the gloves are a little better. Not exactly hygienic, but better.

I try to unwrap the tampon, muttering under my breath as I go. These things are fiddly at the best of times, but when I'm wearing thick rubber gloves, it's next to impossible. Eventually, I pull up my mask and use my teeth to rip the plastic tab, and then carefully, so I don't drop it, pull both ends of the plastic off.

'I'm going to soak up the blood as best I can with this,' I wave the tampon at him, 'and then I'll use another to put some peroxide on it, which will work as a disinfectant.'

'OK.' He sounds nervous. Vulnerable. I hope that's a good thing.

As gently as I can, so he knows I'm not deliberately hurting him, I press the tampon against his forehead, surprised by how much blood is instantly soaked into the white cotton. He winces, quickly drawing in a breath.

'Sorry,' I say, reflexively. I mentally kick myself for continuing to be polite, even with him.

'It's fine,' he says through gritted teeth. 'It just stings. Keep going.'

I do as I'm told, cleaning as much of the blood from his forehead as I can, gradually cleaning his skin enough to see the site of the wound, which is still bleeding. It's about an inch long, a gash deep enough to see a flash of white, of bone, underneath.

My stomach turns. I don't deal well with extreme injuries, never have. In all of my emergency training, it's always been the pictures of blood and gore that I've struggled with the most. For the past few months I've had to face my fear of

150

needles, sometimes injecting myself daily with a cocktail of hormones, but blood still makes me light-headed. And now, on an empty stomach, and feeling as weak as I am, I'm not prepared to deal with something so... gross.

It surprises me, that even in a life-and-death situation like the one I'm in, I'm still squeamish about things like this. Isn't an emergency supposed to give people a new perspective, a resilience they didn't have before?

'Is it bad?' he whispers. His eyes are wide and pleading. My reaction must have been physical. I'm thankful at least that the fabric is covering my nose and mouth, that he didn't see my lips twisted in revulsion, my nose scrunched up against the horror of it.

'Uh... I can see a bit of bone,' I say, blinking forcefully so I don't pass out. 'I'm going to have to close it up. Have you still got that duct tape?'

He hands me the roll, which he'd shoved onto his wrist like a bangle. I place it in my lap, buying a few seconds while I try to take my mind off the white bone that's visible under the mangled, bloodied flesh of his forehead. But it's all I can see, all I can focus on.

'I'm going to put some peroxide on it first,' I tell him, and he moans in anticipation, closing his eyes. I take that as permission.

After struggling to open another tampon, I pour some of the liquid from the old, crusty bottle onto it, and press it against the wound, forcing myself to keep my eyes open, to concentrate on getting this task over and done with so I can forget about looking at his skull. He whimpers as I press the second tampon to his wound, but to his credit, he doesn't flinch. Doesn't move. He's coping with this much better than I am. Although that makes sense, given the number

151

of limbs he's dismembered in the past. He must have an iron stomach.

'OK,' I whisper, throwing the filthy tampons to the edge of the room and tearing off a strip of the duct tape.

Holding my breath, I reach up and squeeze the two sides of his wound together. Blood oozes from between the two edges of flesh. My stomach lurches and my chest heaves. I swallow it down. Breath hisses between the man's teeth, and I feel a small stab of satisfaction at his pain. Then, quickly, so I can get it over with, I stretch the tape across the gash, pressing it down firmly, enjoying his strangled cry.

I let go, and the wound opens again. The gap is smaller now, but it's still oozing blood. The room spins around me.

'Tear off some more,' I instruct, pushing the roll of tape against his chest. He grabs it and does as he's told, ripping a length of it off with his teeth and passing it over. I repeat the process, adding three silver strips to his skin before the cut in his head looks like it's mostly closed, and the blood has slowed to an occasional drip.

'Are you done?' he asks. 'Because I'm feeling—'

He doesn't get to finish his sentence. We hear it at the same time, the low rumble coming from somewhere deep in the belly of the earth. We look at one another. His eyes are wide, filled with understanding and fear, and at exactly the same time, we dive for the safety of the gurney.

Chapter 34

LUCY

One Hour and Forty-Nine Minutes Ago

Lucy sat on the cold concrete and tried to figure out the best tactic for staying alive.

She didn't need to look to know what supplies she had at her disposal. She had water. Dehydration wasn't her problem, but starvation might be. She tried to remember how many days someone could survive without food, if they had water. She thought it might have been weeks, although she really, really hoped that she wouldn't have to put that to the test.

Aside from the water, she had three protein bars – potentially poisoned, and still in their wrappers – which were now lying on the floor beside her. There was a single roll of toilet paper. And a clock. The soft ticking noise was amplified by the smooth, reflective surfaces in the room. At times, the tick-tock was so loud that she was sure it was coming from inside her, taunting her, whispering its reminder that time was running out for her to do something, to take action, to get away.

Quit-ter, it mocked. Quit-ter, quit-ter.

She couldn't stop thinking about Maria's accusation which, she realised with a sudden, gut-wrenching fear, might have been the final conversation she ever had with her best friend. 'Don't just give up', Maria had instructed.

And as much as Lucy wanted to deny it, to let the indignant anger that bloomed in her grow and swell and take root, she wondered if perhaps there was some truth in Maria's words.

Her prepping cupboard, created in a frenzy of energy, had been abandoned at the slightest hint of additional effort. When her conversation with Maria had become too uncomfortable, she'd quit that, too. And then, of course, there had been the business. The real reason why Maria's words had stung.

She'd started that with the same enthusiasm she'd had for her earthquake supplies. The day Maria's art dealer friend had asked Lucy to represent her, several months ago, she'd arrived home almost exploding with excitement.

'I think I can go freelance,' she'd announced to Rhys when she'd walked through the door, her cheeks aching from all the smiling she'd done on the drive home. 'I have my first client.'

'What? Who? That's awesome!'

Rhys had leaped up from the sofa and had lifted her into a dramatic hug. She'd giggled, euphoric. For months she'd talked of starting her own PR company. The firm she worked for had some great clients – a luxury hotel, a boutique fashion brand, a chain of coffee shops – but her boss was of the old school, boys' club ilk, and never gave her credit for her ideas, even when the clients loved them. Again and again she'd watched male colleagues be promoted ahead of her, but the final straw was when she worked out that her boss had been lying about his expenses, claiming far more than he was spending, lining his pockets with client funds.

She couldn't wait to get out, but she also couldn't afford to leave without at least one good client of her own.

'Maria's friend Jo. She's an art dealer, and just made some

big sales. She figured it was time to get some press coverage, so she's asked me to send a proposal next week.'

Rhys had spun her around, they'd opened a nice bottle of wine, ordered takeout, and she'd spent the next week waking up at the crack of dawn to write her proposal before going in to work.

By the time she'd sent the document to Jo, she was already drafting her resignation letter in her head, fantasising about the things she'd say to her boss when she quit, dreaming up names for her new business. She wasn't expecting Jo to come back with so many questions, with demands for services Lucy wasn't certain she could provide.

It wasn't that she'd given up. She'd just realised that perhaps freelancing wasn't the utopia she'd initially imagined. She told herself that she needed more experience before she could take on clients of her own. She convinced herself that she couldn't afford not having a steady pay cheque, even though Rhys assured her that they'd be fine. And finally she got the promotion she'd been asking for. It had all just seemed like too much, too soon, and so she'd told Jo she couldn't proceed with the account.

Maria's disappointment had been the worst part.

'So you're just going to keep working for that asshole because it's, what, easier?'

'It's not that, Maria,' Lucy had defended herself. 'I need more experience.'

'No, you don't. You're brilliant at your job, and they don't deserve you. You're better than that jerk of a boss, and you know it. Stop taking the easy way out.'

Lucy had pleaded with Maria to drop the subject. And she had, but Lucy knew she was still disappointed. Her stomach dropped at the thought of letting her friend down. Then it growled. Loudly.

Lucy sat up. She stared at the protein bars, hunger diminishing her doubts about whether they were safe to eat. It wasn't safe not to eat, she decided, if she was going to get out. Not if, she chided herself. When. She needed her strength for when she got out. She nodded to herself. Maria would approve of her determination.

She figured she could eat half a bar a day, which would last her for six days. She couldn't bear the idea of being trapped any longer than that, couldn't allow herself to believe that she'd still be there in a week. No matter what, she'd be out before then. She had to be.

There were three flavours to choose from: chocolate peanut butter, blueberry, and almond. She figured she'd save the best till last, so she carefully unwrapped the almond bar, removing it and using her thumbnail to draw a line through the middle, where she guessed the halfway point was. She tore the two halves apart, making sure it was an even break, and then wrapped one portion back in its wrapper, placing it next to the two uneaten bars beside her.

She nibbled the edge of her ration warily, and her lips involuntarily turned down. It tasted horrible, like cardboard smothered in sweetener. If she wasn't so desperate for food, she'd never keep eating it. But she was light-headed with hunger, and so she swallowed, waiting to see if there were any side effects: vomiting, drowsiness, pain. When, after a few minutes, no symptoms appeared, she risked another small mouthful. She forced herself to eat slowly, pausing after swallowing to stretch the meal out, and to test its effects. When she'd finished, her stomach still grumbled.

Lucy stood, placing the two and a half remaining protein bars on the shelf so they were out of sight. She wasn't sure how much she could trust her self-control if they were within easy reach.

Then she sat back on the concrete floor and tried to think. She had six days. Six days to find a way out before she starved. Her forehead scrunched in concentration as she desperately waited for an idea – any idea – to pop into her head.

And the clock's hand moved around the stark white face, its soft tick-tock counting the seconds till her death.

Chapter 35

ALICE

The rolling and tilting of the earth reminds me of being at sea and I almost let out a hysterical laugh. I hate being on the open water. I don't want to die feeling seasick.

But I am going to die. I'm certain of it.

My mind, rather than settling on images of my parents, or my brother, or Celia and the twins, or the pregnancy test I should be taking in just a couple of weeks, lingers on Mel. Were her final moments as terrifying as this? The sensations she felt would have been different. She'd inhaled smoke. I'm breathing dust. The heat must have been unbearable for her. For me, it's the trembling and shaking.

The medium is different. But the end result will be the same. I feel just as helpless now as I did when I learned about Mel's death, but with none of the guilt. This isn't my fault. There's only one person to blame, and that's the man who's huddled next to me under a metal table, hoping to avoid being crushed by the falling building.

As I lie under a metal table, unable to tell where my body's trembling begins and the earth's ends, I try to focus on something other than Mel, and her death, and the choices I've made since then that have somehow, inexplicably led me to this place, and instead of letting my mind go where it naturally wants to, I count.

I reach thirty-seven, and then the tremor begins to abate, one of the monsters that's ripping my world apart retreating back to the centre of the earth.

Slowly, gently, I allow my mind to come back into the room, into the present.

And just as slowly, it dawns on me that, somehow, in the midst of the terror and trembling, the killer and I have become intertwined.

I freeze as I realise just how completely we're entangled. My left hand is clinging to one of the legs of the gurney, but my right arm has found its way around his waist, and I'm pulling him towards me, as though I'm craving his closeness. My face is pressed into his chest, so that I can smell his scent – a mix of sweat and some sort of piney deodorant. His heartbeat is fast, panicked, like a hummingbird's wings. Knowing that behind his exterior is a heart, beating just like mine, makes him seem strangely vulnerable, intensely human. His face is buried in my hair. He's whimpering, the sound muffled by the fabric that's covering his face, and the echoes of the rumbling earth.

A strong, muscular arm is wrapped around my back; protective, almost. Our bodies are too close to distinguish from each other's, and for one small, traitorous moment, I'm grateful for the contact. I'm so scared, and feel so alone, that the embrace is comforting.

But as quickly as the urge to cower against him hits me, I'm repulsed, desperate to get him away from me, to escape from his shaking, defenceless frame. I release my hand from the gurney leg and press it flat into his chest. Then I shove with all of my strength, propelling myself away.

He doesn't resist. He simply releases me, then curls up into a foetal position and continues moaning, his self-pity sickening.

Eventually, I can't stand the sound of it, and I move my aching body, crawling out from under the gurney and daring to peer through the dust.

In my shock, I actually let out a gasp.

'What?' The voice from under the gurney trembles. He doesn't deserve to cry. I'm angry now. Whether at myself for momentarily enjoying his comfort, or at him for being so spineless, I'm not certain. I don't let myself think about it, for fear of what the answer might be.

I ignore his question and clamber to a standing position, using the gurney for support.

The room has halved in size. Where the cupboard – and our only source of water – once was, there's now a solid wall of rubble. The building above us must have imploded, landing right here in the basement. Using the mop handle, which was lying beside me during the aftershock, I limp towards the wreckage, needing to see it up close to believe that it's real. My body objects, telling me to stop moving, to rest and recover, but I can't. I reach the edge of the debris and stretch a hand out to touch a pile of brick, higher than my waist. It's real. And it's impenetrable.

I flinch as something to my left creaks and wheezes, and I look over just in time to see a huge chunk of wall collapsing, like the icebergs I've seen on the Discovery Channel, cleaving off the structure of the building and landing with a crash and a billow of dust. The killer emerges from the safety of the gurney.

'No,' he whispers, his voice so quiet that I almost don't hear it. He staggers over and stands beside me.

We look at each other in shock, then look away again. It's too real, now. The fact that we are now living inside our own tomb, that we will slowly be crushed to death by the building we're in, is not just one of many possible outcomes.

160

Looking around the room, I know that it's the only option. There is no escape; this space seems hell-bent on claiming us as its own.

'What now?' he asks, his voice small and nervous. I ignore him.

'Alice,' he says, more urgently this time. 'What now?'

I stare at the ground. I don't answer. There's nothing to say. In all of my training, I've never had to deal with a scenario where there was no solution.

But here we are. Trapped. With no more water source, and no way out.

Chapter 36

Reuters World News

Thousands missing, feared dead, as rescuers search for survivors after Vancouver quake
October 12, 2018 | 11:59 PM GMT

Authorities are yet to release estimates of those killed by this morning's magnitude 9.1 earthquake and subsequent tsunami off the coast of Vancouver, Canada, but experts suggest it could be in the thousands.

'The city of Vancouver has spent millions of dollars creating procedures and infrastructures that would minimise the damage and casualties of an earthquake such as this one,' Los Angeles-based emergency expert Will Mallory explained. 'The city was as prepared as it could be, but with an earthquake of this magnitude, it's impossible for a large metropolitan area to come out unscathed.'

The Canadian city's unique geographic location means that an earthquake can trigger both tsunamis and landslides, with three local mountains rising up from just outside Vancouver's downtown core. This morning's tremors, which included three significant aftershocks, signalled landslides that saw boulders the size of vans plummeting into residential areas already decimated by the quakes.

Operation Panorama, a military operation designed to respond to an earthquake on the Pacific Coast, has been initiated, with reservists across Canada being called to duty as part of the rescue response.

Troops will initially assist emergency services in search and rescue efforts, but may eventually be reassigned to tasks such as providing shelter, supplying clean drinking water, and transport.

Experts suggest that the crucial window for survival of earthquake victims is seventy-two hours. The earthquake hit over seven hours ago, which means the clock is already ticking for those most affected.

To donate to the Red Cross urgent appeal, click here.

Chapter 37

LUCY

Now

In the featureless white room, now eerily still after the rattling aftershock, Lucy opened her eyes. Just a sliver. Just to assess her surroundings, to find the object that had slammed so violently into the back of her head. The light burned her eyes, but she resisted closing them again.

Something had changed. Something had shifted.

The first thing she saw when she lifted her throbbing head was the shelf, still attached to the wall, but barely. One of the brackets had come loose, and the other was completely detached, so the whole thing was being suspended by a single screw. It swayed slightly, a pendulum counting down its own demise.

The shelf wasn't what had hit her. And the bottles of water that were scattered across the floor had already fallen in the first aftershock; they weren't to blame.

The pounding in her head reached an agonising crescendo, and she stopped moving for a few moments, closing her eyes and waiting for the pain, the dizziness, to pass. Eventually it ebbed enough for her to open her eyes again. Slowly, gently, Lucy lifted herself onto her elbows.

She looked around for a protein bar – her energy was waning, and she had no idea how long it had been since she last ate – but as her eyes scanned the room, they landed on something she didn't recognise. Something dark and slightly shiny. It was about the size and shape of a leg. Was it a piece of pipe? She squinted to make sense of it, but she couldn't identify the strange object, which hadn't been there before the last aftershock.

She had tripped on something, hadn't she? That must have been the mystery object, the thing that had assaulted her during the tremor. She placed her palms on the floor and raised herself to her knees. She still felt weak. And a little light-headed. She didn't want to risk standing, in case she passed out, or threw up.

Instead she crawled slowly, like a child, towards the object that had sent her flying across the room. When she reached it, she peered at the inexplicably ominous cylinder. She reached out a hand and touched it. It was cool, and had a fine texture etched into its surface. It was definitely metal, although she couldn't have said what kind. Copper, perhaps? Bronze?

She tried to pick it up. It was too heavy to lift with one hand, so she sat back on her heels and used both hands to scoop it up. She was lucky, she realised as she cradled it firmly. This could have killed her. The tender bump on her head throbbed, as though in agreement.

She turned the lump of metal over, the shape of it becoming clear as she handled it. It wasn't just roughly the size and shape of a leg. It *was* a leg: at least, a sculpture of one. There, in her hands, was a calf and shin and ankle, with tiny indentations of skin, and soft, contoured muscle. She ran her hands over the curves, marvelling at the precision of it. A glimmer of recognition fired in the recesses of her brain. She was no expert on sculpture, but she'd seen something like this before.

She turned it upright, so the top of the leg was facing her.

Etched into the smooth metal, she spotted a signature that made her skin erupt in goose pimples.

This wasn't the work of just any sculptor.

This was the work of The Sculptor.

Chapter 38

BILL

The men and women who swarm around the search and rescue hub aren't showing any signs of exhaustion. They've been trained for this. They've worked hard, pushing their bodies and their minds past breaking point again and again in preparation for a day like today. Their muscles respond to their demands. Their minds block out the horrors of what they've seen, the choices they've had to make. At least for now.

For many of them, the collapse will come tomorrow. Or the next day. Or the one after that, when they're given a break, and their eyes close and the flashbacks fly at them, making them wonder if sleep is really worth it for the visions they'll have to endure. For others, it'll come in the weeks and months following the earthquake.

But now, as they follow orders and placate panicked citizens and stem bleeding and look people in the eye and tell them that they're sorry, but that there's nothing more they can do, they're fighting fit. Running on adrenaline and autopilot and the need to keep going, because if they don't, they can't bear the consequences.

Bill sighs, throws the water bottle he's just drained into the recycling pile and walks towards the Incident Commander's desk, a trestle table covered in paper maps and clipboards for signing in and out, for logging incidents, for requesting equipment.

'Bill Caruthers,' he says as he reaches the table. 'I just finished over at The Keg.'

A steakhouse a few blocks away had caught fire after a gas leak. Thankfully, no one was left inside by the time the flames licked at the building. It had been one of the few jobs today that didn't have a tragic ending for someone.

'OK. There's a kid trapped under some concrete over by the hospital,' he's told. The hospital, which had to be evacuated. Which had partially collapsed. Which should be saving lives, but can't. Bill nods.

'Go see Miranda over there, she'll get you put on the team heading out to the scene. You leave in two.'

He follows the pointed finger and walks towards a woman carrying a clipboard, looking as harried and shocked as everyone else he's encountered today.

'Bill Caruthers,' he repeats when he reaches her. 'Where do you need me?'

Chapter 39

ALICE

'What now?'

'I don't know,' I snap. 'Just give me a chance to think.'

My mind is racing, clutching for a solution where there clearly isn't one. I ease myself onto a piece of rubble, and the palm of my hand stings as it presses on the concrete. It seems almost insulting that I can still feel such an inconsequential injury in addition to the litany of hurts my body has suffered, and yet, the cut caused by that tiny piece of debris I'd clung so tightly to when the killer first woke up is pulsing, demanding my attention.

The piece of debris...

I'd been trying to alert the outside world to my presence, tapping a tiny fragment of the building against the gurney. It was the best I could do while I was still strapped down.

'I have an idea,' I say, picking up the mop handle from the dusty ground next to me. With difficulty, I push myself to a standing position.

'What is it?' he asks. 'Can you even walk? I'll go. Just tell me what I need to do.'

I don't reply. If I tell him my plan, he'll have no reason to keep me alive.

It's harder than ever to make my way across the landscape of rubble. My legs are unsteady, like they belong to someone else, and my arm aches from gripping the mop handle. My body doesn't seem able to communicate with my brain, so every movement is taking too long, each limping, lurching step feels incorrect.

I stumble, and my hands reach out too late, so I fall face first into a pile of bricks. There's an unnatural crunching noise. A searing new pain shoots across my chest. I realise, vaguely, as though it's inconsequential, that one of my ribs has probably snapped. I lay silently, too exhausted to vocalise the hurt.

'What happened?'

Not 'Are you OK?'

I open my mouth to reply, but it feels as though something huge and invisible is being lowered slowly onto my chest, pressing my lungs. I can't fill them properly. I can't breathe. I force a tiny gulp of air, and try to speak.

'...Fell and ... breathe ...'

I struggle against the crushing sensation, but it's useless. I claw at the fabric around my face and pull it off, hoping that its absence will mean I can breathe. But the pressure doesn't ease.

'What are you doing?' he asks, and there's a clatter of rubble as he picks his way over to where I'm lying. Seconds later, he's looming over me.

'What's wrong?' He sounds genuinely frightened.

I press my hand to my throat, and as my fingers connect with my trachea, which is curved strangely, recognition fires somewhere in the recesses of my memory. My eyes widen as I consider what might be happening, and what needs to happen to keep me alive.

I point to my chest, which is tightening, as though a giant hand is wrapped around my ribs, squeezing.

'Can't ... breathe ... help.'

'How? I don't know what's wrong!'

'The needle,' I hiss. 'Get the needle.'

He doesn't move. I can barely breathe, but somehow I find the air to whisper, 'Now!'

Something in my tone, or my face, or the wheezing, pained breaths that are becoming shorter and more laboured, propel him into action. I can't turn my head to see what he's doing, but there's clattering and huffing as he moves towards the needle that feels like miles away, despite it only being a few feet from where I'm lying.

There's a tumbling of debris. He curses, but keeps moving. And suddenly his face is in front of mine again, his nose and mouth covered by the sleeve of his shirt, his eyes wide and glassy. He's kneeling by my side, swaying. I don't know if it's my dizziness or his. Probably both. He's panting, hard. I am trying to force air into my lungs, but my body won't comply.

'Help,' I wheeze through the side of my mouth.

He holds up the needle, filled with my thick, dark blood. I reach out and snatch it from him, pulling the plunger out and spilling my own blood onto the ground beside me. He yelps in protest, but it's half-hearted. Whatever he was going to use it for has to be low on his priority list now. My chest is shrinking, my lungs feel full, like there's no space for anything more, and yet my body is desperate for oxygen. If I'm right about what's happening, I only have a few minutes to live.

I don't have the breath for many words. I'll have to make each of them count. I drop the plunger to the ground, passing the needle back and stretching my left arm across my chest, ignoring the howling pain, until my left hand is clinging onto my right shoulder. Then, with my right hand, I press the spaces between my ribs on my left side, counting

171

down from the top. I reach the third space and leave my finger pressed there.

'Need you—' I wheeze, my head growing light, darkness pressing in on all sides as my body is starved of oxygen – 'inject here. Now.'

I look up at the man who's standing, frozen, the needle hovering in the air. I stare at him, silently pleading with him to do the right thing, to save my life.

I should know better.

The person I'm asking to save me – the only person who can save me – wants me dead.

Chapter 40

THE SCULPTOR

I did not come here today to help.

When I left this morning, when I cast one last glance at the Muse frantically scrambling against the sleek white walls I so carefully designed, trying to find a way out, I was not hunting for a way to assist someone in crisis. I was not seeking an opportunity to become a better person. I was pursuing the completion of what I've been compelled to create.

Whether or not I'm able to help is not really the point. Just because I can make things better for someone doesn't necessarily mean I should. It's not who I am. It's not what I do.

I'm an artist, I want to scream. Of course, that only matters to me. But it really, really matters to me.

It's not just my career, it's who I am, down to my DNA. Using clay and rubber and cement and wax and ceramic and bronze, I take something fleeting and turn it into something eternal. I take the earthly and alter it until it's divine.

That's how I help the world. That's how I offer healing, and comfort.

I don't get involved with the nitty gritty of human suffering. At least, not with the alleviation of it.

And yet, unexpectedly, I've been thrown into a situation where that's exactly what's being asked of me.

It's ironic, isn't it? Me, trapped with my Muse, our suffering shared. Her needing help, me being in a position to provide it. It's a mirror of how things usually are with my Muses, only it's one of those horrible, distorted fairground mirrors, and in this particular one, I'm looking for a way out, too.

So here I am. Here we are. Together. I have two choices: Help, or don't.

Let her live, or let her die. It's all so mundane, isn't it? There's nothing poetic or artistic about a death caused by being crushed by a piece of concrete. Or a death caused by a bystander's apathy. It's not grand or beautiful or worth beholding.

And my Muse, redundant as she now is to me, deserves better. I selected her because I was drawn to her, because I believed she was worthy of being transformed. Because, for whatever reason, I was compelled to her – by her – the way I've been lured in by all of my other Muses, beckoned by an invisible but powerful hand.

In the end, I wanted great things for her.

So... screw it.

It's not really my style, but in this distorted reality, I might as well lend a hand, I suppose.

Chapter 41

LUCY

Lucy stared at the object in her hands for a moment, her brain trying to process what she was seeing, scrambling for an explanation, any explanation, that made some kind of sense.

But all she knew was this: she had, in her hands, a bronze leg that had been created by The Sculptor.

The only reason she even knew about The Sculptor was because of Maria, up-and-coming photographer and all-round art fanatic. Lucy's own artistic abilities were, she was happy to admit, almost non-existent, but living in a city like Portland, it was impossible not to absorb at least a little bit of creative knowledge.

And being around Maria was like taking an art class, only without having to pick up a paintbrush or chisel of her own. She lived and breathed all forms of creativity, and when she wasn't behind the lens she studied everything from street art to classic paintings to sculpture, and plenty in between. If she wasn't dragging Lucy to galleries and specialist book-shops, they'd be hanging out at her apartment, which was really more of a studio, to drink wine and gossip while Maria painted or shot or sketched.

Lucy vividly remembered Maria's sculpture phase. She was photographing pieces from around the city, capturing them in the late-afternoon golden light, shadows dancing across shapes, new art being created from existing art via the lens of an expert. She'd dragged Lucy to an exhibit of modern sculpture at some obscure gallery on the fringes of the city.

Maria had been mesmerised by a piece created by The Sculptor. She wouldn't stop going on about the bronze torso, the curves of the muscles and the tiny, barely visible ridges of skin immortalised in the metal. Lucy had been preoccupied with the burgers they were going to eat afterwards, was already planning her order, trying to decide between rosemary or sweet potato fries.

But she had to admit, even though she'd not really understood the allure of the chunk of bronze on the pedestal in that strange little gallery, she had been intrigued by the mystery of the artist. She'd wondered what kind of person eschewed public affirmation for their achievements, whether that made them incredibly insecure, or enviably confident.

So she knew whose creation she was holding in her hands, but she was left with so many questions. Was she being held captive by some kind of collector? Was it The Sculptor who had taken her? Where had this hunk of metal come from?

She let her gaze slide from the leg in her arms, up to the barely attached shelf, across one stark white wall to the next, where the giant white clock loomed above her. It revealed that the time was four fifty-five. If she had to guess, she'd say it was early morning. But she had a fifty–fifty chance of being wrong about that. Besides, it didn't really matter.

Her eyes continued trailing the walls of the room. It didn't seem to have sustained too much damage – there were no cracks in the walls or floor. The fluorescent strips that lit the room were still intact, clinging to the shiny white ceiling.

Perhaps the earthquake wasn't as severe as it had seemed. Maybe it was too far away to do damage wherever she was. Or maybe the room she was in was just so secure that even an earthquake couldn't destroy it. As her eyes slid across the pristine white wall, something at the back of her mind told her to stop.

The hairs on the back of her neck prickled. What had she just seen? Her subconscious had noticed something, but her brain hadn't processed it yet.

Lucy's eyes flitted back to the clock, and that's when she realised.

The huge round face wasn't quite attached to the wall at three o'clock. It was firmly secured right around the nine o'clock mark, but the other side was swaying. It was almost imperceptible, but there it was: back and forth, slow and steady.

As though the clock was attached by a hinge. As though it was a door.

Chapter 42

ALICE

'Help,' I manage to whisper again.

The words are barely forming now. I'm mouthing them but there's no sound.

He closes his eyes for a split second, then nods.

'OK. OK, what do I do?'

'Top – up—' I gasp, unable to give complete commands, desperately hoping that he understands me, that he does what I tell him to.

He hovers over me for a few seconds, as if deciding whether he wants to help, whether he can, and then he roughly pulls up the ripped hem of my top. I momentarily lift my finger from the spot between my ribs as my torso is exposed, and place it back down on my bare skin.

'I don't – what do I need to do?' he asks, his eyes suddenly serious.

I can't spare the words it would take to tell him that I think I have a tension pneumothorax, a condition I learned about in first aid training, which means that there's air trapped in the pleural space of my lungs. My best guess is that one of my ribs broke and punctured my lung when I fell, so now when I breathe in, the air is leaking into the space outside my lung, with no way of escape. It's pushing my organs around, suffocating me from the inside.

The air needs a way out.

'Needle. Here,' I hiss, my lungs burning, my head spinning. I tap my finger in the space between my ribs, where the needle needs to go, in order to release the pressure that's building quickly – and dangerously – inside me.

A gargled croak leaps from my lips as he bends down to look at where my finger is resting, and I realise what I'm allowing to happen. I can't trust him to operate on me, to save me. I can't put my life – my body – in his hands.

But I'm dying. I need him. My lungs are screaming, my brain is fading, the world is becoming dimmer. If I want to live, I don't have a choice.

The sharp, cold point of the needle rests against my skin, next to my finger. A tear slides down my cheek.

'I just inject it in right here? Like, all the way in?' he asks. I nod frantically. I might only have seconds left.

I look up into his eyes. Streaks mark the fabric that's pulled over his face, damp tributaries where tears flowed when he thought he might lose his life. His eyes are dry now; now, when it's only my life at stake.

He squeezes his eyes closed, then opens them again. Blinks a couple more times, groans, and then rubs his hand over his eyes.

'I'm dizzy,' he murmurs to himself. He sounds scared. This doesn't seem like the same man who taunted me when I was strapped to the gurney, just hours ago. But I know what he's capable of. I know what he might still do.

The needle he's pressing against my skin could pierce my heart, and I wonder if I'd rather just die now than experience a sharp object being forced into one of my vital organs. If he's as dizzy as he claims, he could kill me without meaning to. He could do incredible, irreparable damage to my body, my organs.

But I can't tell him not to perform the surgery. And I can't make him do it. He has no reason to save me, aside from the rudimentary first aid I can offer him, and a plan I – thankfully – haven't disclosed. All I can do is lie here, and hope that whatever happens, it won't hurt too much, and that it'll be over soon.

'OK,' he says. 'I'm ready. Stay still.'

I don't move; I can't. But I try to surrender to whatever will happen, letting my body go limp, the way it's been trying to as I've fought against it.

The seconds tick by. It's excruciating. I am screaming at him in my head, telling him to hurry up or I'll die anyway, but he's just ... paused, his fingers pressing against my skin, his breathing laboured.

'I can't – Alice—'

My mouth is moving, but the words aren't coming out. I keep trying, forcing air that doesn't exist out of my lungs to squeeze out two simple, thin words. 'Do it.'

'All right,' he pants. 'OK. Here goes.'

Chapter 43

LUCY

Lucy dropped the sculpture with a clunk and scrambled to her feet, pushing through the wave of dizziness that hit her.

There wasn't time for her to worry about concussion. She had to escape, and she had to work out how to do it before another tremor hit, or worse: her captor returned.

She stood facing the wall, looking up at the clock, and stretched on her toes to try to reach it. Her fingers brushed nothing but smooth, cool wall. The clock was too high up – probably eight or nine feet above the ground – for her to reach without some kind of assistance.

Only . . . there was nothing in the room that she could use to help her reach it. Lucy took a deep breath, her pulse pounding. It only seemed impossible, she told herself. But there had to be a way.

She looked around. There was almost nothing in the room that she could work with, so she started with the shelf, re-assuringly solid and large.

When it had been properly mounted to the wall, it had been just within reach, as though the water bottles had been taunting her. Just a couple more inches, they'd seemed to mock, and you could die of thirst. But now, with one side detached from the wall, she could reach out and grab it. She stepped over to the wall adjacent to the clock and curled her

181

hands around the shiny white edges of the shelf. Putting one leg out behind her for balance, she pulled. It moved, but not enough. It was still attached to the wall by one bracket, and she didn't have anything to use to lever it off. She'd just have to pull harder.

She took a deep breath, closed her eyes and yanked with all of her strength.

She stumbled backwards, falling to the ground, the shelf smacking her in the mouth as she landed.

Lucy cried out, her hand flying to her face, pain radiating from her chin, her lips, her tongue. She pulled her hand away. It was red. Slick with blood. She groaned and ran her tongue around her mouth. Where there was once a tooth, now there was a gap. Startled, she sat up and looked around, searching for the missing piece of her smile. There it was, on the pristine white floor, surrounded by a tiny puddle of red. She collected the small white tooth and put it in her pocket, zipping it shut so she wouldn't lose it. Then she stood.

She wiped the blood from the corner of the shelf using the bottom of her top, and dragged it across the floor.

Leaning it lengthwise against the wall, Lucy lifted it from the short edge, sliding it up the slick white surface of the wall until it reached the bottom of the clock. Her arms were screaming, and her mouth pulsed aggressively, but she ignored the pain, along with the unsettling sensation that she was drunk, or at least a little tipsy. Was this what concussion felt like? She discarded the thought. There was no time. Her kidnapper could be back at any moment, and the more time she wasted feeling sorry for herself, the closer she was to death.

She just had to slide the shelf behind the clock . . . there! Triumph flared inside her as she used the piece of wood to lever the edge of the clock that wasn't attached to the wall.

Slowly, as though it was resisting giving up its secrets, the clock swung away from the wall, the hinge squeaking softly.

Behind the face was a door. Small and square, like the entrance to a loft. But unmistakeable. And ever-so-slightly ajar.

'Yesss,' she whooped to herself, grinning a gappy, blood-stained smile at no one. 'You did it, Luce, you genius! You did it.'

Her grin slid off her bloodied face as she realised the truth of her situation. She wasn't out of danger yet. Her captor could be back at any moment.

She had found a way out. But it was out of her reach.

Unless she found a way to climb through the door to freedom, she was still as good as dead.

Chapter 44

ALICE

The edges of my consciousness are getting fuzzy, the blackness pushing in. I close my eyes and wait.

There's a sharp prick in my side, along with an aching pressure that I assume is the needle being pushed deeper and deeper into my chest. It stops.

Nothing happens.

And then, all at once, there's a loud hiss of air, and the pressure in my chest lifts.

My eyes fly open, and I gasp reflexively. My lungs fill, and I take huge, deep gulps, sensation flooding my body once again. I half sob, half laugh, as oxygen runs through my bloodstream, filling and rushing out of my lungs.

'Oh my God,' I wheeze. 'It worked.'

I glance up, blinking back spots of light, until a face comes into focus in front of mine. He looks shaken, his hand pressed against his forehead, his eyes planted firmly on the spot where the needle went into my body. I follow his gaze. The needle is still protruding from my ribcage.

'Should I . . . take that out?' he asks, his voice trembling.

'If that comes out, I'll die,' I manage to say. I instantly regret it. I've just given him a way to kill me, one that involves absolutely no effort on his part. But, I remind myself, he saved me, when he could have just done nothing, and I'd have died. Maybe he wants me to stay alive, after all. For now, at least.

'What happened?' he whispers, horrified.

It takes me a minute or two to get my breath back, to be able to talk again. When I can, I try to keep it simple.

'I think there's a hole in my lung somewhere, probably thanks to a broken rib, and air is building up outside of my lungs. The needle is acting as a drain to let air out so that I can breathe normally again.'

'So . . . you're fixed?'

I hold back a laugh, even though my answer is anything but funny. 'Hardly. I'm going to need surgery. My lung is screwed, but this will have to do for now. I just can't make any sudden movements, or I'll risk losing the needle.'

'So what you're saying is,' he pauses, a smugness in his voice that makes me think there's a smile hidden under his makeshift mask, 'that I just saved your life?'

I stare at him, dumbfounded. He raises an eyebrow. I can't respond. I don't know how. I'm not going to thank him, if that's what he thinks. And I'm certainly not going to admit that he saved me. That would mean I'm indebted to him. And as far as I'm concerned, there's no amount of lives he can save that could make up for what he's done.

'I wouldn't say that,' I say hesitantly. This feels like a trap, like whatever I say will be the wrong thing. 'You're the reason I'm so injured in the first place.'

'I'd be careful with your words, if I were you,' he warns. His tone is calm and quiet. It's menacing, and I'm reminded of the shocking pain of his fist meeting my face. I look down at the needle in my side nervously, then back to him. He's tensed, as though he might strike without warning, pull it from my lung, kill me. I'm trembling all of a sudden.

'I mean – I – yes, you did just save my life.'

I hate him. I want to launch myself at him, screaming, and tear him apart. But of course I won't. Instead, I have to grovel, show him how grateful I am. I force myself to swallow down my disgust. It won't keep me alive.

'Well, what do you say when someone saves your life?'

His tone is patronising, like he's speaking to a small, insolent child.

'Thank you,' I mutter between gritted teeth. It pains me to say the words, but I don't want to risk inciting his anger.

'Thank you, what?'

I look at him stupidly, completely at a loss. And I realise for the first time that I don't know his name. In my head, he's 'the killer', or 'the man in the mask' – not a human, not someone with a name and a family and a life outside of this subterranean hell.

'I . . . I don't know your name,' I stutter.

'You don't need to know it,' he snaps. 'I just want to know how grateful you are.'

Fury rises in me as he stares, a frightening glint of depravity in his eyes. I don't know what he wants from me, what this twisted game is that he seems to be playing.

'Thank you . . . very much?' I try, forcing the words out, dignity slipping through my lips along with my gratitude.

He nods, apparently satisfied, then starts limping the few paces back towards the gurney.

'You should have listened to me,' he calls over his shoulder. 'I warned you not to go walking through the rubble.'

I stay where I am, rage coursing through my veins, my skin seething. I force myself to breathe, to focus on the glorious sensation of filling my lungs. They still don't feel like they're working – not properly, not like they used to – but at least I can inhale and exhale, and for that I'm thankful. There's a strange pressure in my left side, which could be the needle that's sticking into my lung, or the rib that punctured it in the first place. I try not to think about what's happening beneath my skin.

When my breathing becomes more rhythmic, and I trust myself to move, I start the arduous process of shifting my body.

Slowly, gently, I attempt to sit upright, rubble clattering around me as I make sure to keep the needle in place. The smallest movement engulfs me in a wave of pain, so it's slow going, made slower by the sharp awareness that the needle can't move or I'll die.

I pull the – now filthy – cotton back over my face, and take a minute to catch my breath before inspecting the tiny piece of medical equipment that's keeping me alive. It's jutting out of my body, just stuck in there, inhibiting the movement of my arm. I marvel that something that was brought here to do me harm has, in fact, saved me. If he hadn't brought the needle, hadn't drawn my blood, I'd be dead. The irony is razor-sharp.

With painstaking movements, I lift my arm and reach around to gently twist the hub of the needle to release it from the syringe. There's a sort of clicking that grinds against my ribs. I grit my teeth and try not to imagine how badly I could get this wrong.

The hub pulls away. I hold my breath. Then, slowly, nervously, I take a sip of air. I let it out. I take another. My body relaxes as I realise that – at least for now, in this particular way – I am OK.

The red plastic hub of the needle is sticking out, poking from my side, keeping me from suffocation. It's not ideal, but it's better than the barrel of the syringe hanging off me. I'll just have to be careful not to knock it or brush it with my arm.

'Alice.' I look up in surprise at the sound of my name, slurred so it comes out as 'Alishh'.

He's curled up beside the gurney, his arms hugging his knees to his chest, his face clearly pale, even in this half-light.

'What?'

'What are we gonna do?' he mumbles. His words are all tripping over one another, stumbling into each other, forming one big, barely comprehensible word: whadaweganado. The gash on his forehead is bleeding a little through the duct tape, but I don't think that's the real problem anymore.

His chin falls to his chest, revealing a fresh wound on the back of his head, slick with blood. He must have been injured in the last shock. I didn't see it before, but that would explain why he was so dizzy when I needed him to stick the needle in my side. And why he's so weak now. The cut is bleeding profusely.

The sight of it makes me both sick and relieved, the latter emotion making me hate myself a little. I know I should help him, offer to dress his injury, make sure he has some water. But we have so little of it – one bottle, propped up between two bricks, quickly dwindling – and I don't want to waste it on him.

'Alisshhh!'

'I don't know, OK? I don't know what the hell we can do. I can barely move, and you're...' I wave my hand at him vaguely. 'Well, I don't think we really have a lot of options at this point.'

I glance over my shoulder at the washing machine I'd been trying to reach when I fell. It's only a few feet away, but I won't be able to make it that far. I don't want to be stranded in the middle of the room, away from our meagre supply of water, and the protection of the gurney.

He mumbles something incoherent, his head lolling onto his chest again. I catch another glimpse of blood glistening at the back of his skull. My eyes flick away, not wanting to look directly at it, in case I throw up, or worse: feel the urge to help.

His head lifts, ever so slightly, then drops again as he emits a low, long groan.

'I think ish . . . concussion,' he mumbles.

'Yeah, well, probably,' I say stubbornly, not willing to give an inch to this man. But I can feel it, the need to help, to step in when someone needs me, simmering just under the surface of my skin, wanting to leap out and lend him a hand. How conditioned I am, I marvel, to want to help the man who almost killed me, who would have definitely sawed me into pieces had the earth not stepped in.

I'm a people-pleaser, always have been. I get anxious if I know that someone's upset with me. Not even upset. Just slightly surprised or put out by my actions. I feel panicked if I think I've let someone down. I apologise when people run into me on the street. I know when I'm being taken advantage of, and I still let it happen. I don't ever want to rock the boat, or displease anyone. And I've dedicated the last twenty years to helping people, to saving them.

But how fucked up am I, that my instinct tells me to help, to nurture, to care? About him.

'Dizz . . .' he mumbles, lifting his head, looking right at me. I meet his gaze, defiant. I will not come to this man's rescue. I will not save him. I will save myself.

Even though he's not saying anything coherent, I understand that he's pleading with me. I feel it, that familiar pinch in my stomach, that pull to avoid disappointing anyone, at all costs. I ignore it. It takes all of my strength, but I push my instincts down.

'Dizzy,' he manages to say, and then his head drops to his chest again. There's a long, low, mournful moan.

And then the room is completely silent. I hold my breath, waiting for him to wake up, to keep mumbling, slurring, begging.

But there's no sign of life. No breathing, no moaning.

Just deathly quiet, and the echo of my guilt.

Chapter 45

LUCY

It had been twenty-three minutes – she knew, because she'd been looking at the stupid, oversized face of the clock the entire time – since Lucy had discovered the trapdoor, and she still hadn't worked out how to get through it. Panic rose up in her as she pictured her abductor returning, getting closer with every passing second.

She stared at the door: just a square, maybe two feet by two feet, made from the same substance as the shiny white wall. Thanks to her shelf levering, it was now gaping open, with nothing but yawning darkness beyond it. She had to find a way through. But she was too short to reach the door, and there was nothing in the room that could be used as a ladder or stool to boost her up.

After she'd forced the trapdoor fully open, using the shelf as an extension of her arm, she'd tried making a sort of pyramid with the six water bottles that were left. As soon as she'd put her weight on them, one of the bottles on the bottom had crumpled and split wide open, its contents spilling onto the shiny grey floor.

She'd then decided to use the shelf as a ramp. She'd leaned it up against the wall, walked to the other side of the room and had run straight at it. When she'd reached the shelf, she'd leaped up, her left foot hitting the shiny surface first, knocking it from its precarious position and onto the floor. She'd flown headlong into the wall, her chin taking the brunt of the impact, before falling into a heap on top of the shelf.

She wished she'd never found the trapdoor. Knowing there was an escape, but not being able to reach it, was worse than having no escape at all. She was crying so hard that she could hardly breathe, her juddering gulps of air only half filling her lungs. She didn't try to calm down, didn't attempt to stop her chest from heaving or her eyes from overflowing. It didn't matter. She was going to die there, in a white box, where no one would ever find her.

The clock continued its march towards the moment when her kidnapper returned to finish whatever it was she'd been brought there for. And as Lucy's sobs lost momentum and her breathing steadied, she heard its derisive rhythm again.

Quit-ter. Quit-ter. Quit-ter.

'No,' she whispered to the clock. To herself.

She might have given up on prepping, on the opportunity to start her own business, on her conversation with Maria. But she wasn't going to give up on surviving. She was going to do everything she could to stay alive.

She closed her eyes and tried to think through her predicament logically.

Whoever was holding her hostage had to have a way in – and out – of the room. The space was pristine. Someone came in to clean, they didn't just throw items in: water, protein bars, kidnapped women. Which meant that if her captor could get back up through that trapdoor, there was a way for her to access it, too. A way that didn't involve superhuman leaps.

She didn't have to get her body up that high. She just

needed to bring whatever it was – a rope, a ladder, maybe – to her. She had to pull it down.

She looked around, her heart beating with renewed determination. What she needed was a pole, or something long and rigid, with a hook on the end. She sighed. What she needed was a genie that granted her three wishes, too. She had to be realistic, work with what she had. It wasn't much, but there had to be a way. She wouldn't allow herself to consider the possibility that there wasn't.

Maybe she could create a kind of lasso, something long that she could throw through the door, with a hook-like implement on the end. That way, if it was lying just inside the door, it would catch and she'd pull it through.

She considered the materials she had to work with. Her entire inventory was paltry: a shelf, five full bottles of water and a broken one, an expensive piece of metal art in the shape of a leg, a roll of toilet paper . . . Lucy furiously willed her brain to solve the puzzle that was in front of her. She tapped her fingers against the crook of her arm, her fingertip brushing a scratch in her leather jacket, which she fiddled with unconsciously as she racked her brain.

Her spine straightened as she realised: her clothes – she could tear up her clothes. She quickly pulled her jacket off and dropped it at her feet. It was made of leather – too thick to tear easily. She pulled her top over her head and then, shivering, slipped her arms back through the sleeves of her jacket. She zipped it closed.

She lifted the wad of slippery blue fabric and whispered 'please work', then bit the hem, on the side of her mouth that didn't have a bloodied gap. She clamped down, ignoring the pain, and pulled.

There was a satisfying ripping sound, and after a few seconds the front of her top had been torn in two, leaving one long piece of fabric. She got to work, tearing it into smaller strips, all mismatched, and then tying them together. When she was done, her makeshift rope was almost the length of the room. Lucy's chest swelled with pride. If only Maria could see her determination.

Scrambling across the floor, she snatched up the bottle that had exploded when she'd put her weight on it. It had split almost entirely through the middle, so she twisted it until it broke into two pieces. Then she tied one end of the rope to the neck of the bottle, leaving the sharp, uneven end exposed. It wasn't sophisticated, but it might just do.

Without hesitating, she threw the bottle end into the dark, gaping mouth of the door. It took a few attempts before the makeshift hook hit its target, but when it did she stood directly underneath, keeping the fabric rope flush against the wall. She tugged gently. The bottle was caught on something. Hope soared inside her. Lucy tugged again, and all at once something dark and heavy tumbled towards her. She ducked just in time, and whatever it was landed on her back with a gentler thud than she'd been expecting, before sliding off.

Stepping away, she looked up and laughed, wincing at the pain in her face as her mouth stretched wide. Just as she'd imagined, there was a ladder, its rope rungs leading into the trapdoor. It was so much easier to access than she'd been expecting.

Lucy didn't wait another second before stepping onto the first rung, heaving herself up by the sides of the rope, scrambling up it and through the trapdoor without wondering what would be waiting for her there.

The space she squeezed herself into was completely dark. Pulling her legs up and out of the white room, Lucy stood and pressed her hand against the wall closest to the trapdoor, sliding it up and down, hoping for a light switch. The wall was bare. She kept moving, knowing that there had to be a light – or another door – somewhere.

Her hand hit something cold and small. She felt for the switch and flicked it up. Light flooded the room, and Lucy was temporarily blinded.

As her vision returned, shapes and colours and features began to come into focus.

And as understanding washed over her, Lucy let out a bloodcurdling scream.

Chapter 46

ALICE

Relief washes over me as silence presses in.

With the killer out of the picture – dead, or maybe just unconscious, I don't really care either way – he can no longer hurt me, threaten me, scare me, taunt me, or kill me. If another tremor hits, I can worry about myself without having to make way for him. The tiny bit of water that's left at the bottom of the bottle is all mine.

I crawl slowly, agonisingly, crossing the few feet from where I collapsed to the gurney, taking my time, stopping as much as I need to. Every time I pause, I look up, just to check. He's still motionless.

Reaching the gurney, I sit, then grab the water bottle and take the smallest sip I can manage. It takes all of my willpower not to gulp the lot, but I have to make this last as long as I can. If I can just stay alive, just keep breathing, keep going, then there's still hope that I can get out of here. I have to believe that. Even if no one knows where I am, even if I'm too weak to alert anyone to my presence.

My thoughts tumble over one another, racing to be the first to morph into some kind of viable plan to get out of here. Nothing materialises, and in the end I rest my head gently against the gurney leg and stare up at what's left of the ceiling, letting my body rest for the first time since this ordeal began.

The yellow light is dim, but as dust particles drift through the air, into the beam, they're lit like flecks of gold; tiny moments of beauty in the midst of all of this horror. I watch the slow, mesmeric waltz of fragments of the building that's closing in around me, and my mind wanders, flitting between memories so vivid that I feel like I could reach out and touch them. Fireflies on family camping trips, smoke curling up to the moon, bursts of light darting between shadowy branches. Stickers on my ceiling, placed carefully to mimic constellations, my eyelids drooping, warm and content and safe. Lying on dewy grass outside Celia's family's cabin, drunk and giggly, her plastic tiara still jaunty on her forehead, promising each other we'd still be friends, even after the wedding.

And then a more recent memory flutters to the surface. More stars, pale yellow felt this time, hanging from strings, alongside a light grey moon and a fluffy white cloud. My stomach twists guiltily as I remember my secret purchase, stuffed hastily under my bed, as though someone would find out if I didn't hide it completely.

I promised Celia, and my parents – the only ones I've told about my IVF – that I wouldn't get my hopes up. That I would just wait patiently, without expectation. After all, as my doctor took pains to tell me time and time again, there were no guarantees. Besides, I didn't have many eggs to begin with. That didn't mean it wouldn't happen for me – some people got lucky. But some people didn't.

And so, in keeping with my promise, I resisted the temptation to start clearing the spare room – a space mostly hidden behind a closed door, the few old albums and books and pieces of abandoned sporting equipment gathering dust – and planning a nursery. I couldn't resist creating a secret Pinterest board though, which I filled with adorable wallpaper and stuffed animals and blankets. It was during one secretive Pinterest scrolling session, on a day when I was tired from treating myself as a human pincushion, so bruised that sitting down made me yelp, that I saw the baby mobile. My heart had stuttered, and my chest had ached with a yearning that confirmed what I'd always known: this would all be worth it.

As soon as I'd hit the purchase button, I'd felt stupid and guilty. I knew better than to get my hopes up. What would I do with it if things didn't go according to plan?

Now, sitting in the wreckage of the basement, I make a promise to myself: if I get out of here, if I make it back to my condo, I'm going to clear out my spare room and set up the nursery, and to hell with not getting my hopes up. What is the point if I don't have hope? Of course, I'm also going to think more carefully about whose DNA I'm going to pass on to my baby, but the one thing I'm not going to do is give up. On my dream of becoming a mother. On surviving.

I need to believe that I'll get out of here. And if I can make it out of this alive, then anything's possible.

I just need to find a way out.

I'm weak and slow, but without anyone else to worry about, I consider whether I could somehow dig my way to freedom. I don't have any tools, and the mop handle is hardly strong enough to break through rubble. I'd need a hammer, or a shovel.

And then I remember the saw. It won't be much use for moving huge chunks of rubble away, but it has to be useful for something. It's surely better than nothing.

I reach for my backpack, which I'd strategically placed over the tool, and pull it towards me with my foot. As it slides across the grimy floor, metal shrieks across concrete. I keep pulling until it's within reach, and grab the nylon handle, tossing the bag aside.

The disappointment is physical. The saw, once a weapon, a tool, is now a useless pile of shards, shattered into multiple pieces, none of them useful. Frustrated, I swipe at them with the mop handle, and fragments bounce and skitter across the floor, tinkling harmlessly.

I check to see if the noise was enough to disturb the figure slouched over himself, but he hasn't moved. I watch for a long time, looking for signs of life, for any indication that he's just unconscious. Nothing happens. I don't want to acknowledge that he is, in all likelihood, dead. It's in my best interest for him to be gone, but it's also horrifying. Because if he couldn't make it . . . can I?

I push the thought aside. I don't need to be thinking like that. It won't do me any good. Especially now that I'm here alone. With a corpse.

Silence presses in on me, the same kind of silence that had terrified me when the earthquake ended, all those hours ago. And it dawns on me that this is it. This silence, this void, is all that's left. If I die here, I will die alone, with no one but a dead killer for company.

Goosebumps erupt on my skin. Panic crawls up my chest. My breathing becomes shallow, strained.

My survival is now all up to me. There's no one else to share the burden with, no one else to give me hope, or motivate me, or terrify me into action. I have to get the attention of someone – anyone – outside. To do so, I have to find the strength to get back across the room. I have to dress my own wounds. And if I fall again, or move the wrong way, and the needle that's keeping me alive falls out . . . that will be the end. I can't operate on myself.

Loneliness and fear overwhelm me, and I wonder if I should have tried harder to save him.

After all, he saved me when he didn't have to. He literally saved my life, just minutes ago. And yes, he's a murderer, but he also stuck a needle in my side and stopped me from suffocating to death. He actively saved my life. I passively let him die. So which of us is the real monster?

Him, I remind myself angrily. Of course it's him. He's the whole reason I'm even trapped here. He wouldn't have had to save me if he hadn't kept me strapped down to the gurney while the room assaulted me. And, most importantly, I've never killed anyone.

Until now, a small inner voice chides me.

I shake my head.

'No,' I whisper.

But it's insistent. The guilt gnaws at my stomach like acid, and the relief I felt when silence pressed in around me turns to dread. I can't move around like he could. I can't hit the washing machine to draw attention to myself. Without him, how long will I survive? Besides, I don't want to spend days trapped in this tomb with a dead body. What if he starts to decompose? What if his spirit is restless and he haunts me? What if he holds me responsible for his death? I didn't kill him, but then again, I knew that he was in trouble, and I didn't help. What if I'm no better than him?

I'm frozen in fear, too scared to move, to make a sound, to disturb his soul, to face my own.

And then he moans, the sound loud and clear and unmistakeable, and my heart leaps.

There's only one thing I can do, only one way forward.

I have to save him. It's the only way to save myself.

Chapter 47

LUCY

It was so much worse than she could ever have imagined. And she was good at imagining.

When Rhys had left to go on a week-long hiking trip with some of his oldest friends over the summer, Lucy had waved him off with a kiss and the instruction to have a great time. She was happy for him to be hanging out with his friends and doing something he loved, but she was also happy for herself. With him out of the apartment, she could indulge in her favourite things: eating nothing but mushrooms on toast or cookies and cream ice cream for every meal, taking long, lazy baths while re-watching *Gossip Girl* for the hundredth time, sleeping till midday on Saturday without feeling guilty.

The first few days had flown by. Maria had come over with a bottle of rosé one evening, and they'd played cards till the small hours of the morning, falling asleep on the sofa and waking late, venturing out heavy-headed in search of a greasy brunch. But the following night, the novelty of her solitude wearing off, she started hearing things. A scratch on the window. The squeak of a door she was certain she'd closed. A whisper. She told herself she was being stupid, that there was nothing to be scared of, that her imagination was running wild.

But she'd struggled to fall asleep, only managing to drift

off after she'd turned all the lights on and played music that drowned out her thoughts. The next day, she didn't hear from Rhys. He was hiking in the wilderness, she reminded herself. He might not have a phone signal. There was nothing to worry about.

But when she went to bed, the noises began again, and she managed, in the darkest hours of the night, to convince herself that Rhys had been killed – by a bear, or by falling into a fast-flowing river, or after stumbling into a ravine – and was trying to communicate with her from . . . beyond.

Of course, he'd texted first thing the next day to say he was having a great time, and she'd felt ridiculous for the story she'd created out of fear. She never did tell Rhys what she'd thought. And she never heard the strange noises again.

She'd always conjured strange, twisted things in her mind. But never, in her most gruesome thoughts, could she have imagined this.

As the scream died in her throat, Lucy turned a slow circle, taking it all in, her stomach writhing, bile crawling up her throat.

Strip away a few key details, and Lucy would be looking at a modern, clean, well-equipped artist's studio, the kind Maria would lose her mind over. There was an antique wooden drafting table against the wall to Lucy's right, a lamp hovering above the scattering of papers that covered the worn surface. Next to that was a matching drafting cabinet, its thin drawers concealing hundreds of sheets of paper, some blank, others scribbled on in haste, still others carefully etched upon, line by meticulous line.

To her left, in the middle of the room, a pedestal held a half-finished sculpture of some as-yet unidentifiable shape. Behind it was a pallet on wheels, topped by a miniature tiger made out of clay, its muscles practically rippling as it crouched, poised to strike. A few more tables, some on tripods, others on wheels, dotted the clean white floor space, each topped with a sculpture in progress. Lumps of wax or clay, smooth legs or arms or hands, and intricately detailed pieces just waiting to be cast in bronze. A TV hung from the far end of the wall to Lucy's left, and closer to her, a peg-board held various instruments: a saw, chisels, pliers, brushes, files and a handful of tiny, intricate tools, the purpose of which Lucy could only guess at.

Just a normal, well-equipped sculptor's studio.

Except it was anything but normal.

Above the desk was a series of photos of a young woman. Lucy recognised her. She was the woman who went missing up in Washington, the one whose body was discovered just a few days before Lucy was whisked away in the night. The latest victim of The Coastline Killer. Carla. Only in these photos she wasn't the happy, smiling ballerina that Lucy had seen on news sites and Twitter in the weeks and months after the woman's disappearance.

In these pictures, taped to the wall in rows of five, Carla was screaming, writhing in pain or fear on the ground, crying, banging on walls, standing on her toes as though reaching for invisible help. Some of the images were of her face, twisted in fear and rage and pain and longing. But others were close-ups of her skin, her muscles, her legs against a smooth concrete floor. Lucy knew that floor. She knew exactly where the photos had been taken. Her chest contracted as understanding flooded her. Carla had been held in the room Lucy had just escaped from. She'd been watched, observed, her body studied intricately and then disposed of in the waters of Annas Bay.

Lucy understood, with terrifying clarity, who it was that had taken her. She understood the danger she was in. And she knew something else that no one else knew. She knew who The Sculptor was. She'd seen the elusive artist with her own eyes. But she still couldn't quite make all of these facts fit together, couldn't see the full picture.

For the briefest moment, she considered throwing herself back through the trapdoor into the white room, just to get away from the horror she'd discovered when she turned on the lights. She swallowed, looked away, knew she could never go back there.

Her eyes fell instead on the shelves lining the opposite wall – all perfectly lit, as though displaying a collection curated to be admired, to be boasted about – where the room's real horrors were held. A few of the items on the shelves had rattled off during the quake, but many still remained in place. The tremors mustn't have been that bad after all. Just bad enough to rattle a bronze leg from its shelf above the trapdoor. Like a gruesome clue for her to follow.

More sculptures dotted the wooden shelves, some finished, others half-done. There were arms, torsos, feet, hands, individual fingers, toes, knees. Bones. It was an anatomical study in bronze and wax.

Her gaze settled on a shelf at eye level. She squinted at a sculpture of an arm. It wasn't made of metal – plaster, perhaps? – and it had what looked like a bone sticking out from the top. She stepped closer and, against the voice in her head telling her to run, to close her eyes, to stay ignorant, peered at the plaster arm with the bone protruding from the end, unable to make sense of what she was seeing.

Why would...?

A whimper escaped her lips. The sculptures.

They weren't just meticulously carved to look like human limbs.

They contained human limbs.

She stumbled backwards, tripping and falling, landing heavily and awkwardly onto something. She didn't want to know what it was, didn't want to see. Lucy made herself look forward, focusing on nothing but escape. With trembling arms she pushed herself up, got back onto her feet and looked for a door. She had to get out.

If she didn't escape immediately, if The Sculptor came back, she'd end up inside expensive bronze statues that art students admired and studied and tried to replicate.

She couldn't let that happen.

The door wasn't difficult to find, once she peeled her eyes from the horror of what surrounded her. An apron, rubber, and black, and covered in plaster dust and wax and she didn't want to think about what else, hung from the back of it. She turned the handle. Miraculously, it opened.

Lucy had found her way out.

She knew who The Coastline Killer was, and why pieces of young women were being hacked away. She knew The Sculptor's secret, even if she didn't have a name.

And she was going to tell the world.

Chapter 48

ALICE

'Hey,' I say. 'Hey, stay awake, OK?'

Clambering over the rubble, I reach him in just a few seconds. Carefully, like he's a wild animal that might bite, I pull down his fabric mask and lift the bottle to his mouth, tipping it gently so the tiniest bit of our meagre supply touches his lips.

He doesn't move. There's no response.

'Hey,' I say again, louder this time. 'I know you're still alive. So open your eyes, OK? I'm going to help. But you need to fight this. Just don't die, all right? Come on, I can't do all the work here.'

I try again, tipping the bottle ever so slightly. This time, when the water hits his lips, his tongue appears. He licks his lips. Relief swells inside me as I tip the bottle a little more. He opens his mouth and sips. His Adam's apple bobs up and down as he swallows. I let him drink for a few seconds, and then I take the bottle away, setting it down between the two bricks that kept it upright.

He moans in complaint.

'That's all we have,' I say firmly. 'I'm not giving you all the water. Now will you please open your eyes?'

There's a pause. I clap in front of his face.

'Hey!'

His eyes flicker open. He looks at me for a second, although his gaze is empty, like he's escaped this pit and is somewhere else entirely. Then his eyelids flutter closed.

'Nope,' I say loudly. 'No way. You have to stay awake, do you understand? If you fall asleep, you might not wake up, and I don't want to deal with your corpse. Besides, as much as I hate to admit this, neither of us is getting out of here alone. You hear me? I need you to be alive, which means that I need you to talk to me.'

He mumbles something incoherent. He's not saying real words. It's just a jumble of syllables, a sound that trails into nothing.

'Let's start small, all right? You know who I am, but I don't even know your name after all of this. What's your name?'

His head moves, only the tiniest movement, side to side. No.

'Come on,' I say, exasperated. 'You really think right now is the time to worry about your identity? You don't talk to me, and you'll probably die anyway. So what difference does it make if I know your name?'

Silence.

'OK. Fine. I'm going to call you Dwayne, then. Hey, Dwayne. It's been awful to meet you. How's your head?'

He opens his eyes again, this time focusing on me. His brown eyes meet my own. I hold his gaze, despite the shiver that runs up my spine. He licks his lips.

'Not Dwayne,' he whispers. 'Ricky.'

Despite myself, I laugh. Loudly.

'Ricky? Are you kidding me?'

Ricky is not the name of a serial killer. Ricky is the name of the neighbour who makes dad jokes every time you walk past, or the kid at high school who always had the freshest sneakers and made sure everyone else knew it.

And, apparently, a man responsible for scores of sickening crimes.

I laugh again. I know his name, now, incongruous as it may be. That's more ammunition for when I get out. More to tell the police.

'You don't deserve such a harmless name, Ricky. You don't deserve to stay alive, either, but I do. And as I think I might need your help to get out, I'll be patching up your head for you.'

The words that are tumbling from my mouth sound like they're coming from a stranger's lips. I'm giddy with relief, nervous about the consequences of helping him, mad at myself for babbling so foolishly. Part of me is glad to have a task to focus on, something to work towards. Without one, all that's left is to think about how I'm completely helpless, how I'm really just waiting to die.

And then I wonder if I'm losing my mind, expending my tiny reserve of energy on saving this man. There's no time to untangle my knot of emotions right now, so I keep talking instead.

'Will you try to stay awake and not die while I do that?'

He mumbles, a non-committal sound that I take to be a yes, and I reach over for the duct tape that's on the floor beside him, wincing with the movement. It's incredible that even in this amount of pain, I can function. If I was hurt this badly in my everyday life, I'd be completely useless.

Now, though, I don't have a choice. Every movement is excruciating, and yet not moving is not an option. So I move, and I hurt, and I keep moving. Locating the inside-out rubber gloves, now covered in blood and grime, I pull them on, trying to touch them as little as possible.

I stand behind him, and gently push his head down so I can see the injury better. My stomach turns, but I swallow and force myself to carry on. I look closer. His hair is all matted with the blood, making it hard to know where the wound begins and ends. As gently as I can, I pull the hair aside, revealing a gash the length of my middle finger. The blood is running freely down his neck and onto his back. No wonder he's struggling to stay conscious.

There's no time to search for the final unused tampon and attempt to clean this gaping hole in his head. If I don't stop the bleeding, sterilising it isn't going to help at all. Using my teeth, I rip a piece of duct tape from the roll and plaster it roughly along the length of the gash. The killer – Ricky – lets out a roar.

'Oh good,' I say cruelly. 'You're awake.'

He just hums, a low, animal noise, his body going limp again.

I rip another strip off the roll, and place it across the one I've already stuck to the back of his head. I'm going to need a lot of tape to stop the bleeding. I wish I had a razor blade, to get rid of the hair so that the tape could stick neatly to his skin, but then again, if I was being granted wishes, a razor blade would be pretty low on my list.

I keep tearing pieces of tape with my teeth, sticking them down, creating a bigger and bigger patch across his head. Eventually, the flow of blood down the back of his neck seems to slow. I stick the end of the tape to his forehead and pull the roll all the way around his head, covering both wounds, keeping all of the duct tape tightly in place.

He must be in agony, and I almost – for the briefest of moments – feel sorry for him. Thankfully, that feeling is fleeting.

'OK,' I say. 'You can have another – small – sip of water.'

I hand him the bottle and he manages to lift it to his lips, tipping it slowly and taking a long sip.

'That's enough,' I snap, snatching it from him. I might not have let him die, but I'm also not going to sacrifice myself, or my water, for him.

'Thank you,' he whispers.

'Well, let's just say I didn't do it for you,' I reply. 'And I also didn't look at all that blood and gore for you to die on me now. So I have to keep you talking. OK?'

He nods.

'So, Ricky,' I say, lowering myself to the ground. 'What do you want to talk about?'

Chapter 49

ALICE

'And I've never been to Paris,' the man I now know as Ricky says wistfully, as though somehow that's the thing he should be most regretful of in this life.

'Paris would be nice,' I say, not meaning it particularly – although I'm sure Paris is lovely – but wanting to keep him talking so he doesn't die on me. 'Have you travelled much?'

'A bit,' he says, waving his hand non-committally. 'Y'know. Italy. Greece. London. Spain. Mexico. That sort of thing.'

'That's loads,' I say, surprised. Travel is supposed to expand your horizons, make you a better person. I guess that doesn't apply to everyone. 'You ever been to Germany? I have a brother who lives there.'

'Where?'

'Berlin.'

He nods. 'Berlin. So much history.'

I keep feeling like I'm trapped in some sort of surreal nightmare. This can't be really happening. I can't be casually talking with this lunatic – a man who was intent on murdering me, who I've chosen to try to keep alive – about his travels. And yet, here we are, chatting about travel destinations like we're just two people who have met at a networking event and who are enjoying some cultured small talk.

I feel sick at the thought of what I'm doing, what I'm saying, who I'm saying it to. But I know if I just stood by and let him die because I refused to talk, refused to keep him conscious, that I'd never be able to live with myself. Assuming I do, in fact, live.

Silence descends on us.

'So,' I say, scrabbling for more conversation. 'Where are you from?'

He shakes his head.

'What?'

'No,' he says. His voice is clearer now. He seems to be gaining strength. 'Next question.'

'Fine,' I sigh. Then: 'Siblings?'

'Next.'

'OK, fine. But I'm running out of topics, here. Help me out?'

He thinks for a second. 'Baseball?'

I groan. 'Pass.'

I'm out of ideas. I'm cold, I'm tired, and the aching in my body seems to have reached a crescendo.

My guard is down. Without thinking, I blurt out the question that's been playing on a loop in my head almost since the moment I woke up in this room.

'Why do you kill people?'

Ricky's head snaps up. His eyes meet mine. Fear ripples through me but I hold his gaze, reminding myself that he's got bad concussion, that he's saved my life before, that he's more interested in saving himself than hurting me. It doesn't help. My insides are like liquid, swirling violently. My body knows that I should run, even if I can't.

After a few seconds, he sighs, and drops his focus to somewhere just in front of his feet. There's a pause, as though maybe he's never really, truly considered why, like he's having to search himself for a reason.

'You wouldn't understand,' he says with a small shake of his head.

I grimace. He's probably right. But still. Now that I've dared to ask, I have to know. I have to make sense of who he is, what he's done. What he wanted to do to me.

'Try me.'

'There's ...' he trails off, his eyes glazing over, sliding off me and into the dark, his mind somewhere else entirely. I watch as his hands curl into tight fists. He takes a deep breath, and then looks back at me. The loathing in his eyes makes me want to shrink, to become invisible. I regret asking. I don't want to know any more.

'I did what I did for a reason. That's all you need to know.'

He's seething, the anger radiating off him in waves. I can't tell if it's directed at me, or at someone else, someone who hurt him, maybe. I don't know. And before I can convince myself that it's a terrible idea, my mouth is opening and the words are tumbling out.

'But why me?'

The question sounds whiny and pathetic, even to me. But I have to understand. Even if he won't tell me why he kills, surely I deserve to know why it had to be me, why my life was deemed worthless to him?

He stares at me, anger still simmering behind his eyes, and for a moment I think he'll just brush me off, refuse to answer. But then something in him softens, and he begins to speak.

'I know this doesn't really make a difference, but it really wasn't personal.'

I'm aghast. How could this not be personal?

'It's personal to me!'

'I know,' he says, the fury gone from his voice. 'But what I mean is that I didn't pick you because ... I mean, you didn't personally ... upset me, or something.'

'Then why?' I demand. 'There has to be a reason.'

'You just—' he sighs – 'match.'

'Match what?'

'The requirements.'

'What requirements?'

I'm incensed, my voice shrill, caution abandoned. Fury is burning brighter than my fear.

'It wasn't ... I just ...' He trails off for a moment. Then he seems to settle on a thought.

'You seem to know about The Coastline Killer,' he says, like this is obvious, like I should be an expert on my own murderer. 'So you know that there's a certain type of woman that ... matches.'

'OK,' I say slowly, trying to make sense of what he's saying. 'So I fit some physical requirements? There must be thousands of women in Vancouver who you could say the same thing about. I'm not exactly unique like that. So why me?'

'I spotted you on the bus,' he blurts out impatiently. 'And you fit, you looked right, you just – it was easy. And I followed you, and looked you up online, and I made sure I knew your routines and patterns.'

Currents of fear and revulsion ripple up and down my spine. I don't have time to process what he's said, what it means, the violation of it, because he's still talking.

'And honestly,' he seems to have found his flow, 'your routine was pretty predictable. I mean, you didn't really do anything. It was easy to follow you. Easy to plan how to take you.'

214

'So I deserved to be murdered because, what, my life's boring to you?'

'I didn't say you deserved to be murdered.'

'Oh, OK, but you're happy to murder me, anyway?'

'You don't understand,' he shouts, flecks of spit flying from his lips. 'You can't understand because it's bigger than you. It's not about you!'

He's right. I don't understand – won't ever understand. How could I understand something that makes no sense? There can be no legitimate reason for what he's done, no justification. I want answers, but I should have known I wouldn't get any from him, none that make sense, anyway. Because, in the end, it comes down to pure, awful chance. I was on the wrong bus, at the wrong time. That's all it is.

A sense of bleak hopelessness fills me. Perhaps I do want him to die, after all. Maybe it was a mistake to keep this wounded, twisted man alive for a moment longer. Maybe I could still kill him.

Silence falls on us once more. And then, in a voice so small I almost miss his words, Ricky speaks again.

'It wasn't meant to be like this.'

Chapter 50

LUCY

Lucy stumbled through the door and found herself in another dark, cold room with a concrete floor. She blinked a few times to let her eyes adjust to the darkness. As she waited, she listened for signs of life, signals of danger.

But the silence was resounding. Shapes began to form in the darkness. She seemed to be in a shed of sorts. There was a roller door to her left, and a workbench covered in more tools ahead of her. The middle of the room was empty, but for an oil stain on the concrete. So it was a garage. And if that was where The Sculptor's car was kept, and the car was gone, then perhaps she really was alone.

She spun around to see where she'd come from. The door she'd climbed through was one of eight, the same size and shape, made to look like a long, built-in cupboard system. She didn't stop to look in the other doors. She didn't want to know.

All she wanted was to escape, to get as far away from the white room and the studio as possible, to find someone who could help her. Her eyes swept the room for a phone, or computer, or any other means of communication, but there was nothing useful. Just the kind of junk found in garages across the world: boxes of forgotten belongings, disused appliances, gardening equipment, cans of oil.

Lucy stepped towards the roller door, her heart pounding, her mouth dry. Even though The Sculptor's car was gone, she had no idea what lay on the other side of that thin sheet of metal. A murderer might not be there, but who – or what – else was?

Moving cautiously and listening for any sounds that could indicate danger, Lucy curled her fingers under the tiny gap below the edge of the door and pulled gently to test its movement. It gave, just a little, but as it slid up it let out a shrill squeal, the metal rusted and old.

She froze.

A few seconds passed without another sound; no rush of someone coming to recapture her, no shout of surprise. She debated with herself over whether to pull the door up all at once, like pulling off a Band-Aid, and risk a loud, unmissable wail, or to go slowly, keeping the squealing under control.

In the end, she decided that her nerves couldn't cope with the slow torture of the latter. She just wanted to get away. Closing her eyes, and willing there to be no one around to hear it, she counted to three and then hoisted the door up. The unearthly screeching noise that surrounded her set her teeth on edge, but she didn't stop until she knew she could fit under the gap she'd created.

The fresh air that rushed to her was heady and delicious. She smelled pine and dirt, and she had to resist stopping to just breathe it in, in deep, greedy gulps.

But there was no time for that. She didn't wait to find out if anyone had heard her. Without letting herself think about what would come next, she dropped to her belly on the cold concrete and rolled underneath, wincing as something sharp dug into the soft flesh of her neck.

She rolled twice, then sprung into a crouching position, poised to flee.

The air was still. And silent. Lucy was completely blanketed in darkness. She held her hand up in front of her face, and could only just make out a pale shape against the inky night. After a few moments, she began to make out more shapes, more details, in the scene around her.

She shivered. Slowly, quietly, she stood and turned in a circle, taking in what little she could see. With her back to the garage, there was nothing before her but darkness, punctuated by long, slender shapes she supposed were trees. It was the same to her left and right. Behind her was the garage she'd emerged from. And beside it, visible in the dim moonlight, was a small cottage, like a lumberjack's cabin.

If anyone had been inside, they'd likely have been crushed by the ancient tree, which had toppled onto one side of the wooden roof. A portion of the structure was intact, but most of it was destroyed.

Shivering, Lucy decided that she couldn't run. It was too dark, and she had no idea where she was, or which way she needed to go. For a split second she considered ducking back under the garage door, huddling inside until dawn and then making a dash for freedom when she could see more clearly.

But she had to try to get help, or work out where she was so she could find her way out before The Sculptor came back. There was no phone, nothing of use, inside the garage. Perhaps there would be something inside the cabin that could help.

Fear tore through her as she considered what she might find inside: a dead killer, or worse – an injured one. She shuddered. She had nothing to protect herself with, but she had to work on the assumption that if she'd managed to escape without someone stopping her, there wasn't anyone in the immediate area who *could* stop her. Not yet, anyway.

Moving as quietly as she could, wincing at every twig cracking underfoot, Lucy closed the distance between herself and the cabin, her eyes wide, her every muscle tensed, ready to run if someone appeared.

But no one did. The cabin remained broken and forlorn, one half of it crumpled like a discarded candy wrapper. She made her way around the base of the tree, its roots reaching high into the night sky like fingers beckoning her onwards. Or signalling for her to stop, to stay back. On the other side of the tree was a door. It was still intact, but the frame around it had buckled in the collapse, leaving the door ajar. She swallowed, trembling with fear but knowing that she had to keep going no matter what. Quitting now was no longer a matter of pride. It was life or death.

Her stomach churning, Lucy stepped across the threshold into the ruins of the cabin. It was darker inside without the moonlight to help, but she didn't dare try the lights. If someone was around, the last thing she wanted to do was alert them to her presence. In the gloom she could make out a table, a sink, a fridge. She stepped towards the sink, wincing as glass and other debris popped like gunshots beneath her feet, and opened the cabinet beneath it, feeling her way in the dark, hoping to find a flashlight.

Her fingers touched nothing more than plastic grocery bags. Groping in the dark, she found the kitchen drawers, and opened the top one. Cutlery. Frustrated, Lucy slid the second drawer open and reached inside. She winced as her palm met the sharp point of something cool and metallic. Her heart leaped. It was a knife! Carefully, she felt for the handle, then gripped it tightly. Having a weapon gave her a surge of confidence. She kept rummaging through the drawers until her fingers wrapped around a small cardboard box. She shook it and heard the reassuring rattle of matches.

Placing the knife down for a moment, she opened the box with shaking hands and struck a match against the edge. The bright light that flared in her hand was blinding, and for a moment, Lucy looked away. The room, for just a few seconds, was visible, and she took in as much as she could. Directly ahead of her was the tree trunk, surrounded by piles of broken furniture, walls, a crushed sofa. To her left, beyond the kitchen table and a high, stacked bookshelf, was a door that looked as though it led to another room.

The match burned close to her fingers, the heat at first welcome before quickly becoming unbearable. She shook it until the flame extinguished, then lit another one, looking more carefully this time. She couldn't see a phone on any of the walls. Disappointed, she shook the match and was plunged into darkness again.

Sliding the box into her pocket, Lucy picked up the knife and shuffled carefully across the kitchen towards the open door. Her shin connected with something low and solid, and she bit back a yelp as pain shot up her leg. She stopped at the bookcase to rub her stinging shin, then reached into her pocket and pulled out the matches. Perhaps the bookcase would hold some kind of clue – a map of the local area, discarded letters that disclosed the address of the cabin – anything.

As the light flared in front of her, Lucy's eyes focused on a photo in a silver frame. She froze. In the image, a man with brown hair and dark eyes had his arm slung across the shoulders of a woman with light brown hair, pulled up into a loose topknot. They were standing with their backs to a beautiful, sweeping bay, the water so blue it looked fake.

The man was laughing, his eyes fixed on the woman, who was beaming at the camera like she'd never been happier.

The hairs on the back of Lucy's neck prickled. She was looking, once again, at The Coastline Killer.

Chapter 51

ALICE

The cold creeps in, somehow seeping through cracks we can't see, or we'd have tried to squeeze through them ourselves. It fills the room, although it doesn't bring with it the fresh air we so desperately need. It settles on me, permeating my skin and settling in my bones, making me fantasise about fire and blankets and hot water bottles.

I can't stop shivering.

It started as a small tremble, a delicate quiver. That was a few hours ago. I can't control it anymore. It's taken over me, causing me to convulse, a violent shaking that amplifies every ache and pain in my body. My teeth chatter, the noise so loud it resounds like a drumroll in my tender skull. No matter how brutally I rub my skin, I can't warm up. I'm tired. I need my body to be still, to rest, to recover. But it won't obey.

Ricky's shaking too, his whole body shuddering from the dramatic temperature drop. I look around, knowing there's nothing that can help me, but hoping against facts that somehow, magically, a blanket or scarf or sweater will have appeared on the ground.

There's nothing but dust and rubble.

'I'm ... It's c-cold,' he says through the chattering of his teeth.

I nod feebly in agreement.

'We're going to g-get hypothermia,' he says. 'We need to sit together. B-body heat. It's the only way to keep our temperature up.'

I shake my head, curling my fingers up against my mouth and breathing on them. The tiny puff of warmth from my lungs does nothing to combat the chill in my fingertips.

'I'm n-not offering,' he says. 'I'm telling y-you. Our bodies will sh-shut down if we get any colder. I'm n-not dying here.'

'No,' I say, as firmly as I can manage. It sounds weak.

'Really? You'd rather d-die than touch me?'

I glare at him, but I'm not sure if he can see it in the weak light. The truth is, I'm not sure what the answer to that question is. Of course I don't want to die. But I might not have a choice, whether we huddle together or not. The last thing I want is to be pressed up against him in my final moments.

Besides, the complete hideousness of being so close to him aside, if we're able to share body heat, we're close enough for him to kill me effortlessly; to snap my neck, or pull the needle from my side, or choke me. There's no way I'm giving him that kind of advantage.

He starts shuffling towards me, his movements clumsy and imprecise. With his duct tape helmet and jerky motion, he looks like a character from a horror film. *Undead*. Mummified. I shake my head. My thoughts have been jumbled, incoherent. I can't seem to string a logical idea together. I'm losing control. First, my body. Now my mind.

When Ricky has crossed the tiny distance between us he sits down next to me, shuffling across the slab of concrete until his thigh is touching mine. I want to pull away, to tear my body from his, but I don't have the strength. My stomach churns, but I'm at his mercy, and the idea frightens me so much that a gurgle of terror escapes from between my lips.

'St-stop it,' he says. He's so close that I can see his thin lips, which have turned an alarming shade of blue. 'I need warmth as much as you do, and you're the only one wh-who can provide it. B-besides, if you're d-dead, you're useless to me. OK?'

I want to show my disgust, to fight him off, or at least move away, but I don't have the energy. I didn't think it was possible to feel any chillier, but the temperature seems to drop a few degrees lower as I understand how little agency I have in this situation.

'I'm going to p-pull you to the ground. No, before y-you object, I'll be careful. We j-just need as much body contact as we can get, to generate heat. And then, I have my apron just here.'

He gestures somewhere to his left, out of my sight.

'And I'm going to c-cover us with that, and it'll trap our body heat and keep us as warm as possible. I know you don't want me touching you, but I promise you, I'm not touching you like that. Besides, I'm a m-married man.'

I suddenly find the energy for my head to snap around, for my eyes to widen. He's married? He has a wife? I'm suddenly brimming with questions.

Ricky laughs. It's bitter, completely devoid of humour.

'Yeah, that's r-right. At least, legally speaking, I am. I'm guessing the divorce p-papers are on their way. And before you ask, she doesn't know about . . . anything. Of course she doesn't. She's a good woman—'

At this, his voice cracks. He swallows a couple of times, looks down at his feet. Takes a deep breath.

'OK-K. Here we g-go.'

Ricky doesn't wait for my permission. To him, I'm nothing more than a human-shaped hot water bottle. Something to be used, a resource to be depleted. Tears of frustration and fear flow down my cheeks but I don't resist – can't resist – as his right arm finds its way around my back, his left snaking around my stomach, his hands linking by my side, keeping me in place. Everything in me tenses, and my rigid body is moved against my will, both of us falling clumsily to the ground.

He inhales sharply as we hit the rubble, and I find myself hoping that he's hit his head again, that he's opened up his wound, or added a new one. Because then, weak as I am, I could crawl away from him. But he's still moving, wriggling his arm free from me, sweeping the ground for his apron.

He pulls it over us, and then pulls me close to him again.

Tears keep rolling down my face, their heat too fleeting to offer comfort. I try not to think about our closeness, the complete absence of space between us, his chest pushing against mine as his lungs fill, mine pushing back as his empty. I try to clear my mind completely as I'm forced to provide body heat to the bastard who saved me.

Instead of thinking, I count. I control each breath in, and each breath out. I don't notice the temperature changing as we lie there, codependent. And somehow, against every instinct screaming at me to stay alert, I must slip into a dazed kind of sleep, because suddenly I'm awake again, and I'm not shivering anymore.

I'm cold, but my body has stopped shuddering, my breathing shallow and steady, matching Ricky's.

I'm alive. And I'm no longer on the verge of hypothermia.

225

I wish I was strong enough to refuse to give him warmth. But if I do that, I'll lose his.

And so I let my eyes droop, and wonder if I'll ever wake up.

Chapter 52

ALICE

The snatches of sleep that come to me are anything but restful.

Warmth seeps into my skin from Ricky's torso and, eventually, flows back to him. Simultaneously, I hate myself for surviving this way, for relying on him, listening to his heartbeat that soothes me like a twisted lullaby, and recognise that it's the only way that I can possibly survive.

If I have to take his body heat to stay alive, then I'll do what it takes to get it.

But still. Although I fall quickly into a kind of sleep that verges on unconsciousness, I wake again in what feels like just moments. The pain is too acute to ignore, and breathing is still a struggle. Every new breath fills my chest with a slicing pain, and each lungful of air is a reminder of the needle sticking out of my side, the tiny pieces of metal and plastic that are keeping me alive. When I do drift off, it's in short, horror-filled bursts, where my mind takes me to places more terrifying than the dark, shrinking cave I'm trapped in, and the person I'm sharing it with.

Eventually, I give up on trying. Instead, I close my eyes, and I let my thoughts drift. I think about the fact that Ricky is married, and I wonder what sort of person his wife thinks he is. Does he treat her kindly? Do they throw dinner parties for their friends, who think he's just a nice, normal guy? Nice. Normal. It's what I'd wanted from a donor, what I hunted for between the sparse lines of information included in so many profiles they'd all started to blur together. The father of my future child, I'd eventually decided, would be a man named Alvin. I don't know if the sperm bank uses their real names, but in any case, Alvin is forty-one, and an accountant. He runs marathons, apparently dresses well, and loves baking cakes. Nice. Normal.

At least, that's what he told them, what he'd led them to believe. But if Ricky could fool a woman into marrying him, surely it wouldn't be difficult for a guy who just wanted a bit of extra cash to make up some details about himself. My mind whirrs with new questions. Am I crazy for even thinking about bringing a child into the world without fully considering the genes they'll be inheriting? Is it irresponsible of me, selfish even, to have a child this way, simply because I want one? Shouldn't I be grateful for my amazing career, my friends and family, my lovely condo? Who am I to think I can have it all, to think that something won't go terribly, horribly wrong, if I try?

I imagine what Celia would say if she could hear my thoughts, if she knew the way I was thinking. She'd be appalled.

'Alice,' she'd said, when I'd first broached the subject of IVF with her. 'You will be a brilliant Mom, and any kid would be lucky to have you as their parent.'

'But I work full time,' I'd argued, as though trying to talk myself out of the idea.

'So? What's that got to do with anything?'

'Do you think it'd be unfair to them, if I wasn't even there? I mean, you left your job when you had the twins.'

She'd laughed. 'I despised that job, Al. I was good at it,

228

sure, but you know I wasn't happy there. I'd just convinced myself that I had to be grateful. You, on the other hand, my God. You should see your face light up whenever someone so much as mentions an emergency bloody exit. You were born for that job.'

We'd laughed, but I'd known, deep down, that she was right. I love my job. I'm great at it, I'm passionate about it, and if I quit, I'd feel unfulfilled. No matter how fulfilled being a mom might make me, I don't want a child *instead* of a career. I want both.

And, I realise with a sense of triumph, if I somehow make it out of here alive, if I survive a killer and an earthquake and being trapped underground, cold and injured and afraid, then I can do anything. I can accept my dream job. And I can have a baby.

The odds might be seriously stacked against me, but if I somehow make it out of here, I'm not going to keep questioning whether I deserve good things. And I'm going to stop worrying that I'm not capable.

Gathering my strength, I lift myself from the floor. Ricky stirs next to me, but he doesn't wake fully. Slowly, gingerly, I crawl out from under the insulation of the rubber apron, shivering as the cold hits me anew.

Logic tells me that I should stay where I am, save my energy, wait for rescue to come. But another voice – equally logical, and far more insistent – tells me that, unless I do something now, unless I move, and keep fighting, rescue will never arrive.

The effort of crossing the room makes me sweat, and the heat feels like a small mercy, a tiny reward for all of the pain.

I stare at the metallic box of the washing machine, wondering how to find the strength to stand unassisted by the mop handle, how I'll lift it, and bring it down again, making enough noise for someone on the outside to hear. I'm so tired. I don't think I can do it.

But I have to. I know I don't have a choice. Not really.

Gritting my teeth, I raise the handle up and bring it down with all the force I can summon onto the top of the washing machine.

When the plastic connects with the metal it creates an almighty crash, which echoes in the tiny space, a tinny ringing that fills my head and pierces my bones. Ricky's voice reaches me – shouts of surprise and complaint, I think – but without stopping, I bash the handle on the washing machine again. And again. And as I do, I scream, long and loud and full of fury and pain and confusion and self-pity.

And then, just as quickly as the energy bubbled up inside me, it dissipates, and I'm left panting, my whole body on fire, too weak to lift the mop handle anymore. I slide down the side of the washing machine, the ringing still reverberating in my ears.

And then there's nothing. Just a long, steady silence.

Chapter 53

ALICE

The banging stops.

I hit that damn washing machine for as long as I could before I dropped, spent, onto the dusty ground. Ricky, fully awake by that point, had screamed, threatened, demanded that I keep going, but my body wouldn't allow it. Eventually, he'd crawled over and had wrenched the mop handle from my limp hand, smashing the machine himself, his own energy depleted in minutes.

We'd taken it in turns after that, bashing as much as we were able to before collapsing and allowing the other to take over. I don't know how long it's been since I had the strength to stand, to lift my arms, but every few minutes, Ricky finds a source of energy – I don't know where it's coming from – and he bashes the washing machine for thirty seconds or so. At least, it was thirty seconds, when he first started. Now it's more like fifteen.

'Ricky?'

It's the first word I've spoken in what feels like hours, and my voice comes out hoarse and cracked, punctuated by the chattering of my teeth.

Ricky's head snaps up. He's as surprised as I am to hear his name coming from my lips.

'What?'

'Do you think they're coming?'

It's a pitiful thing to ask. They're not coming. Of course they're not. No one knows we're here. Emergency services will be stretched beyond capacity, and most people will be too focused on their own survival to go looking for people trapped in abandoned buildings. But despite knowing the answer to my own question, I need reassurance. Because I'm scared that down here, in my final hours or minutes or however long I have left before the infection or dehydration takes me, I'll lose hope. I'm worried that the fear will grip me and take hold and not let go so that when I die, I'll be tangled in the hands of terror.

I can't let that happen.

Ricky doesn't answer immediately. But when he does, his voice is full of false, bright cheer.

'Of course they are,' he says, a smile in his words. It's exactly what I need, even though I know he's playing the same game that I am. 'They've heard us already, I bet. They know we're here, and they're just looking for a way to get to us. It won't be long now.'

I nod, my muscles contracting in constant, wracking shudders. I believe him. I believe him because I have to. Because not believing him is too terrifying to consider.

'Do you think they'll have water for us?'

I look down at the bottle, now empty, and consider tipping it up above my tongue again. But that hasn't worked for a few hours, now. It's all gone, every last drop, and continuing to believe there's a tiny bit at the bottom of the bottle is more exhausting than just accepting that we've run out.

It's all I can think about, now. My mouth is so dry that swallowing has become unnecessary. My body still tries to do it automatically, and every time it does, it's like sandpaper is being dragged along the back of my throat.

'Oh,' Ricky laughs, 'they will have so much water. Bottles and bottles of it. Fresh and clean. And they'll have blankets, too. Clean ones. Imagine that! Something not covered in dust!'

I laugh, a rasping, choking sound.

'And food,' I offer. 'We'll get something that two days ago we'd have turned our noses up at, and it will be the most delicious thing we've ever eaten.'

'Coffee,' he adds. 'They will give us coffee.'

I let out a groan of longing.

'Oh my God. Coffee.'

Ricky chuckles.

'I swear I will never take any of that for granted again. Water. Food.'

My laughter dies in my throat.

Ricky doesn't deserve to take anything for granted again. The women he's killed don't get that opportunity, and neither should he. I don't reply. There's nothing to say.

Instead, I close my eyes and dream, not of coffee or blankets or food, but of Ricky being led away in handcuffs, never to be free again. A smile plays at the corners of my mouth.

There's a moment of complete silence. And then the bashing begins again.

Chapter 54

BILL

'Caruthers,' a voice calls from behind him.

Bill spins and comes face-to-face with the Incident Commander, clipboard in hand.

'We just got a call from a few blocks away,' she says, breathless. 'A woman thinks she heard some banging from underneath an old abandoned house. Geissler's there now, and he agrees with her. Think you can go check it out and let me know if you need more of us over there?'

'Sure thing,' Bill says, hope sparking in his chest again. He needs this. He needs a win. It doesn't matter how small, or how impossible it will be for one rescue to erase all the people he couldn't save, he wants to cling to it, to let it take over his mind, push out all of the darkness. 'What's the address?'

The Incident Commander gives him the name of a street Bill knows is close by, and he starts running immediately, powered by adrenaline and the knowledge that every second he cuts off his journey is a second he can use to save someone.

He sees Geissler before the young fireman sees him.

'Geissler,' he yells as he runs towards him in the darkness of the early morning. The man spins, starts waving his arms.

'Caruthers,' he calls back. 'I think we've got something over here.'

Bill breaks into a sprint, covering the last few feet between them with ease. There's a woman standing next to Geissler, looking tired and shaken up and grimy, but otherwise unharmed.

'Caruthers,' his colleague says when he reaches them. 'This is Moira.'

Bill shakes her hand and nods at her, curious.

'She lives a couple of blocks away. She was on her way home when she thought she heard something. A metallic tapping sound. And a scream. I think I can hear the tapping, although it's intermittent, but I haven't heard any screams—'

'Shhhh,' Moira waves her hands to silence them, 'there it is.'

Bill stands still, his head cocked to one side. He can't hear anything. 'I don't—'

'Wait. Just listen.'

He does as the woman instructs, cynicism blossoming inside him. He waits, but he can't hear a sound. He tells himself he'll give it thirty seconds before he lets them down. Maybe they imagined it. Maybe their brains conjured it because, like Bill, they need a win. But he can't stand here waiting for something that doesn't exist. A couple of birds chirp from a nearby tree, but apart from that, the street is silent. There isn't even the regular hiss of traffic, now that so many of the roads are unusable.

Bill opens his mouth to tell his colleague and the neighbour woman that he's going to have to get back to the hub, when he freezes.

His heart pounds. His head snaps up, his eyes wide, meeting those of Lleyton Geissler.

'Hear it?' the rookie asks.

Bill nods. He strains to catch it again, to identify exactly what it is. It's faint, but definitely audible. It's inconsistent, too, which means it's not mechanical.

'Do you really think it could be ... ?'

'That's exactly what I think, gents,' Moira says. 'But listen ... I haven't been home since this all started, and I need to know if my husband is OK. I just wanted to make sure whoever is down there is going to be all right.'

'Of course,' Bill replies, patting her shoulder. 'Thank you. We've got it from here.'

He tries to tamp down the bubble of hope that's building behind his ribs. He knows better than to believe that just because somebody survived the quake, they'll make it out of there alive. The past few hours have proved that. Besides, they don't know the condition of whoever it is who's down there, or whether they can be reached without the usual equipment.

And yet it feels like a triumph already, like perhaps all is not lost. Like maybe he can make a difference, after all.

Geissler is already on the radio, letting the captain know that there's definitely someone down there, and that they need a backup team.

While his colleague is on the radio, Bill starts wading through the wreckage towards the house, trying to get a feel for the situation, to work out their best way forward.

'Careful,' Geissler calls from behind him. Bill waves an acknowledgement over his shoulder and keeps stepping closer to the shell of a home.

The entire property seems to have folded in on itself, as though something huge and heavy fell from the sky, landing neatly in the middle of it. The radius of damage is massive, with debris strewn across the yard, into the road, and even

236

onto the neighbour's yard across the road. A nearby pylon has cracked in two, the top half mercifully missing the bulk of the property, and landing instead on a pile of displaced rubble.

But that isn't what Bill is fixated on. He can't stop staring at the front left corner of the house, which seems to have inverted in the quake, creating a hole filled with rubble. His best guess is that the basement has collapsed, pulling a corner of the house inside. He shakes his head. If there's someone down there, it really is a miracle they've survived.

He picks his way around to the back of the house, where the damage is less severe. There's little more than a skeleton where a house once stood, but at least from the back of the property, Bill can imagine that there had been a building. At the front, that isn't so clear.

There's a pipe protruding from the back corner of the house, presumably some kind of ventilation from the basement. He pulls the flashlight from his belt, and whacks it against the pipe.

Then he waits.

Chapter 55

ALICE

'Alice!'

'Mmmm?'

I'm so tired. And once again, I'm so very cold. My body won't stop shivering, even though I know that the shudders are using up valuable energy; energy I can't afford to lose. My body isn't mine – it's doing its own thing, which right now I think might be just plain old shutting down. I don't have anything left in me with which to fight.

'Did you hear that?'

Hear what? I want to ask. But my mouth is so dry, and my head so heavy, and parting my lips to try to speak feels like too big a task to even bother attempting. So what comes out is a low, soft groan.

'I think someone's here!'

I know what he's doing. And, while I appreciated it a little while ago, when I desperately needed reassurance, it's too late now. I'm beyond optimism, beyond fear, even. Fear takes energy. I don't have the strength to tell him not to pretend that we're going to be rescued.

There's a burning pain across my side, which I'm pretty certain is the infection I feared. The needle wasn't hygienic when it was buried between my ribs, and now goodness-knows-what is pulsing through my bloodstream, circulating around my body, poisoning my veins.

The bright side, though – what I've been telling myself – is that I'll probably get a fever before I actually die, and then I won't really know what's happening, anyway. Surely, that's a good thing? Not knowing. It must be better that way.

'Alice!'

He's yelling now. I crack an eye open, just a tiny bit. He's standing. Waving his arms.

Maybe *he's* got a fever, I think. Maybe he's lost it, and he's only a little way away from death.

But then there's a clang.

I freeze. I will my body to stop shivering, as though the trembling is affecting my hearing. I hold my breath.

Clang.

My eyes fly all the way open. Whatever made that noise was loud. And so clear. And suddenly, I discover a source of energy I didn't think existed, and I'm propped up on my elbows, scrambling to stand, and screaming as loudly as I possibly can.

'Help! We're down here! We're trapped! Help!'

Ricky's joining in, too, his voice as hoarse as mine, but filled with hope and excitement and a kind of vigour that neither of us believed was left in us.

He's smashing the mop handle on the washing machine and screaming and sobbing, and I'm shouting and waving, even though no one can see me.

And then I stop. I touch Ricky's arm. He pauses.

'What?'

'We can't hear them if we keep screaming. We need to listen. They know we're here now.'

We stand, facing each other, in total silence.

Then, suddenly, there are three rapid clangs, followed by three slower ones, and another three in quick succession.

I half laugh, half sob.

'SOS,' I gasp. 'It's Morse code. SOS. They know we're here. We're being rescued.'

Ricky's eyes are shining. He flings his arms around me and I weep into his chest, clutching his back, relief coursing through me, warm and sweet.

And then the spell is broken. I realise what I'm doing, and I jerk away from him, crossing my arms over my body, protective. I mumble something, not real words, and retreat ever so slightly. The pain comes crashing over me again, and I sit heavily.

But now, there's a lightness in my chest. Someone is here.

I let the reality of that sink in, the hopelessness that had consumed me lifting all at once. I will myself to survive, to push through the infection and the thirst for long enough for us to be lifted out of here to safety.

I've survived so much already. I can hold on a little longer.

Silence descends again, and panic rises up in me.

'They do know we're here, don't they?' I ask, my voice high-pitched and strained. 'They haven't left, have they? What if they've gone?'

The idea of being so close, of communicating with someone on the outside via metallic banging, only to have them walk away, thinking they heard something but then deciding it had been in their imagination after all, that's too terrifying to consider.

'No, they heard us,' Ricky says. 'They did. I know they did. And they're coming back. They'll need to get tools to dig through, to make a hole in this building big enough to get us out.'

I picture a hole being created in the side of the building,

seeing sunlight filtering in, and fresh air. I'm certain my chest will explode with how badly I want that, how desperate I am for escape.

Silence swells, and along with it, my panic. Ricky's words have done nothing to calm my sense that we've missed out by a hair's breadth, that we almost saw freedom, but that it's slipped through our fingers. I want to sob, to throw myself at the walls and bash them with my fists until I break through. But all I can do is wait. And hope.

And then, in a glorious burst of noise, the drilling begins.

Chapter 56

ALICE

The drilling and hammering has been going for what feels like hours.

At first I thought I might faint with happiness and hope. I had stood, then sat, then limped weakly for a couple of steps, a pathetic attempt at pacing, until exhaustion had won and I'd slumped onto the ground again.

I'd wanted to help. It was impossible, just sitting there passively, waiting for the strangers outside to reach us. I felt lazy, like I should be playing my part. But there was nothing I could do.

And so now I sit, and I listen to the drilling and smashing and, occasionally, a yell. Those moments have felt close to euphoric. Another human! Another voice. The first time it happened, Ricky's head snapped towards me. We'd stared, smiles painted on our dusty, grimy faces – our mouth coverings abandoned, too dusty themselves to be effective – our eyes shining in the dimming light.

But since then, Ricky's smile has faded, overtaken by a frown that I'm certain has been brought on by the realisation that we're getting out of here.

That we're both getting out of here. Alive.

As this truth settles on me, I realise how easily he could still kill me. He might not have much strength left in him, but it wouldn't take a lot. He wouldn't even need to do anything violent. He could just reach over and pluck the needle from my side, and I'd be dead in minutes. He could tell the rescuers that I died because the needle fell out when I moved.

He wouldn't even have to mention me at all. He could hide my body on the other side of the room and pretend it was just him down here all along.

When the earthquake had first hit, all my attention had been on surviving the natural disaster. Then, when I'd realised that the man in the mask was still alive, I'd had to put all my energy into being useful, convincing him that I was worth keeping around. And when the room had shrunk and our water source had been destroyed and it seemed inevitable that we were both going to die down here, all I'd wanted was to let someone – anyone – on the outside know that we were here.

I had a plan for getting the attention of someone outside. But I don't have one for how I'm going to stay alive for long enough to tell the world who Ricky is. Because he's not just going to let me walk away from here. I know his name. I've seen his face. I could destroy him.

I'd thought – naively, I understand now – that my fight was over. He saved me, after all. He's been saying *we* when he's talked about getting out. He hasn't tried to kill me for a while.

But right now, just before our rescue, I'm in as much danger as I was the moment I woke up in this room. I might as well be strapped down to the gurney again, the rusted blade of a saw being wielded by an anonymous man in a creepy plastic mask.

I try to breathe deeply and slowly, to stay calm. I just need to convince him that I'm not a threat. I have to make him believe that I won't spill his secrets.

'When we get out,' I begin, but it seems that he's already one step ahead of me. Without any warning, he's moving, heaving his body up from the ground, determination in his jaw, tension written in the hunching of his shoulders, like a quarterback ready to pounce.

In the seconds it'll take for him to reach me, I have to choose. I can try to lie my way out of this, try to make him believe that I'm on his side, that I'm so grateful to him for keeping me alive that I'll never talk. Or I can fight.

I'm weak, but so is he. He should be able to overpower me effortlessly, but he's still swaying. He doesn't seem to be able to focus properly, or keep his eyes open for longer than a few seconds without them drooping closed. He's weaponless. I have the mop handle, which is on the ground, off to my right. Within reach if I'm fast enough. If he doesn't stop me.

He's lurching towards me. My brain tries to calculate, tries to see the future, to predict the consequences of fighting, or talking. My decision is made, a split-second choice that I know, even as I make it, could be a terrible mistake. I heave my body to the right, my arm shooting out to grab the mop handle before he reaches me.

Ricky laughs and closes the gap between us, stomping on my arm just below my elbow. I cry out and my fingers reflexively curl into a fist, clutching nothing but air.

With his foot still pressing into my arm, the pressure so great I'm certain I'll hear a snap any second, he reaches down and picks up the mop handle. He stands and presses the jagged end into the soft flesh of my neck. My stomach flips over.

'I won't tell,' I whisper, the movement of my breath in my

throat intensifying the pressure of the sharp plastic against my flesh. 'I promise.'

'I can't risk it,' he says, pressing harder. I still have the use of my left arm, but I'm scared that if I move, he'll just finish me, right here on the ground. There's no reason for him not to. I was stupid to think I could appeal to his better nature, stupid to think he even had one.

'Your wife,' I gasp, desperate for a way to get through to him. 'What would she think of this?'

His laugh comes out like a bark.

'Well, she'd have to be thinking of me,' he says. 'And trust me, she's not.'

'Why not?'

The mop handle is pressed ever so slightly more firmly into my throat. I'm pretty sure it's broken through the skin now, but I try not to let on that I'm in pain.

'That's none of your business.'

'No,' I squeak, 'but if you're going to kill me anyway, you might as well get whatever this is off your chest.'

'This isn't some kind of confession,' he spits. 'I didn't do anything wrong. She left me. She left me for that—'

My left hand flies up to grab the mop handle and, in one movement, I push it up, off my neck, taking him by surprise. I roll out of harm's way. He cries out and lunges for me, but I've rolled again, and then I sweep my leg out and kick him right on his kneecap as he's moving forward. The shock of it, and the momentum of his body, causes him to trip. He falls heavily, and there's a hollow thud as his head connects with a chunk of rubble the size of a shoebox.

The mop handle flies out of his hand and onto the ground, where I grab it and point it at him, trying to ignore the roaring pain where my already-damaged leg connected with his knee. He moans. I clamber to my feet and press the sharp end that was, moments ago, about to impale my neck, into his throat.

He looks at me, and then his body goes slack. I could kill him right now.

'I'll do it,' I threaten. My voice is raspy, almost threatening.

In that moment, I almost believe my own words. My heart is pounding furiously as I grapple with my options, as I press the mop handle a fraction more into the soft flesh of his neck. Ricky's eyes bulge.

Flickers of smug satisfaction lick at my ribs. Now he knows how it feels to be terrified, to be vulnerable, to be at the mercy of someone else. The emotion scares me, though. I'm not a murderer. I'm not like him. I saved him from the brink of death, after all. Could I really kill him now, after everything?

This would be self-defence ... wouldn't it? After all, he did attack me first, he held the mop handle to my neck and would have pressed down if I hadn't swiped his knee. So if I pressed just a little harder, made all of my problems go away, would that be justifiable?

His groan reverberates through the mop handle, vibrating in my palms. I can feel his panic. His life is in my hands. I stare into his brown eyes, my own narrowed, frantically trying to decide whether I could take him out. Whether I want to.

I want him gone. But not badly enough to commit murder, not when I'm so close to freedom. He isn't worth it. And besides, he doesn't deserve a quick death.

'If you so much as move in a way I haven't approved,' I growl, 'I will take you out. And I will scream what I know about you so loud that the rescuers will know everything

246

before you have a chance to come near me. Do you understand?'

Ricky's lip curls up into a tiny, triumphant smile. I press harder. A tiny trickle of blood slides down his neck. He whimpers, and his whole body tenses. His smile drops.

'OK,' he breathes. 'OK, you win. You win. Please.'

I lift the mop handle enough for him to roll over, but I remain tense, ready to use it again. I won't kill him, if it comes to that. But I will defend myself.

I sit, facing Ricky, watching him carefully for signs of movement. He's lying still, groaning and sniffing, but I can't let my guard down. I'm not stupid enough to believe I've bested him altogether.

More drilling filters through the ceiling, followed by buzzing and clanking. I don't know what the noises mean.

I just know they need to get to us, and fast.

Chapter 57

LUCY

It might have been the changing light that woke her, although it was probably the noise – a bird outside was angrily defending its territory at just the right pitch to pierce Lucy's sleep.

It was panic she felt first: sheer, blind panic. She was supposed to be escaping, not napping. How could she have let herself lose focus like that? She tried to recall the moment her terror had waned enough to allow her body to rest.

There had been the photo – The Coastline Killer, the Uber driver from the gallery, smiling so casually, looking carefree and happy and not at all like the kind of person who chopped women up and stuffed them into sculptures. Lucy's spine had hummed with fear, just a glimpse of her kidnapper sending signals to her brain that she needed to flee. But she stayed, and she stared, and she wondered how anyone could be that close to a murderer without suspecting what was really going on behind those deep brown eyes.

She'd grabbed the frame and smashed it against the side of the bookshelf, shaking the glass away and pawing at the photo until it slid out. She'd folded it carefully, trying to touch only the edges, and making sure the pair's faces weren't obscured, then shoved it into her jeans pocket.

She only had a few matches left by then. She'd rummaged

through every drawer and cupboard she saw, eventually finding a flashlight, which saved her fingers from the constant burning of the open flame. She had found a phone in the bedroom, and for just a moment Lucy imagined the relief of unburdening herself onto a stranger, having her problem become theirs, waiting for them to arrive. But when she picked up the receiver, there was no dial tone. She swore, hit the hang-up button, and tried again. But the line must have been damaged by the fallen tree. If she couldn't bring help to her, she'd have to go in search of it.

Still clutching the knife, she'd rummaged through a pine wardrobe and found an old, oversized jacket that smelled of wax and grease, the memory of the wax statues in the studio making her heave. She swallowed it down. She needed warmth, and she couldn't be fussy about how she got it.

Back in the kitchen, she opened the fridge and found it almost bare. There was a can of Coke on the shelf in the door, which she had cracked open, greedily gulping down the sugary liquid, feeling her strength returning and clarity coming back to her thoughts. She ate fistfuls of Cheerios from the box she'd found in one of the cupboards, and then sat heavily at the small kitchen table, knowing she needed to make a plan, but not knowing where to start.

Her body had won over, sleep coming fast and deep, her head falling onto the wooden surface in front of her, a handful of Cheerios rolling onto the floor and then bouncing and skittering away. Night slipped by and the world was bathed in soft, muted light by the time the birds shocked her from her accidental sleep.

Without thinking or planning, but knowing she had to get away as quickly as possible, Lucy gripped the knife and took one last look around the room. In the dim dawn light, she could see the full extent of the wreckage. Debris was littered across the kitchen and into the room beyond. She was amazed that the bookcase had survived.

She couldn't see anything that could help her, and she didn't want to waste any more time looking. Her captor could arrive back at any moment, and she wanted to make sure she was as far away as possible when that happened. Lucy shoved the flashlight into one of the jacket's deep pockets, and stepped over the glass and rubble to the door she'd walked through in the middle of the night.

She peered outside and, confident that she was alone, dashed across the clearing and hid behind a majestic fir. She held the knife out in front of her chest, the volume of her panting making it impossible to listen for other noises. She forced herself to calm down, to take in her surroundings.

Lucy shivered. It was cold in the early morning, and the jacket wasn't thick enough to keep her warm. She needed to move. She couldn't see a car, a bike, or any other mode of transport that would help her reach safety faster. She'd have to walk. Or run.

Creeping out of the safety of the tree's shadow, she moved as stealthily as she could towards the other side of the garage she'd emerged from in the night. Maybe there was something at the back of the property – other signs of life, a town in the distance ... anything to show Lucy which way she should go.

Attached to the side of the garage there was a huge metal barrel, like the copper still she'd seen on the gin tasting tour Rhys had booked for her last birthday. But this wasn't copper. And she had a feeling it wasn't used for gin. Understanding shimmered at the edges of her mind, but she shoved it back down. She didn't want to know. Knowing wouldn't help her.

Trembling, she kept walking, stopping when she got to the corner of the garage. What she saw crushed her spirits.

There was nothing on that side of the property, either. The ground sloped upwards, and in the distance she saw snow-topped mountain peaks, like she was trapped in a Christmas card. But there was nothing magical about where she was.

Without giving herself time to second-guess her own thought process, she made a decision. Downhill would mean heading, in some vague way, towards the coast, towards civilisation, assuming that she was still somewhere near home, which she also couldn't be sure of. She didn't know how far she was from someone who could help. All she had for protection – from bears, or a butcher of women, who also happened to be a world-famous artist – was a small kitchen knife.

She didn't like her chances in a combat. Which meant her best option was to simply not come across anything that could hurt her. Speed was her best chance of survival.

And so Lucy turned on her heel, stepping on the hard ground above the spot where she'd been trapped, and broke into a run.

The woods swallowed her up without a sound.

Chapter 58

ALICE

'Hello?'

My heart stops for a split-second at the sound of another human's voice. And then I shout, my voice hoarse.

'Down here! Hello? Help us!'

Us.

I need them to know that I'm here. I need them to hear me. I need to be part of this story so that if Ricky tries anything again, they'll ask questions.

I've thought this through, and I've decided that there are only a few ways it could go. As long as they know I'm here, as long as I can communicate with them, make them aware that I'm alive and OK, then Ricky can't kill me without drawing attention to himself, without the rescuers wanting to know what happened. Without them coming to find me, and looking into my death.

He won't want that. My biggest risk at this point is that he'll attack me and make it look like an accident. I have to stay on my guard, keep the mop handle close, make sure he doesn't try anything.

Once we get out, I'll be safe. As soon as I've breathed fresh air, I will tell my rescuer that I need to be protected from Ricky. The rest will take care of itself. I'll be able to alert the authorities. He won't be able to touch me. He'll be arrested before he can even think about coming for me.

'Hello?' The voice is muffled. 'Who's down there?'

It's male, I think. But it's hard to tell. It's coming through the layers of rubble which means it's hard to make out clearly, but it's more than what we could hear before. Which means they're closer.

'Hello?!' Ricky calls out. 'Can you hear us?'

Us. So he's playing this game, too.

Since his fumbled attack, he's been lying on the ground, holding his head and groaning. I think being overpowered by me really made him understand how dire his situation is. The way I see it, there's no way this ends without him in prison. Unless something goes terribly wrong which, of course, it still could.

'We're sending something down,' the voice calls again, filtered through wood and plaster and brick and whatever else lies at the heart of a building.

Ricky glances up at me. He looks as confused as I feel. We don't need them to send things to us. We need them to get us out.

There's another whine of a drill and I wince, afraid that the already-fragile room will collapse. But it's short-lived, and it only causes a tiny trickle of debris to tumble down, from a spot just above us. I duck, but it's nothing more than a dusting of something soft and powdery.

Ricky hauls himself into a sitting position. I tense, tightening my grip on my plastic weapon.

Something bashes inside the ceiling in the corner that collapsed, and seems to work its way along the ceiling. And then there's a tiny hole in the corner, a few feet from the gurney. There's another shower of insulation and dust, and

253

I cough as it forms a cloud around me. I stare expectantly through the gap.

It's just darkness. The basement is filled with a scraping sound, like something's being dragged in the space above us. Then a clatter, a distant yell. My heart is thrumming, with anticipation or fear or excitement, or maybe all three.

And then something appears in the space above us. It's not a person. It's . . . a plastic bucket. Shiny, and sunshine yellow. It tips, and something rattles inside it. There's another rustle of movement, and then the bucket falls. I flinch as it jerks suddenly, and then stops in mid-air, suspended by a rope.

Ricky, who's by now managed to stand and walk a few steps towards the bucket, looks at me, as though asking for permission. I gesture with the mop handle for him to approach it. He reaches the bucket and dips his hand inside. I hold the mop handle out, ready to strike if he tries to attack again. Instead, he looks back at me, beaming with joy.

'What?'

He pulls out a bottle of water, triumphant. I let out a puff of air, a sigh of disbelief and delight. He throws it over to me and I catch it, cradling it to my chest for a moment like it's a small, precious child. Then he pulls out another. I could cry with relief. Instead, I twist the top off and gulp the whole bottle down in a couple of seconds, letting out a satisfied 'ahhhh' when it's finished. Ricky does the same thing, then wipes his mouth with the back of his hand. He grins.

'God, that tastes amazing.'

I smile broadly, forgetting for a moment that we're prepared to kill each other. At least, that he's prepared to kill me, and I'm prepared to stop him.

Because he's right. It's sweet and pure and delicious, and I want more.

He reaches back inside the bucket and pulls out a piece of paper. His hand is shaking.

'We're working hard to get you out,' he reads from the single white sheet. 'But the building is unstable, so we're waiting for an engineer. How many of you are down there, and what's your condition? Let us know if we can send anything else down.'

'Something for my fever,' I say immediately, energised by the water, and thrilled at the idea of being able to make requests. 'And more water. Food, maybe?'

It feels like I'm asking too much, like all of those luxuries shouldn't be available to me. Ricky nods.

'And a first aid kit,' I add. 'We need to dress our wounds properly.'

He reaches into the bucket and retrieves a pen. Leaning on the gurney, he scribbles for a few seconds, my weapon pointed carefully at him the whole time, and then puts the pen and paper back inside. He gives the bucket a couple of sharp tugs, and a few seconds later it jerks upwards, disappearing into the space above us.

I feel a sharp sense of loss, as though the bucket was a companion, and now it's left us. It was the first contact we've had with the outside world, and its appearance felt like a breakthrough, like I was allowed to really, truly hope that we would get out of here. Now that it's gone I feel lost. Abandoned. Ridiculous, I know. But I feel it anyway, a heavy stone in my stomach, an ache beneath my ribs.

It isn't until a few minutes have passed, and I've talked myself out of grieving for the bucket, that it hits me.

I didn't see what Ricky wrote on that paper. I don't know if he's acknowledged my existence. I don't know what he's told them about me.

I berate myself for the slip. I'd been so distracted by the

255

water, and the promise of more supplies, that I forgot who I'm with. I'd let him take control of our communication. I'd let him dictate the terms of our rescue.

And now I don't even know if it will be our rescue, or if he was just orchestrating his own. Alarmed, I realise that my one tiny moment of distraction may have just cost me my life.

Chapter 59

THE SCULPTOR

There's a lot on my mind.

For starters, it looks like I actually might make it out of here.

It was touch and go for a while there. The night was freezing, and hypothermia threatened to creep in. I've never shivered so much before, and I found myself longing for my camping equipment. I'll never take a sleeping bag for granted again.

I'm glad to be getting out.

But, of course, freedom presents its own problems.

I haven't yet worked out how I will slip away from here unnoticed. But, however I do it, I need to get away.

And even if I can escape, that's just the beginning of my challenges.

I need to get back to my cabin. I need to know what's happened to the Muse in the white room.

That'll determine whether I need to flee immediately, or if I have to fix my mistakes first.

All that would need to have happened, for the Muse in the white room to escape, is for the trapdoor to have come slightly ajar – which, given the force of the earthquake, isn't impossible – and she'd see it.

There's nothing else in that room, nowhere to hide something as obvious as a trapdoor. If the clock falls, or swings away from the wall, that'll be it. She'll know the way out. Of course, she'd still have to work out how to reach it, but that wouldn't be impossible. Not if she's desperate enough, which, at a guess, I'd say she is.

And if she finds a way through that trapdoor, well, then she'll know everything. She'll know that I'm not just The Sculptor. She'll know that I'm not just The Coastline Killer. She'll know all of my secrets, my entire process, the secret ingredient that makes my sculptures so much more important than any others. She'll see evidence – solid, prosecutable evidence – of who I am, and what I've done.

My stomach churns at the thought. If she knows, then she'll have run. Making it out of my atelier won't be hard; it's the white room that's practically impossible to escape, especially when I'm there, watching.

Only one Muse has ever come close to discovering the exit before. She was part of Clio in Pieces, an arm. She had beautiful fingers, which I moulded into a delicate point, as though she was holding an invisible pen, a scribe, recording the history of the world as she saw it.

Before she was immortalised in bronze, my Muse woke up one night when I was stealing into the white room to bring her supplies. I had fresh bottles of water, food, and more toilet paper – everything she needed to stay healthy, alive, and for her muscles to become lean and pliable.

Her water had been laced with sleeping pills, so I was obviously startled when she'd woken up, and said groggily, 'Where am I?'

I've never climbed that ladder as quickly as I did that night, and by the following morning I'd accelerated my plan so that she wouldn't attempt an escape. I'll never know how much she saw. I don't know how much she understood about what was happening. But I wasn't going to take any risks.

I'd worked through the night to make sure my clay model was perfect, and she was silenced the next day, ready to be taken to the ocean, miles away, where she would drift before landing on some beach in California.

That's the closest I've come to being discovered. Until now.

I keep thinking about what will happen to my work if anyone discovers who I am, what my methods are. I'll go to prison, of course. But that's not the thing that bothers me the most. The thing that's burning inside me is the realisation that people won't understand. They won't even try to.

It won't matter what I tell them. Even if I can find the words to explain my work, and the force that draws me to my Muses, the sense I have every time, that this is the way to create meaningful work, they'll just see me as a monster. No matter how much I insist that I don't have a choice, that I'm powerless to stop the Muses from luring me, like sirens in a dark, stormy ocean, that I have tried to stop, but that I can't, I don't have an option . . . they won't believe me. They won't listen. At best, they'll call me crazy. At worst, a calculating psychopath.

I'm neither. I'm cursed. I'm blessed. I've been handed a gift from above, and I'm nothing more than a steward of it, a servant following instructions.

I'm not an idiot, though. I know how the world works. And I know that, if I'm caught, my creations will be relegated to some morbid collectors' basement, or an evidence locker, never to be seen or appreciated by the world.

I deserve more than that.

So, no matter what it takes, I will get away from here undetected. I will hunt the Muse from the white room down. She will never spill my secrets.

Chapter 60

ALICE

'You know,' Ricky says as I carefully lift the bottom of my shirt to expose the needle, wincing and sucking air sharply through my teeth with a hiss. The whole area around it feels like it's on fire, my usually olive skin now flaming red. I grit my teeth and let the pain seep out of me in a flood of silent tears. 'It's going to be... difficult... to explain what we're doing down here.' There's a pause. 'When we get out.'

I turn my head sharply to look at him, and reach instinctively for the mop handle, which is beside me, out of Ricky's reach, within mine. I'm vulnerable while I'm tending to my wound. I made him stand a few feet away, and thankfully, he complied. Now he's looking right at me, his jaw set, determined.

The rescue team sent us another bucket, and another note. There was a small bottle of Advil and a first aid kit, as requested, along with four fresh bottles of water and a couple of candy bars, which we gobbled up immediately. The instant boost to our strength was incredible, the simplest of sustenance alleviating much of the pain I'd been in and clearing the dense fog that had been filling my head. I still have injuries to tend to, but I no longer feel like I'm at death's door.

After we'd eaten the candy and sipped some of the water,

Ricky had passed the first aid kit to me. I'd unzipped it in a frenzy, my chest swelling with excitement when I saw its contents. There were bandages, sterilising wipes, tape, gloves, a foil blanket, and a pair of trauma shears – which I'd quickly tucked into the waistband of my leggings.

Then he'd reached into the bucket and pulled out a new note.

'Glad to hear you guys are doing OK,' he'd read. My heart had skipped. 'You guys'? So they had heard our shouts, and he'd been honest in his note. They knew that I existed.

My blood had fizzed with relief: he was going to let me be rescued. And then fear had flowed quickly through my veins, drowning out my joy. Why would he just let me live? It didn't make sense.

'We're working as quickly as we can,' Ricky had continued reading. 'The engineer is here and drawing up a plan to get to you both safely. We're trying to get a helicopter in so we can airlift you to a hospital as soon as you get out. Hang in there. We're coming for you.'

We'd both grinned, and then I'd ordered him to stand away from me while I cleaned up my infected skin.

Now he's finally addressing the problem we're going to have to sort out before we get out of here.

I've tried to imagine the moment when I'll be pulled free from this nightmarish basement – how I'll react, what I'll say. All I know is that I'll find the closest rescuer, I'll cling to them for dear life, and I'll make it known that the man rescued with me is dangerous.

I've racked my brain, but I don't think there's anything else I can do. Letting the rescuers know who he is before we get out is far too dangerous for me. And letting me out is – surely – far too dangerous for him.

'We could say we were having an affair?' he suggests

262

weakly. He's embarrassed by his own words. He should be. Anger rises in me, hot and fast.

'Absolutely not! There's no way in hell that I'll—'

'OK, OK,' he holds up his hands in surrender. 'OK. I know. But look, Alice. We have to tell them something...'

'I was thinking maybe the truth.' The words slip out before I've thought them through. Stupid, stupid Alice, I think. I'm getting too bold, now that I have the mop handle, now that I overpowered him, now that rescue is within reach. But he has more to lose than I do. And I know what he's willing to do to me. Maybe he's prepared to be questioned by the rescuers about my death. Maybe he's just that brazen.

I hold my breath and watch him nervously for a reaction, my fingers curled around my plastic weapon.

He sighs. 'Alice,' he says slowly. 'Don't make me do this.'

'Do what?' My voice comes out as a pathetic squeak. He knows I'm completely and utterly afraid of him, of the power he has over me. He'd be an idiot not to see how the balance has shifted again. Whether he's able to act on it, that's the part I'm not sure about. Now that we've got Ibuprofen, water and food in us, his strength will be returning. Perhaps we're no longer so evenly matched.

His head wound is still bleeding, red seeping through the strips of silver. I've promised to clean him up once I'm done with my own injuries. But perhaps that's not enough reason to keep me alive anymore. Not with help on its way.

'If you tell the truth, my life will be over.'

'What about those women you killed? They didn't get to choose whether their lives were over. Why should you?'

'Alice, listen to me. You don't understand—'

'No, you listen,' I hiss, my fear morphing back into rage. It gives me courage, my anger. Makes me say stupid, unsafe things. I should be promising my silence. Not arguing. And

263

yet, when I think about the women who died at his hands, hands that have saved me but maimed so many others, I can't hold it in. I need to speak up for them, because they can't. Because somehow, against all odds, I can.

'You don't get to suddenly be given a fresh start, even if being down here has changed your perspective on things. You don't get to walk away from what you've done, and not have to face the consequences, even if you've had a change of heart.' I pause for a moment. 'Especially if you've had a change of heart,' I add. 'You should want to give those families closure. You should want to do the right thing.'

I'm panting, the exertion of my outburst more than I really have the strength for. By contrast, Ricky doesn't seem distressed, or angry, or emotional. He's calm. Eerily so. His eyes meet mine, his expression unreadable. The silence is thick with tension. Eventually, he speaks, his voice low.

'You think you know me.'

He stares at me. I stare straight back, unflinching.

I shrug. 'I know everything I need to know.'

There's a rumbling sound overhead. We both cower, our arms instinctively reaching over our heads. There's a clang, and a growl that could be an engine. Or another aftershock. Small pieces of plaster and wood and insulation rain over us. In the corner of the room, something bigger and heavier falls.

Eventually, the crumbling around us settles. The engine sound stops abruptly.

'I understand what you're saying,' Ricky says after a long pause.

I almost forget what we've just been talking about. Almost.

He's looking right at me, his deep brown eyes intense and clear. 'But I need you to understand this. I am getting out of here, and I'm going back to my real life. To my home, maybe even to my wife, if I can patch things up with her. You have to remember, Alice: I was watching you before I took you. I know where you live. I know where your parents live. I know where your friend Celia and her lovely little twins live.'

Fear rips through me. But I don't back down.

'Fuck you,' I spit. 'You can't do anything if you're in prison.'

'Alice.'

His voice is calm. Terrifyingly even. There's no emotion in his words. And I realise that he does have a plan. He's not worried about what I'll do when we get out because he's still in control.

'It's your word against mine,' he continues evenly, 'and believe me, there is no evidence pointing to me as any kind of criminal.'

'Why else would I be here?'

He ignores the question.

'And even if – and as I say, it's not going to happen, but if – I was in prison, I promise you, if it was you who put me there, I would find you. I would destroy your family and friends, one by one, so you would know exactly what was happening. And then I would kill you.'

I feel sick. Why did I think I could beat this guy? Why did I open my stupid mouth? I should have agreed to whatever he wanted. Anything to get out of here safely, with my friends and family safe, too.

'You ... how?'

He laughs, and the sound is like tiny little knives of fear slicing down my spine.

'Believe me,' he says. 'I can. And I will. I have the means. I know you think you'll be safe if I'm behind bars, but I need you to understand that if you breathe a word of this, to anyone – anyone – I will know. And I will kill you, don't think I won't.'

Tears spring to my eyes. I hate myself for showing my fear, my weakness, because that's exactly what he wants. But I can't stop them from welling up. It's automatic, my body's reaction to his threats. He might be bluffing. But what if he isn't?

'I don't want to kill you,' his voice warms, softens somehow. 'I really don't. You saved my life, and I owe you for that. You might not think I deserve it, but even so, I'd be dead if you hadn't helped. So I'd rather that we both get out. Alive. Which is why we're going to tell them that we're having an affair. Got it?'

He's so calm. So measured. I want to pull the scissors from my waistband and plunge them right into his eye, through his psychotic brain. I want to watch the blood pouring out of him, spilling onto the floor, mingling with the dust.

But I won't.

So then where does that leave me? My family, my friends? Can I really keep this quiet, to protect us all? If I do, other women will die. If I don't, I could lose everyone I love. I don't know how to make that kind of choice. I don't want to be put in this position.

'Got it?' he repeats, and I nod. For now, at least, I have to play by his rules. I have to get out alive. I have to find my family and Celia, and then I have to make sure that they're protected. I can't even think about stopping him unless I can be certain that they'll be OK.

Will I have to move away from the city I love? Get a new identity? Face him in a trial? Could I risk even trying to bring a child into a world where there's a target on my back? The idea fills my chest with dread. I can't think that far ahead, though. I have to concentrate on making it out of here.

Which means that, at least until I know that I'm safe, I have no choice but to keep my mouth shut, and pretend that I'm sleeping with the man who almost killed me.

Chapter 61

ALICE

'Well, hey there, folks.'

I jump, the unexpected voice startling me. I'm on edge as it is, unnerved every time Ricky so much as blinks.

Looking up to where the voice came from, there's a man's face, as dirty as ours, peering through the same hole where the bucket had appeared from.

I drop the roll of medical tape in my hands and eagerly stumble over a pile of rubble to stand underneath him.

Only . . . the man doesn't reach his arms down, doesn't instruct me on where to stand or what to do.

'I'm Bill,' he says. 'You must be Alice. And Ricky.'

The men nod at one another. I want to scream in frustration. Why are we doing introductions when we could be getting pulled out of here?

'We're going to get you folks out as soon as we can,' Bill explains, 'but we're just making sure we can do it safely. This building's in pretty bad shape, as I'm sure you know better than anyone, but we're doing what we can to make it as safe as possible.'

I nod, not really understanding what he means. All I need to know is when I'm getting out.

'So in the next few minutes we should have a bit of a makeshift winch situation sorted out here. The engineer is up there making sure we're all good, and we should be able to start lifting soon, once I get the OK from them. In the meantime, Alice, is it? I'd finish up dressing those wounds of his.'

His face disappears. I don't know what else to do, so I follow his instructions, my hands shaking so badly the dressing barely covers the gash on Ricky's forehead. After he'd threatened to kill everyone I love – which, apparently, he can do somehow, even if he's locked away – he demanded that I patch up his head wounds using our new supplies. I've been unwrapping, cleaning and redressing them, while trying to keep the mop handle within reach, and watching him closely for any sudden movement. I just want this to be over.

A few minutes of walkie-talkie crackle later, Bill's face reappears. 'So ... who's going first, eh?'

He looks at me expectantly, but Ricky steps in front of me.

'I will,' he says.

I gape.

'Better test the way, make sure it's safe,' he adds.

How chivalrous.

'Okey-dokey,' Bill says cheerfully, not showing any sign that what Ricky just did was unbelievably selfish. Perhaps if he knew exactly who he was rescuing he might not be so upbeat.

I consider yelling out, 'He's The Coastline Killer', just getting the truth out there now, while there's a witness, and while freedom is within reach. But what if he just kills me on the spot? Or what if he doesn't, and instead he makes good on his promise of killing the people I love? I don't understand how he would, but he's got away with the murders of so many women over the past few years – he's clearly smart, and well-organised. I can't risk it.

269

'I need you two to step back for a minute, please,' our rescuer instructs. We both do as we're told. He retreats again and we hear his voice floating down to us from the darkness, communicating with the others outside.

While we're alone, Ricky hisses at me.

'Remember what I told you, OK? Silence, and we both get out of here alive.'

I stare at him, my eyes narrowed. I clench my fists, but I nod.

'I just have to widen this hole,' Bill calls from above, 'so prepare for some banging noises and a bit of debris, OK?'

Neither of us responds, but we move as far away as we can. There's a series of loud, terror-inducing noises, and then a bundle of straps is fed through the freshly widened hole.

The building is creaking and groaning as though it's about to crumble around us, and I will the rescuers to hurry up. I'm so tense, my muscles so tight I feel like they could snap.

'Right-e-o,' Bill says, his positivity almost making me believe that everything will be OK. 'The boys are all set up, and they're ready to lift the first one of you out. So – Ricky?'

Ricky steps forward. Bill glances at me, not saying anything, but the question written across his face: Are you sure? I nod, almost imperceptibly, but he sees it.

'All right, my man. If you just step through these two loops . . .'

He guides Ricky through the process of attaching the harness, making sure it's tight around his legs and waist. He explains that Ricky will be lifted through the hole, that from where Bill is lying, there's a sort of tunnel through the wreckage that will lead them to the outside. That he'll be right there, right beside him, guiding him through it all. That he's in safe hands.

Despite the chilly air, beads of sweat have broken out

across my upper lip and my forehead. My breathing is shallow. I take a deep breath and tell myself that this is almost over.

My stomach is still writhing, but I am strong. I've survived this far. I can make it another few minutes, even if, for those few minutes, I'll be left down here completely alone.

Ricky's strapped in, and there's another burst of static, voices coming from Bill's radio.

'Ready?'

'Ready.'

With a jerk, my almost-murderer is lifted from the ground. He rises slowly, with small twitches and starts. His body sways in the harness. He looks at me gleefully. I glare back at him.

And then, when he's almost within reach of the hole, he stops. He's still grinning, but after a few seconds the smile drops from his face.

'What's happening?'

'Hold on.'

There's another explosion of static as Bill communicates with the unseen crew above us. I can't hear his words, but his voice is urgent, animated. My stomach clenches. Ricky glances at me, worry painted across his dusty face.

'Right,' Bill calls out. 'There's a bit of a problem with the winch mechanism. They're just working on getting—'

He doesn't get a chance to finish his sentence. The hole in the ceiling begins to crumble, pieces of wood and plaster and cement raining down on Ricky. I fling myself to the ground, hands over my head. My name is being screamed, and there's a loud moaning, like metal being stretched beyond its limits. Then there's more crumbling, tumbling, crashing, smashing, coming from all around me.

271

'Alice,' Ricky yells, his voice breaking through my fear. 'I'll pull you up! Give me your hands! I'll pull you up!'

I stand, shielding my head, and leap over a pile of rubble to reach the spot beneath him. His head is bleeding heavily now – he must have been hit again. There's a terrifying crash and, when I look behind me, the space where I had just been lying is gone, replaced by a huge chunk of building. The whole space is trembling. It's not an earthquake, though. This is different. It's not the ground beneath us. It's the building, giving up, willing to take us with it.

Ricky's arms are outstretched, reaching down towards me. I lift my hands, screaming as my ribs are pulled apart. I grip his wrists, and he grips mine, pulling me up with a strength I'd never have guessed he still had. An almighty noise billows around me. A cloud envelops us. I scream, or maybe it's Ricky.

Bill's voice reaches me through the cacophony. It sounds distant, like it's coming through layers of steel.

'Ricky!' he screams. 'Now! I need you to grab my hand now or you're not getting out of here.'

In that split second, I know.

He'll save himself.

This is the end.

And then the hole widens, and I'm caught in a shower of debris and dust and chaos.

Chapter 62

ALICE

The sunlight is blinding, the fresh air sharp on my scoured lungs.

I gasp, then cough, then groan. Then I laugh. It's glorious. Bright, and so colourful it hurts. It's not just the unbelievably vivid surroundings, though – everything hurts. I blink the world into focus and discover that I'm lying on soft, green grass, the blades tickling my face. Beside me, a man in beige is wheezing. He's covered in dust and wearing a hard hat.

Lifting my head, I squint against the harsh daylight. Ahead of me is a ruined building, a heap of splinters and bricks and shards. My mouth opens. That's what I escaped from? Shapes move around me, hover over me, ask me questions I can't quite make out.

'Where's Ricky?' I manage to croak.

'You just stay where you are,' a male voice says from somewhere close to me. I blink again, hard. The shapes become humans, and I search the faces frantically, needing to know that Ricky hasn't run away.

I struggle to prop myself up on my elbows. A strong hand presses on my shoulder, but I twist away.

'Take it easy,' another voice says. 'Help is on its way. I need you to stay where you are.'

'No,' I gasp, struggling to roll over.

'Hey!'

I look up. A firefighter is crouching down so he's almost at my level.

'I'm Lleyton. I'm going to make sure that someone takes a look at your injuries, OK? But I need you to stay where you are. You're safe now, all right? You're out of danger.'

He has no idea.

'But Ricky . . .' I'm breathless. I can't explain everything until I know that he's here, that he will be arrested, that he hasn't escaped.

'Your friend?' Lleyton asks. He's suddenly looking anywhere but directly at me. Over my shoulder, behind him, at the ground. He licks his lips.

'I'm so sorry,' he says in a small, quiet voice. 'We tried to get him out, too, but the building collapsed. We only just got you out. I'm afraid he didn't make it.'

'No,' I say. I don't believe him. Ricky didn't die. He got away, he's running, and he's going to kill again. I heave my body up, ignoring Lleyton's pleas, wriggling free of his hands.

I begin to stagger towards the wreckage, rebelling against my body's protests. My injuries can wait.

'Ricky!' I scream. Gloved hands grab at my arms. I wrestle them away. 'No!'

'Alice, it's too dangerous,' Lleyton insists. 'You can't go any closer.'

I'm quickly overpowered, despite my struggle. I can't get past the man who's gripping my elbow, but I'm desperate to make him understand, frantic in my need to stop Ricky. The truth bursts out of me, before I have time to consider the consequences.

'He's The Coastline Killer,' I gasp. 'Ricky. He's The Coast-line Killer. You can't let him get away.'

I look up at Lleyton. His eyebrows are drawn together, and for a moment I'm convinced that he won't believe me, he'll think I'm crazy, confused, concussed. But then his eyes widen, and his mouth forms an O. He stays frozen like that for a second, and then, when he speaks, his voice is slow, his words clear.

'Are you telling me that the man you were trapped with is a serial killer?'

'Yes,' I sob, relief, pain and fear pulsing through me. 'He tried to kill me. He can't get away.'

'He didn't get away, Alice.' His voice is gentler, now. 'The building collapsed on him.'

I shake my head, tears streaming down my cheeks. He's not clinging to me anymore.

'I have to see. I have to see his body.'

I make a break for it, but Lleyton curls an arm around my waist and pulls me back, with no effort at all. I collapse, gasping and crying and shouting: 'I have to see.'

Lleyton sinks to his knees beside me. 'OK, look,' he says. I lift my head and try to plead with him without words. He has kind eyes. 'We'll see if we can recover his body, all right? But I need you to stay here. It's not safe near the building, not in the state you're in. A helicopter's on the way to pick you up, along with my buddy Bill, there, who pulled you out.'

He points to the man on the ground, who I was lying beside just moments ago. A small crowd has gathered around him.

'If you go wait with him while we look, you can get your-self patched up. There might be another Twix in it for you.'

I offer him a watery smile.

275

'And Alice?'

'Yeah.'

'I'll make sure we find him. OK?'

'Thank you,' I whisper. Lleyton calls to someone, and I allow myself to be led by a stranger back to the cluster of rescuers.

I'm quickly engulfed, wrapped in a foil blanket, given water and hot, sweet tea and the promised Twix. I tell them my name, my address, my parents' phone number. I don't tell anyone else about Ricky, though. I told Lleyton. He believed me, but if the man I was trapped with did manage to escape, somehow, then the firefighter is in as much danger as I am, as my friends and family are. I'm not going to put anyone else at risk.

As I sit, accepting the kindness of strangers, I begin to notice my surroundings. I'm in a suburb, but there are no identifying landmarks. I could be anywhere. The damage here isn't immediately visible, aside from the destroyed building I emerged from. But then I see the downed power line. A deep crack across the front of a house across the road. A shattered window.

Someone comes to inspect me for injuries. I tell them I'm fine, although I'm not sure that's true. Hands gently move my foot back and forth, and an ice pack is applied to what I'm told is a sprained ankle. The rest, they say, will be taken care of at the hospital.

The dull rattle of a helicopter fills the air, and panic rises in my chest. I stand up. A woman with grey hair tries to push me back into the camp chair I've been sitting in, but I shove her aside, lurching towards the ruins of the building I was trapped in.

'Lleyton!' I shout. 'Lleyton!'

Once the helicopter arrives, they'll want to take me to

276

hospital immediately. They might be able to show me photos of a body that looks like Ricky's, but I know I won't believe them. He's evaded the law for so long. I can't be certain that he doesn't have a way to disappear. Not unless I see him with my own eyes.

A helmet pops up out of the rubble. A face follows.

'Alice,' he shouts over the noise of the approaching chopper. 'Stay back!'

'I can't leave! I have to see him.'

'I know! We've found him, we're just trying to pull him up. Just stay where you are, OK?'

There's a gust of wind as the helicopter approaches. I look up, squinting against the sun, and watch it descending behind a row of houses. There's a school football pitch that it can land on, apparently. I shift my weight impatiently, but balancing on my good leg is challenging, and after a few seconds I sit awkwardly on the grass beside a huge piece of splintered wood.

I grab fistfuls of grass and tear them up anxiously, thinking about Ricky's threats, wondering if Lleyton has really found him. There's movement from the detritus of the building, which must have been someone's home once, followed by a burst of activity, shouts I can't decipher, machinery squealing.

After a few seconds, something large is hauled from the ruins, held by webbing and lifted by a pulley. One of the firefighters is guiding their find towards the grass.

I struggle to my feet, wishing I still had the mop handle, and lurch towards it. As I get closer, it's lowered to the ground and I can tell that it's a body. My heart stammers. I let out a cry and trip, landing sprawled out beside the corpse.

Ricky's corpse.

It's him. I know it's him immediately, although every inch

277

of him is covered in thick, dark dust. There's more blood, a huge patch of it seeping across his chest where a piece of metal shredded his torso. It's still partially embedded, glinting in the light. One sleeve of his top is missing, the sleeve he tore off to use as a mask, and my makeshift head dressing is still intact, now covered in grit and blood.

I stare at the face that filled me with terror, and wonder if I'll ever be able to shake the feeling that he's out to get me. But I can't deny that this is him, that this is the man I was trapped with.

The Coastline Killer is dead.

I drop my head and sob. Arms find their way around me. I feel myself being picked up, and I don't resist as I'm carried to the helicopter, lifted inside and gently laid on a stretcher. My tears don't stop as we take off, or as we glide through the air. I cry harder as a needle is pressed into the soft skin on the inside of my elbow – my right arm, this time – and I allow myself to let go of the fear I've felt every second since waking up in the basement.

I'm free. I'm safe. I let my head fall back on the pillow, and I drop into an instant, deep, dreamless sleep.

Chapter 63

BBC News Online

**Remarkable rescue effort from Vancouver quake
wreckage
13 October, 2018
Eleven minutes ago**

More stories of hope are emerging from Vancouver
after yesterday's devastating earthquake, including a
rescue effort this morning that authorities are calling
'miraculous'. We are yet to receive details on the
survivor or survivors, as their identities have not yet been
confirmed, but reports from those close to the operation
have suggested that a male and female adult were pulled
from the site.

   Matthew Donoghue, team leader of Red Cross
Western Canada, who is overseeing the fleet of
helicopters being sent into the Vancouver disaster area
to take victims in need of critical medical attention to
working hospitals nearby, said of the rescue, 'It was
unbelievable.'

   'We're hearing stories like this from all over
the Vancouver metropolitan area,' he told a BBC
correspondent. 'The civilian and emergency services
rescue efforts have been truly inspiring. Without a

formal structure, they're coming together and meeting the needs of victims in their local areas. Many of the roads are damaged beyond use, so rescue efforts from outside are struggling to reach the places where they're needed most. We can get helicopters in, but we only have so many of those, so our priority has to be victims who need the most urgent medical attention. In the case of this particular rescue effort, some of the injuries sustained were so bad we're all shocked that there were any survivors at all. Credit goes to all of those who assisted in this incredible effort.'

At least one patient was airlifted from the site, a collapsed building in Vancouver's suburbs, to Kelowna General Hospital in British Columbia, one of only a few operational hospitals in the region.

The discovery of survivors trapped in the basement of an abandoned building in the Vancouver neighbourhood of Burnaby was made earlier this morning. Rescuers believed that whoever was down there had been trapped for almost twenty-six hours.

It is believed that a rescuer was injured in the effort, although their identity has not been confirmed. It is not known whether there was anyone else trapped in the building, or whether there were any other casualties in the rescue effort.

Follow more news of the Vancouver earthquake here.

Chapter 64

LUCY

The tiredness that pulsed through Lucy's bones was making her weak.

She'd been running for hours without seeing a single human, or sign of life. She wasn't certain which direction she was travelling in, or whether she was even going anywhere. Sometimes she was sure she was just going around in circles. Often she knew that she could go no further. But she'd pressed on anyway, defying her exhausted body and frightened mind. Now it was dark again and any sense of direction she felt that she'd had disappeared as the day had faded into the yawning jaws of night.

Throughout her flight, she'd heard things.

Things that made her blood fizz in her veins. That made the hairs on the back of her neck prickle. Screams, at first. She wondered for a terrible second if they were human, but she quickly realised they came from a frightened, hunted animal.

After the screaming came the howls. Bloodcurdling appeals to the moon, which she couldn't see behind the clouds, but whose light emitted a soft, eerie glow upon the forest. Light enough to see shapes and shadows. Too dark to know what they were.

To Lucy, every branch, every trunk, looked like a predator coming for her.

She wanted to cry. But she didn't have the energy. She was too cold to continue, the sharp air biting the tip of her nose, the tops of her ears, nipping at her bones. The batteries in her flashlight had given up hours ago, the panic rising in Lucy's chest as the beam faded to black.

Her legs buckled, twigs snapping and leaves crunching under her weight. She knew she had to keep going, that it was too dangerous to stop. She could die out there in the cold, exposed to the elements. She had no idea what time it was, only that it was night, only that she'd been running all day without finding rescue.

Everything inside her was telling her to stop, to rest for a bit. Dawn was surely on its way, and when it arrived, she'd have the strength to keep going, to continue to search for help, for someone she could tell her secrets to. But if she stopped, there was no guarantee that she'd still be alive when the sun found its way over the horizon.

She pressed herself up onto her hands and knees, shoving the knife into a jacket pocket, and began crawling, stumbling as she went, her face falling into the dirt, her mouth filling with blood and leaves and soil. She was exhausted, in pain, dehydrated. Lost. But she pushed on, regardless.

Something cracked nearby, and her head snapped in the direction of the noise, her hand reaching automatically for the handle of the knife. She looked around. There was nothing. At least nothing she could see. She took a deep breath, and forced herself onwards, even as things rustled and snapped around her.

Her eyes were heavy, but her heart was pounding. She needed rest. But she also needed to stay alive. She couldn't have both.

Eventually, her body won the fight. She slumped onto the forest floor, sleep coming in short, hard bursts, interrupted by a howl or a hoot or a crack that split the air around her. Every time, her eyes would snap open in alarm, and she'd try to clamber back onto her hands and knees, desperate to keep going, to find help, to get as far away as possible from that awful cabin. But then her trembling arms would betray her, her head would fall against the leaves that littered the ground, and she'd tumble into a dreamless, restless sleep.

Another crack, this one louder than the rest.

Her head shot up, smacking the trunk she'd collapsed against with a hollow thud. There it was again – a cracking of leaves and twigs, loud and clear, closer this time.

Something heavy was coming her way. She saw the light before she spotted the intruder. A beam, yellow and bright, juddering across the leaves. A flashlight.

'Help,' she whispered, her voice hoarse from the cold.

A crack. A rustle.

'Help,' she repeated, louder this time.

'Hello?' The voice was like a warm blanket, soothing and safe. Friendly. A saviour. 'Hello, is someone there?'

Lucy whimpered.

'Oh my God,' the voice said. 'Are you OK?'

Something warm pressed against her cheek. A gloved hand. Lucy tried to speak, but the exhaustion was pulling at her, calling her into sleep. She was safe now. She didn't need to fight. Someone was there.

Arms clasped at her, under her armpits, lifting her. Her body responded, her legs scrambling for purchase against the dirt.

A breeze breathed against her face.

She was standing. Her eyes battled to open. As they found

focus, the clouds overhead parted. Barely, imperceptibly, but enough to light up the forest for a split second.

And in that second, Lucy's eyes fixed on the face in front of her.

Her knees buckled.

It was over.

Chapter 65

ALICE

I'm aware that I'm in a hospital before I'm fully conscious.

The beeps, the smells, the nurses talking in low, soothing voices, telling me how well I'm doing; I'm aware of it all, and somehow not really awake.

So it's no surprise when my eyes finally open and my mind sharpens, to discover that I'm in a hospital room. I'm alone, and I'm plugged into a bunch of machines. My mouth is so dry that I can't swallow. I lift my head a little, to see if I can call someone, and spot a button near my hand, the back of which has a needle protruding from it. I lift my finger to hit the button, and let my head fall.

In films, people who wake up in hospitals struggle to remember. Memories come to them in snatches, snippets. Mine don't. They're right there, at the front of my mind, from the moment I wake up. The basement. The mask. The earthquake. A serial killer threatening my life. His body.

I press the button again, and then again. I'm desperate for information. And to make sure that the police know who Ricky was. I'm sure Lleyton has passed on what I said, but I need to know. I need this to be over.

Soft footsteps approach.

'Oh hello there, hun.' The nurse's voice oozes warmth.

She's short, wearing sky-blue scrubs, a huge smile painted across her face. I let my body relax a little. I open my mouth, but all that comes out is a croak. My throat is so dry, my tongue so much like sandpaper, that words are impossible.

'We thought you might wake up soon. You've been asleep for quite some time. Here.'

She holds out a paper cup. With monumental effort, I take it from her, everything aching as my muscles work to obey my brain. I lift the cup to my lips and take small, delicious sips. My mouth feels infinitely better.

'Thank you,' I whisper, dropping my arm, the paper cup falling onto my stomach. The nurse collects it and begins adjusting something above me that I can't see.

'My name's Poorna, by the way.'

'Poorna,' I say. 'I'm Alice.'

'I know, love. We have all your details, thanks to your rescuers. How are you feeling, Alice?'

'Uh...' I try to find the right word, and settle on, 'sore.'

'I bet,' she says sympathetically. 'You've been through a lot, but you'll be pleased to hear your recovery is going exceptionally well, considering. You suffered a tension pneumothorax, which means there was air in the pleural space outside of your lungs, thanks to a broken rib. But you were really lucky – whoever inserted that needle did an amazing job. Could have just as easily killed you.'

I shudder at the memory. I resist the urge to tell her that the person who did the amazing job also very nearly did kill me. Besides, Poorna doesn't give me a chance to tell her. She keeps talking in that same cheerful voice that's soothing to my soul.

'So we had to do some emergency surgery on your lungs, which was a huge success. As I said, you broke a rib, and you have a few other minor fractures and lacerations here and there, as well as a pretty nasty sprained ankle. We've also been treating you for an infection. The needle in your side was pretty dirty, so your body rejected it, but you're recovering well.'

I nod, then let my head fall back on the pillow. After a second, I lift it again, panicked.

'Is . . . will my injuries stop me from getting pregnant?'

I can barely breathe at the thought of it. Poorna gives me a small smile that I can't read.

'I can't say for certain, but I shouldn't think so, no. Your injuries were mostly around your chest, not your abdomen. You'd need some tests to say for certain, but there's no reason to believe you couldn't conceive.'

I could weep with relief, but there's no time. I'm still bursting with questions.

'Where am I?'

'Kelowna General Hospital,' she says. 'You were brought here by helicopter yesterday. The roads were unusable and the hospitals in the Vancouver area are totally overloaded, or completely destroyed. Poor things.'

And then I realise: I have no idea if my family is OK, if they survived the quake, how bad the damage was outside of my tiny, grimy bubble.

'My family,' I say, trying to sit up. Poorna rests a hand gently on my shoulder, pushing me back down.

'I've spoken to your mom,' she says, then quickly adds, 'they're both fine.'

I exhale sharply.

'I'll give them a call now; they'll be glad to hear you're awake. You can talk to them soon, but the police asked to be notified when you're able to talk. Should I let them know you're awake? They said they'd want to come and question you.'

She looks concerned, like perhaps I'm in trouble and need protection from the police.

'It's OK,' I say with a small smile. 'I need to talk to them as soon as I can.'

'All right,' she says hesitantly. She opens her mouth, as if to ask me something, then thinks better of it. 'Be right back.'

Her steps fade into the hum of background noise, and I try to untangle my thoughts, so that when the police arrive, I'll be able to tell them what happened without it sounding like a babbled mess.

There's a knock at the door and I flinch in surprise. It's not Ricky, I remind myself. He's dead.

A figure rounds the door. I don't know this person. He's huge – all muscle, his bulk filling the door frame. Fear wraps itself around my heart and squeezes. Is this the resource Ricky mentioned, the person who he promised would come for me and my family, even if Ricky himself was in prison – or dead? But how would he know? My finger reaches for the call button.

'Hey, Alice.'

The fear whooshes out of me all at once. I might not recognise his face, but I will never forget the voice of the man who rescued me.

'Bill!'

He limps towards me, and now that my vision isn't clouded by fear I notice that he has a cast on his arm, and some kind of brace around his head, with metal rods going into his skull. His head is shaved, and there's bruising all across his eyes. I didn't really get a good look at him in the moments after my rescue; he was surrounded by people, and so was I. But he's in a bad way.

'Sit down,' I say, waving towards the chair next to me. 'Are you OK?'

'I'm alive,' he replies with a grimace. 'And I'll be OK, yeah. Just a few injuries to keep me on my toes. How about you?'

'I think I'm all right,' I say. 'I've been out since the helicopter. I just woke up, so I haven't tried to walk or anything yet. But I'm happy to be alive. And out of that basement.'

'I bet,' Bill says. Then his gaze drops. 'I'm sorry about Ricky.'

I stare right at him, my stomach tying itself into a thousand knots. Doesn't he know? Perhaps Lleyton didn't tell him. There were more pressing issues, like getting us to hospital.

'I'm not,' I say. The shock on Bill's face tells me everything I need to know.

'He wasn't a good person,' I say, by way of explanation. Bill's eyebrows meet in the middle as he frowns.

'Well, I can't speak about that, but I can say that what he did for you . . .' He trails off.

'What did he do for me?' I ask, surprised.

'He saved your life.'

A laugh bubbles up and erupts from me. Bill looks like I've just slapped him in the face.

'Hardly!'

'He did. I saw it, Alice. I was there.'

I stare in disbelief at the man who pulled me from the rubble. I can't remember the specifics of the rescue. Ricky had insisted on being pulled out first, and he was being lifted in the harness when the building began to collapse. There was stuff flying everywhere. Shouting. Chaos.

'He pushed you up through the hole in the ceiling,' Bill tells me. 'I was retreating, but he kept forcing you up, so I had to take you. He saved your life, when he could have saved his own. He must have known he'd die when he did that. The building was crumbling around us.'

I stare at Bill. I don't know how to react. I have no idea how I'm supposed to feel, but I suspect I'm supposed to feel something. Instead, I'm numb. And so incredibly tired.

'Look,' my rescuer says gently, 'I'm sorry. I know this must be difficult, but I just thought you should know that, no matter who he was, what he did, not many people would have done that; believe me. I just thought you should know so that you can tell his family.'

His family. He had a wife. Possibly kids, I don't know. Whoever was in his life, they're about to learn the truth about him; the real truth. No matter what Bill believes, the man who died in that building wasn't a hero.

As I remember the body stretched out on the grass in front of me, my stomach flutters with emotions too tangled to identify. I'm angry that there won't be any real justice for the women he killed. I'm grateful that I don't have to look over my shoulder, that I can tell the truth without fear. And there's something else, too. Something empty; hollow.

Because the one person who truly understood what I went through down there – the only person who knows what we endured – is gone. Those memories are now mine alone to wrestle with, to come to terms with. They're my sole responsibility.

'Thank you,' I say eventually, smiling. Not for the information about Ricky. 'Thank you for rescuing me. For saving me.'

'Ah, it's my pleasure.' He smiles. 'I needed a good news

story, after everything I saw after the quake. I needed you to survive.'

Poorna breezes back into the room, her smile falling when she sees that I have company.

'Everything OK, Alice?'

'This is Bill,' I tell her. 'He rescued me.'

Poorna beams and introduces herself.

'Your parents are over the moon to hear that you're awake. They wanted to speak to you right away but I told them you'd have to call them back in a bit. They told me to tell you that Celia's fine, too.'

'Thank God,' I breathe. 'Thank you.'

'Of course, love. And the police are on their way.'

'The police?' Bill asks with a frown. I wave his question away.

'Oh. Never mind,' I say. I need to tell the police first, and I don't know if I have the strength to say the words out loud more than once. Not yet, anyway.

'I think visiting time is over for today,' Poorna says gently. Bill turns his body slowly – his pain evident – to her, then back to me. He smiles.

'I'll come and see you tomorrow, if that's OK?'

'I'd like that.'

He grins and shuffles out of the room, looking surprisingly fragile for a man of his size.

'You OK, hun?' Poorna asks.

I grimace. 'I'm tired,' I admit.

She looks at me for a moment, assessing me. 'You sure you're up for talking to the police? They'll be here in ten minutes or so, but I can ask them to come back—'

'No,' I interrupt, sounding much more confident than I feel. 'I need to do it now.'

Ricky's identity is no longer my burden to bear. I'll gladly offload the truth to the police, and let them do whatever needs to be done. He might be part of my past, but he's sure as hell not going to be part of my future.

Chapter 66

ALICE

'Well, we just got our electricity back this morning,' my mom tells me, the receiver of the phone Poorna managed to sneak into my room pressed to my ear. 'Although it's still patchy.'

I smile, relief that they're safe from the earthquake flooding me afresh.

It's strange, hearing about the extent of the destruction without seeing it with my own eyes. It's hard to understand the enormity of what's happened. My parents have tried to share some of the details: the estimated death tolls, the state of the roads and buildings and services, but I feel disconnected from it, as though the natural disaster I experienced was an entirely different event.

Emergency services personnel have been flown in from all over the country and across the world. Aid workers and disaster relief teams rushed to sites most affected by the earthquake – Vancouver Island, Vancouver, Seattle – and have set up medical facilities and shelters for those whose homes have been destroyed, of which there are so, so many.

Mom and Dad have taken in a couple from down the road, whose house caught fire when electrical wires sparked. They lost everything.

I don't know who's been affected, and who hasn't. Who's lost loved ones, and who's homeless.

But I don't need to know everything just yet. Right now, I'm just grateful to be speaking to my mom again.

'Don't forget, Mom, there might still be aftershocks, OK? Promise me you'll be careful?'

'This coming from the woman who had to be airlifted out of the rubble? I think I can take care of myself, thank you.'

There's a smile in her voice. I try to keep my voice steady when I say, 'I know you can, Mom.'

'Have you heard anything more from the police?'

'Not really,' I sigh. 'Someone else came to question me earlier today, from the FBI this time. I told them the same thing I told the officers yesterday, but they wanted to hear it for themselves, I guess.'

'Do they know who he is?'

'I think so,' I say. 'They showed me a picture, and it was definitely him. They didn't tell me his name though. So I guess now they'll look into him, I don't know. They weren't too keen on telling me much.'

'Well, I suppose it's in their hands, now.'

'Yes.'

Someone shouts in the background.

'Alice, I have to run. A group of us are rebuilding the Branstons' front room, and I came in here to grab the hammer when you called. I'd better get back to it.'

I smile. 'OK, Mom. Speak soon. I love you.'

'Love you, Al.'

After she hangs up, my mind races. I know I should try to get some sleep, but I can't turn my thoughts off – flashes of moments in the basement, Ricky saying, 'You think you know me', Bill's adamance that Ricky sacrificed himself for me – and my emotions are all over the place. I'm weepy, although I can't understand why. I'm angry. I'm relieved. I'm still trying to process everything that happened.

I reach for the TV remote and switch it on, needing a distraction. I know it'll probably just be more images of Vancouver razed by the cracking open of the earth, entire buildings now little more than powder settling on the ground. But even that, even the horror of what happened to my home city, is better than facing the complex tangle of emotions I'm feeling.

The screen flickers into life.

A newsreader is standing in what looks like a small harbour, white boats bobbing in the water behind her, and blue skies stretching out above her.

'I'm Cara Reid, reporting live for Channel Six News from the town of Astoria in Oregon. It was here, in this small fishing harbour, that a woman's body was discovered in the early hours of this morning by a local fisherman. Witnesses describe her as missing an arm, which has led to speculation that The Coastline Killer has struck again . . .'

My eyes widen and my spine tingles. How could he have struck again? He's dead. I saw his body for myself.

'—leading locals to wonder if the woman found here today could be missing Portland woman, Lucy Tran, who was reported missing on October ninth.'

Perhaps he killed her before he came to me. Perhaps she was his last murder.

'An autopsy is yet to be carried out, but a source close to the police has said that it looked as though the woman was killed within the past twelve hours, leading the police to believe that The Coastline Killer may be continuing his work of destruction along the Pacific Northwest.'

My blood turns to ice.

Chapter 67

ALICE

Sixteen Days Later

The doorbell rings. I don't attempt to get up.

I'm still struggling to walk, although I can make it a few steps at a time, assisted by crutches. It's a huge improvement, but even so, the smallest things tire me out and set my lungs on fire. The doctors tell me that I was lucky, that I got off lightly, that I'll heal, eventually. I'm impatient, though. I want to be able to walk unassisted, to get out there and help with the rebuilding of my city. I want to go home.

'I'll get it,' Dad calls from the kitchen. Mom looks up from her book and smiles at me.

'What are you up to, love?'

'Just – emailing James about the job,' I say, the lie warming my cheeks. Mom, who's always known when I'm not telling the truth, just nods.

'So you heard back from him then. Do you know when they want you to start?'

I shake my head. 'It's still too soon. They're still recovering, and they've said I can take as much time as I need to heal. I'm just trying to get a job description so I can prepare in the meantime. It's not like I have much to do.'

That part, at least, is true. As soon as I got back to Vancouver, and the Wi-Fi was restored, I'd emailed James to ask if his offer was still on the table. He'd replied and said that the job was all mine, that they needed me more than ever. We haven't negotiated a starting date yet. The city is still reeling from its losses, and regular work – unless you're in demolition or construction – is not on many people's minds. It's been days since I last emailed James.

What I'm not telling my mom is that I'm flipping between the two tabs I have open in my browser. The first is Alvin's donor profile. When I'd originally been searching for a donor, I'd paid the sperm bank for access to extended profiles, which had included baby photos and personality test results and a write-up of what staff at the centre had thought of him when he came in. I've been reading and re-reading it for days now, desperate for clues that he is who he says he is, but so far I haven't found anything that can tell me with any certainty that he's a good person. That he's not a psychopath.

There's no urgency. Even if I was in a condition to be thinking about trying to get pregnant – which the doctors tell me won't be for months – the clinic was badly damaged and will take time to get back up and running. The good news is that my eggs are being stored at a facility in Alberta, which wasn't affected by the quake. The bad news is that there weren't many to begin with, and the ones that were sent to the clinic for my IVF were ruined.

So I don't have many chances. I have to make sure that when I do try again, it's with full confidence that I've selected the right donor.

The second tab I have open is the Facebook profile of Richard Tremblay. Or, as I knew him, Ricky.

In the end, the police had shared his name.

'We have an update on the case,' they'd told me, sitting beside my hospital bed, two of them; serious, and clearly exhausted.

I'd been relieved. Since the news report about the woman, Lucy, who had been murdered after Ricky had died, I'd felt like I was going insane. Ricky was The Coastline Killer. But Ricky was dead. So how could both of those things be true? Turns out, apparently, they weren't.

'We're eliminating Richard Tremblay as a suspect in The Coastline Killer investigation,' one of the officers had told me.

'Ricky? His name is Richard Trem—'

'Tremblay. Yes.'

'Wait,' I say, trying to absorb everything they've just said. 'You're eliminating him?'

'As a suspect for these specific crimes, yes.'

'But he was going to saw my arm off! He was going to leave me in the water!'

'We understand that,' the officer had said patiently, 'and we're not disputing your account. But we believe he may have been a copycat. In any case, he wasn't The Coastline Killer.'

'What if the person who killed that Lucy woman is the copycat?'

'We can't discuss specific details of an ongoing investigation with you, but we can assure you, we've looked into that possibility and ruled it out.'

I'd stared at them, stunned into silence, waiting for everything I'd believed about Ricky, about our time in the basement, about his threats, to shift and re-settle in my mind.

Since then, I've stalked him obsessively. He didn't have a big social media presence, but he did have a Facebook profile. I learned that he lived in Minnesota. That his wife's name is Michelle. That they never had kids.

I've tried to stop clicking the refresh button, knowing that nothing new is going to appear, but I can't resist. Because nothing makes sense. If he wasn't The Coastline Killer, then why did he take me? Why had he threatened to hurt my family if I talked? Why did he, as Bill claims, save me in the end? And was he born a killer, was it in his genes, or did something happen that made him the way he was? His Facebook profile isn't giving me the answers I need.

'Al?'

Dad's head pokes out from behind the door.

'Yeah?'

'It's . . . someone's here to see you.'

Alarm bells chime in my head. There's something in his tone, in his inability to meet my eye.

'Who is it?'

'I think it's best if she explains that to you. I'm going to send her in. Gail?'

He makes a jerking motion with his head, signalling for my mom to leave. She looks flustered for a second, then gets up and follows him up the stairs, just as a woman with an immaculate blond bob walks in. An electric current ripples through my veins.

I know this woman. I've seen her on Facebook. I take her in: her delicate features, her perfectly contoured cheekbones, her expensive-looking pantsuit.

'Michelle.'

'I—' She pauses. I've thrown her off. She didn't expect me to recognise her. 'Yes, I'm Michelle. Alice?'

I nod, sliding my laptop onto the coffee table.

'I, um . . . sorry, is it OK if I sit?'

She gestures towards the armchair my mom vacated just moments ago. I shrug. My head is buzzing.

'So,' I say. 'You're Ricky's—'

'Wife, yes,' she finishes my question before I've finished asking it. She sits, placing her huge designer purse on her knees. 'Well, I was. I sent the divorce papers, but I guess he never got them.'

Silence settles over us. She touches her hair, the locket around her neck, her wrist.

'I felt like I should meet you,' she says eventually, as though that explains her presence.

'Why?'

My harsh tone conceals the truth: I understand why she's here. I suspect she's just as curious about me as I am about her, about what she can tell me about the man who supposedly died to save me.

'I don't know,' she says, her voice small. 'I suppose I just wanted to understand.'

'Yeah,' I sigh after a pause. 'Me too.'

She offers me a weak, apologetic smile, which I return.

A hundred different questions clamour in my brain, but they all get tangled up, so I'm left speechless, staring at the woman who was married to the man I believed was The Coastline Killer. Eventually, one of the questions bursts out of me.

'Did you know?' I ask bluntly. 'I mean, what he was capable of. Did you know?'

She stares at me for a few seconds, her expression unreadable. Then she seems to deflate.

'I knew he wasn't – well, in the end he wasn't a good man. I just never thought he was capable of . . .' she trails off and waves in my general direction, as though I'm a blemish that's tarnishing her husband's good name. 'But whatever he did to you, it was the first time. I'm certain of that.'

'I know what the police have said.' I speak slowly, choosing my words carefully, aware that I'm wading into murky, conspiratorial waters. 'But he still might have been The

Coastline Killer. The coroner could have been wrong about Lucy's time of death, or that could have been a copycat.'

'No,' Michelle shakes her head. 'He wasn't.'

She pauses. I look up.

'I can prove it.'

Chapter 68

ALICE

Michelle rummages in her purse for a moment. She pulls out a wad of papers and a notebook, and slides the pile of documents across the coffee table between us.

'Look.'

I shake my head at her, needing more of an explanation.

She gets up, placing her purse carefully on the carpet. Grabbing a piece of paper from the top of the pile, she comes to sit beside me on the sofa. She smells like jasmine. I bristle at her closeness.

'This is the paperwork that shows he was in hospital on the date when one of the girls went missing. A . . .'

She opens her notebook, flips through a few pages.

'Sandy Grosman. August first, twenty-fifteen. Ricky had appendicitis. His appendix ruptured and he needed emergency surgery. He was in hospital for three days; July thirty-first to August second.'

I look at the paper she's shoved under my face. Then I pull my laptop towards me, quickly clicking away from her husband's Facebook profile before she can see, and google Sandy Grosman. I open the Murderpedia page that appears near the top of the search results and compare the dates.

She's right. They match. I open my mouth to tell her that it's not enough proof, but she's on a roll.

'And here,' she says, waggling a glossy photo in front of my face. I snatch it from her, annoyed, and peer at the faces. My heart races. Ricky is there, but that's not what's made my pulse quicken and my palms sweat. It's the woman next to him. The woman who's now next to me. Michelle, looking younger – and completely different.

'Your hair,' I whisper.

'Oh yeah, I've changed it,' she says, touching her bob, which was chestnut brown and curly when the photo was taken.

It's not just the hair, though. Her face is make-up free, and she's wearing casual clothes – a cream-knit sweater and a pair of jeans. The resemblance is striking.

She looks just like me. Or, I suppose, I look just like her.

When I asked Ricky why he'd targeted me, of all the women in the city, he'd shrugged my question off. He made it seem like I was just picked for convenience, that I was simply the first woman he saw who fit a specific profile. But now I'm not so sure. If I didn't resemble his ex, would he still have targeted me, or was there another woman on that bus he'd have taken instead?

'This was Thanksgiving at my parents' last year,' Michelle is saying. She doesn't seem to notice how distracted I am, and if she sees the similarities in our appearance, she doesn't mention them. I struggle to focus on her words. But I need to know what she's saying. I need answers.

'See? The date's right there.'

She points to the bottom-right corner of the photo, where there's a date printed in a sort of 1970s orange colour. I squint to read it. The date was 11/23/2017.

I force myself to tear my eyes away from the image, and click back to Google to check the date of American Thanksgiving last year. It matches. I look up. The transformed Michelle flips through her notebook again.

'Janine Cook,' she says.

I take the photo from her and get the internet to verify. There's an article dated 24 November of last year, talking about the woman who went missing on Thanksgiving Day from a small community in Washington. Her body was found, according to another article pasted alongside it, two months later, missing a leg.

'It couldn't have been him,' Michelle says matter of factly. 'I'm not saying that you're lying. That he didn't go to Vancouver to—' she swallows. 'Well, I'm not saying that that part's not true. I know what he was like. I know he had his – issues. I'm just saying he wasn't The Coastline Killer. That wasn't Ricky.'

'Could he have been working with someone? Like, were they a team?'

I know I'm clutching at straws, even as the words leave my mouth. To her credit, Michelle doesn't look at me with pity.

'I suppose anything is possible.' She shrugs. 'But there wasn't anyone close enough to him to be involved in something so complicated and sophisticated. And I don't know what they told you, but the FBI did a pretty thorough search on him. They'd have found some evidence, if any pointed to him being The Coastline Killer.'

I nod, and put the photo on the table, face down. Ricky's smile taunts me, like he holds the answers that I need in order to move on, to be free from him.

I look up at Michelle. She's waiting patiently for me to process everything she's told me, for me to come to terms with the truth. I ask the only question that's left, the question I'm now certain she has the answer to.

'If he wasn't The Coastline Killer, then what the hell was he doing?'

Chapter 69

ALICE

Michelle stands up and walks back to where she left her purse. She pulls out a huge folder. It looks like a photo album, and for a horrible second I imagine that it's their wedding pictures. She drops it on the coffee table, where it lands with a thump. I look up at her, but she just stares at the album as though daring me to refuse to open it. Nervously, I place the laptop next to it and lift the black leather cover.

The page is full of hand-scribbled words, newspaper clippings and print-outs from news websites and Wikipedia pages.

'It was hidden at the bottom of his filing cabinet,' she says, her voice wobbling. 'I didn't... I didn't know anything about it until the police found it and asked me what I knew.'

She sits heavily next to me as I keep turning the pages silently, my mind reeling, my stomach squeezing tighter and tighter with every page.

It's a scrapbook. Or maybe it would be more accurate to call it a portfolio. Pages of reports, photos that make my skin crawl, autopsy findings. Crime-junkie theories.

Page after page, showcasing the work of The Coastline Killer, in intricate detail.

'So he was...?'

I leave the question hanging in the air. This feels like proof, but Michelle's just shown me that he couldn't possibly have been The Coastline Killer.

'He was obsessed,' Michelle sighs. 'I mean, I didn't know that he was this obsessed. I just thought he was into true crime, you know? I have friends, colleagues, who have gone mad for, like, *Making a Murderer*, or *Serial*, those sorts of things. It's entertainment these days, isn't it? So I just thought it was like that. He'd sit and read about The Coastline Killer for hours, watch anything he could about the murders. I didn't like it, obviously. But there was a lot I didn't like, so it was just one more thing I was too tired to fight about.'

I turn to look at her. Her lips are pressed together, forming a straight, thin line. Her jaw is clenched, the muscles at the side of her face pulsing. I wonder how much she saw of Ricky's anger, the rage that rippled under his skin. She says that she didn't know, that she didn't think him capable of what he did. But is that really true?

'You were getting a divorce.' It's a question, housed in a statement.

'Yes,' she says quickly, as though desperate to get that off her chest, to distance herself from the man who created the book in my hands. 'Yes, I'd left already. I'd moved to California. I – well, I met someone. I mean, I didn't meet him, I already knew him, we just reconnected. It was Ricky's old business partner, Drew.'

'OK,' I say, wondering if that alone could make Ricky want to kill her. Or someone who looks a bit like her.

'I didn't want him to know about Drew, because I knew it would stir all of that stuff up again. They started a business together, years ago. They were room-mates at college; best friends. Neither of them had siblings, so they were like

307

brothers, I guess. Drew's incredibly smart, and he invented a sort of memory chip to go into Blackberry phones. Ricky was the business-minded one of the two of them, could talk a good game, got some early investors, that kind of thing.

'Only Ricky was obsessed with getting rich, like, that was his whole aim. He felt like he had something to prove because he grew up poor, so he didn't care how he did it, as long as he made money. He made some pretty bad decisions to get ahead, lying to investors, falsifying financial records. Stuff that could have got them in a whole heap of trouble. When Drew found out, he was furious. He didn't report Ricky to the police, but he did fire him. Took him a good few years to get himself out of the mess Ricky had made, too.

'Ricky and I had only been dating a couple of years by then, but I stuck by him, even though I knew that he was to blame for the hole he'd found himself in. I just figured it was the pressure of his student debt piling up, and maybe just, I don't know, inexperience. I didn't see it as a red flag. He never did take responsibility, though, pointing the finger at Drew, convincing himself that Drew stole the life he deserved. He even tried to sue him – his best friend! He was so bitter about the whole situation, especially when the business took off and Drew made millions. And he lost the case. And all of our savings. He never recovered; not really.'

She breathes in deeply through her nose, as though trying to compose herself.

'He did try to make a go of it, for a while. But without Drew, it just didn't work. He didn't have a business partner who balanced him out, and so none of his ideas ever took off. I guess bitterness just . . . took over, in the end. He used to be so adventurous, so much fun. But then he started acting really weirdly with me. Hot and cold, being really patronising or controlling. I didn't understand it, but we

308

just drifted apart. Eventually, we separated. We were living completely separate lives at that point.

'So yeah. I knew that he'd be upset once he found out about Drew and I. I wasn't trying to hurt him. It just – happened. I never expected him to snap, for it to make him go out and do something so – so insane.'

'I'm sorry,' I say, confused. 'I don't understand. I mean, I get that he was mad at you, and at his old best friend. But why would he pretend to be The Coastline Killer? Just because he was obsessed? That doesn't make any sense.'

'No,' she says, reaching across me to flip through more pages of the scrapbook. The jumbled Coastline Killer-themed articles end abruptly, and the pages that follow look far more organised, as though they've been put together by someone else entirely.

I peer at the page Michelle's stopped at, trying to make sense of it. At the top, in thick, black capital letters is the date *7 MAR 2017*, followed by a name I recognise: *JENNIFER GUTIERREZ*.

Below this is a print-out of a calendar, with a flight number and time underneath.

'This is one of The Coastline Killer's victims,' Michelle says. I nod. I already knew that.

'And that,' she says, placing a finger on the calendar entry, 'is a copy of Drew's diary, showing that he was in Oregon on the day she went missing.'

I look at her, my eyes wide.

'Ricky thought . . . ?'

'I don't think he actually believed that Drew was The Coastline Killer,' she says quickly. 'I just think he thought he could make it look like he was.'

My forehead scrunches up as I try to absorb what she's saying. I flip through a few more pages. There's one for every victim, and for each woman, there's corresponding information about Drew's whereabouts – Facebook and Instagram posts, calendar entries, receipts.

'How would he ... how did ...?' My brain isn't keeping up with all of the information she's hurling at me. I'm struggling to understand how I fit into this.

'The police think he was paying someone that he found online – the dark Web, most likely – to hack into Drew's records. He scans all of his receipts so they're all kept on a digital system. Same with his calendar. It's all online, although it's pretty secure, so it'd have taken a pro to access them.'

'But if he found all this evidence on Drew, couldn't he be The Coastline Killer? Couldn't they have worked together?'

Michelle shakes her head, her vehemence making her blond hair swish back and forth across her face.

'No. The thing is, for some of the cases, Drew was where those women were taken. He travels all up and down the Pacific Northwest for work these days, and so he just happened to be in close proximity to a few of the victims. It's coincidence. Nothing more. There are a number of cases—' She flips through the scrapbook, pausing at pages where the date and name are scrawled across the top, but where there's no information about Drew underneath. 'Like here,' she says. 'And here. These dates, Drew has alibis for.'

I raise my eyebrows, doubtful. Of course she'd say that. She's with the guy.

'The police checked him out,' she says, reading my scepticism. 'They cleared him. Obviously. I wouldn't stay with a guy who might do – that.' She gives a little shudder.

I don't point out that she was married to a guy who tried to do exactly that. There's an awkward pause. She's watching me, as though waiting for a reaction. I'm scrambling to see how it all fits together, how it changes anything at all, but I can't get there. My brain is too slow.

'The police and FBI think that Ricky was trying to frame Drew,' she says eventually. 'They were asking me if he had a medical background. They said that he took some of your blood, right?'

I nod, frowning. 'It was the first thing he did.'

'He had no idea about medicine. They think he was taking your blood to plant on Drew, somehow. In his car, or his clothes, or something. I don't know. Maybe he was going to plant something on your – on you.'

She corrects herself, but not quickly enough. On my body. That's what she was going to say. He was going to plant something on my body that implicated the man who had taken his business and his wife.

I was nothing but a tool for him to pin the murders of nineteen women on a man he hated, for revenge. And, as a bonus, I got to be the punching bag for him to take out all the rage he felt towards his wife. I close my eyes and attempt to let her words sink in.

'Why Vancouver? Why not closer to where this Drew guy lives?'

'Drew had a meeting,' she explains. 'It had been in his diary for months. He was in Vancouver the day before the earthquake, and he was due to stay an extra day, but got called back for something happening back at head office. He was supposed to be there that day.'

'Ricky took a couple of trips out there before that last one,' she tells me. 'I found the booking details when I went through his emails. He was there in August, and again in September. So my best guess is that he'd been planning this for a while.'

'But Drew wasn't even there,' I say hollowly.

'I'm sorry,' she whispers.

It dawns on me, as I try to conjure some kind of emotion, that The Coastline Killer – the real Coastline Killer – is still out there, still hunting women, still evading capture. I try to feel something – anything – about that fact. But all I feel is tired.

'I . . . I didn't know.' Michelle is still talking, even though there's really nothing left to say. Ricky's reason for doing what he did is so much smaller and more pathetic than I ever could have imagined. Everything I went through, it was all for a sad, bitter man's revenge.

'If I'd had any idea what he was doing, if I'd known that this – that you—'

'This isn't your fault,' I say woodenly. And, whether she'd seen his dark side before or not, it's still true. How could she have known what was happening when she was estranged from her husband, when she lived halfway across the country?

She couldn't have predicted this any more than I could have.

We sit in silence. Something upstairs creaks. I suspect my parents are on the landing, listening to every word. I want her to leave, so I can process what she's told me. But she shifts, like she wants to say something. I wait.

'They told me that he saved you.' Her voice is shaking. It's not a question, but I know the answer she's looking for. The answer she needs. I don't know if I'm going to give it to her or not. Don't know if she deserves it.

'He did,' I say in the end, because it's the truth. 'And that's the bit that doesn't make any sense to me. Because he was going to kill me. I don't have any doubt about that.'

She looks away, her eyes glinting.

'But, for whatever reason, he did save me. And for what

it's worth, I'm grateful to him for it. I don't forgive him for what he did, and I don't think I'll ever be able to. But he did, right at the end at least, do the right thing.'

Michelle stares at the page of the scrapbook that's lying open. Then she gently, carefully, closes it and stands.

'Thanks for your time,' she whispers. She looks even more shaken than I feel, but I don't have the energy or inclination to comfort her.

It's only after she's gathered her things and seen herself out that I realise: Ricky never actually claimed to be The Coastline Killer. He hinted at it, and he didn't correct me when I announced to him that that's who he was. But he never said it himself. And although he said he was going to kill me, I can't actually prove that he was going to go through with it. I believed he was. There was nothing to suggest that he wouldn't. But ultimately, he didn't. If the earth hadn't intervened, would he really have killed me?

I close my eyes.

What evidence is there? He threatened me. But, again, there's no way to prove whether he would have actually done what he told me he'd do. Because even if he'd survived, and I'd told the police what I thought I knew, he'd have shown them the evidence that Michelle just showed me. He wouldn't have been charged as The Coastline Killer. He wouldn't have been charged with murder. The worst he would have been charged for was kidnapping me. Maybe some kind of assault. It's bad, obviously. But not serial-killer bad.

I reach instinctively for my arm, brushing the small raised bump on the inside of my elbow. I can feel it through the fabric of my sweater, a physical reminder of what the earthquake saved me from, what I believed it saved me from. In that moment, when Ricky was standing over me, masked

313

and gloved and aproned, the teeth of his rusted saw gnawing against the flesh of my arm, when the earth rumbled and knocked him off his feet, I'd thought that he'd said 'Oh my God.'

But now, in the light of what I know, perhaps that wasn't what I'd heard at all.

Did he, in fact, breathe 'Oh, thank God'?

Was he just as relieved as I was for a way out of the murder?

I won't ever know.

Without warning I feel sad for Ricky. And then I feel guilty for feeling sad, because what am I, some victim with Stockholm Syndrome? But he did save my life, regardless of whether he put me in that situation.

He wasn't born a psychopath. He made some terrible choices, let bitterness corrode his humanity until it almost disappeared. But in the end, he found it. Too late to redeem himself, but perhaps in time to give me a glimmer of hope.

I reach over and close the lid of my laptop.

I don't know whether Alvin the accountant is truly a good person or not. I barely know anything about him, and I never will. But I know myself, and I've learned that I'm so much more capable than I ever knew.

Before the quake, I spent so much energy worrying that I wasn't good enough, that I wasn't the expert I claimed to be, that I couldn't possibly have it all.

But against all odds, I survived. I'm still here. I've been given another chance.

And there's no way in hell I'm going to waste it.

Chapter 70

BBC News Online

Human skeleton discovered inside bronze sculpture created by mysterious artist The Sculptor
16 November, 2018
Twenty-eight minutes ago

Police are asking for the public's help in identifying an anonymous artist known only as The Sculptor, after human remains were discovered inside one of the mysterious sculptor's creations.

Los Angeles radiography student Bryce Mayfield made the grisly discovery in October, after X-raying the bronze arm, which belonged to a relative, for an art project.

'I was just trying to make some art, you know?' Mayfield explained in a YouTube video he created for his channel after reporting the discovery to police in London, where he was staying to complete an internship. 'I was X-raying random objects I found in my uncle's place, and one of them was this sculpture he'd just paid an obscene amount of money for at some pretentious auction.

'I took the X-ray, expecting it just to be hollow, which was kind of the point of my project, you know, like, show the empty nature of these material possessions? What I definitely wasn't expecting was a skeleton inside it. I freaked out. I called my mom back home and told her about it, and she called Tom, that's my uncle, and he called the police. I'm just glad I'm nowhere near that creepy house anymore.'

Police haven't released any details that point to the identity of the skeleton, and so far they are focusing their attention on speaking to The Sculptor.

'We can't be certain that there's been a crime,' a spokesperson from Scotland Yard explained, 'but these are highly unusual circumstances, and we're looking to speak to the artist calling themselves The Sculptor immediately to understand what's happened here. Until today, we've kept details of the case from the public, but we're now asking anyone who owns a piece by this artist, or anyone who has any information as to their identity, to get in touch so that we can run tests and find out whether there are more pieces to investigate.'

The Sculptor is famous throughout the art world for remaining anonymous. No one knows the identity of this bronze sculptor, whose work has been compared with that of French artist Auguste Rodin. Many have tried to work out who is behind the life-like human figures in the artist's collection, but, so far, no one has been successful.

If you have information that could help, please contact Crimestoppers on 0800 555 111.

Chapter 71

ALICE

Seventeen Days Later

'You don't have to do this,' Celia tells me again, her hands gripping the steering wheel, her eyes fixed straight ahead, even though the car is stationary and the engine is off.

I don't reply. It's been over six hours since Celia picked me up at my parents' house in the inky black of early morning, and at least once every thirty minutes since then, she's repeated the same words, a mantra that holds absolutely no power over me. I've tried explaining, but it's no use. Because, in the end, it doesn't make any sense to me, either.

I try not to be impatient with her. After all, she did drive me all the way down here without understanding my reasons. She convinced my parents to let me go, as though I'm still a teenager who needs their permission, and not a grown woman. She stopped the car – multiple times – to let me stretch my aching legs. So I don't begrudge her insistence that I don't have to do what I've come all this way to do.

I reach over and pull her into an awkward hug.

'Thank you,' I whisper into her hair. 'For everything.'

'You're welcome,' she murmurs. 'But you owe me, like, a year's worth of Saturday-night babysitting.'

I laugh and pull away. 'Deal.'

'Do you want me to wait here, or . . . ?'

'It's OK.' I shake my head. 'If you want to go do something for a bit, I can call you when it's over?'

'I might just go for a walk around here,' she says. 'I need a stretch, and it's beautiful.'

She's right. The park is stunning, the trees mostly bare, with a few fiery leaves still clinging on, trembling with the effort of resisting the soft breeze. The sky is a diluted cornflower-blue, just a couple of soft clouds lazily drifting across the wide expanse. Peeking through the tops of the trees is a snow-sprinkled mountain peak, majestic and threatening all at once. It might be dormant, but it still contains the power to destroy the city beneath it.

I try to turn my thoughts to more positive things, but it's difficult, given where I am, and why I'm here.

Sighing, I open the door and gently swing my legs out. Celia rushes from the car, opening the back door, grabbing my walking stick and dashing around to my side to hand it to me. I take it gratefully. I could have collected it myself, but I know that today is going to stretch my limits as it is. I'll take all the help I can get.

'Thanks. See you in a bit?'

'Yeah, just message me when you're done. You sure you don't need me to walk with you?'

She glances, concerned, at the path that winds up a slight incline and out of sight, and then back to my leg. I'm concerned, too, but I don't want to worry her. The doctors insisted that I let my lungs recover before focusing on my muscles, so my legs, although they are healing, are stiff and painful. Walking is difficult, although it's been getting a little easier every day.

'I'll be fine,' I say. 'The doctor told me that I need to start walking again.'

That, at least, is true. I am supposed to be building my

strength, little by little. I'm not entirely sure that this is what the doctor had in mind, but with a promise to Celia that I'll call her if I need her, I start hobbling up the path, trailing behind a couple, their heads bowed, their bodies pressed close together, as though they might be able to absorb one another.

Keeping up with them is impossible. My progress is slow and limping, but I follow the clusters of blue paper lanterns that are tied to tree trunks at intervals, and by the time I reach the clearing, I'm exhausted. And late.

I stand on the path, trying to pant quietly as I watch the tight knot of mourners in various shades of blue who are gathered around a makeshift stage. There are a couple of wooden pallets, placed side by side, that provide a few inches of extra height. On the platform is a woman in a long, floaty blue dress. Beside her is an easel, on which rests a larger-than-life portrait of a smiling woman, her teeth gleaming, her eyes practically sparkling with life.

Above this, slung between two majestic trees, is a cord strung with more blue paper lanterns. The effect is festive. The mood is anything but. The occasional sniff drifts through the cool air towards me. I stay completely still, unsure where to look or how to hold my body, feeling like an intruder, even though the Facebook event declared that the memorial was open to anyone.

'The last thing I said to Lucy,' the woman says, her voice thick with emotion, 'was that she was a quitter.'

Her voice breaks on the final word. She swallows, visibly fighting her emotions. When she speaks again, though, her voice is steady.

'I told her she was giving up on her dreams, which I can see now was a pretty dramatic accusation to make about a stupid work thing. She walked away from me, then. She

319

was angry, and I'll always regret that our last interaction was that one. But as she left, I told her that I loved her, and I know she heard.

'The thing is, I've known Lucy since we were fourteen. She was this crazy outgoing, funny kid in school, and I was the weird girl who'd rather be in the art room than out playing sports. There was no reason we should have been friends, but one day I was walking around the school taking pictures for my photography class, and I came across Lucy smoking a joint outside the library, wearing her Docs and a leather jacket. She was just on her own, like, totally OK in her own company, which basically made her an exotic creature to me. Most of the kids at school would have done anything to avoid being by themselves. So I took some pictures of her which, in the end, won me a photography prize. Indirectly, Lucy kick-started my photography career.'

Movement from a few yards away catches my eye. I spot a woman standing at the edge of the clearing, just a little way around from where I am, almost tucked behind a tree. Her eyes dart from my face to my leg, then back up, past my walking stick, until our gazes meet. I stretch my lips into a kind of half-smile, an acknowledgement that we're both hovering awkwardly on the fringes of the memorial.

I wonder what her story is, why she's not huddled with the rest of the group, sharing her grief, absorbing theirs. Maybe she's a relative who had a falling-out with the family. Perhaps she only knew Lucy peripherally, not well enough to talk about her with the people who loved her most. She's in jeans, a blue plaid shirt and practical work boots, her hair pulled up into a messy bun. She's dressed far more casually than anyone else in the group, but clearly she saw the note in the invitation about the colour theme. The woman looks away, and I turn my attention back to the ceremony.

'We somehow became best friends, even though we were really like chalk and cheese. We've had some amazing times together.'

Lucy's friend stops for a moment, staring above our heads, into the distance, as though seeing her memories playing out in front of her.

'There are too many moments to talk about in just a few minutes. So I won't share anything specific, although I will say that there were meals and road trips and tears and break-ups and laughter, and far too many bottles of wine. But today I want to say this about my darling friend Lucy Tran. She was absolutely, undeniably, not a quitter. I was with Mr and Mrs Tran when they received the devastating news that Lucy had been found. And what the police told us was that she fought. She fought like hell. She was missing a tooth, she had a broken nose, and she had probably been crawling through some kind of forest.'

There's another pause as the woman pulls a tissue from the pocket in her dress and dabs at her eyes.

'I'm sorry. I know that those details are hard to hear. But I'm not telling you any of this to upset you. I'm telling you this so you can understand who Lucy was. She was a fighter. She didn't give up. Even when she must have been so scared, and in so much pain. She—'

At this, she dissolves into gut-wrenching sobs, the kind that make my eyes well up in sympathy. An older woman steps onto the makeshift stage and snakes her arm around the speaker's waist, guiding her into a cluster of weeping mourners.

My own heart crumbles a little, and I wonder what I really thought being here would achieve.

After speaking to Michelle, and learning that Ricky wasn't The Coastline Killer – wasn't a killer at all, technically – I knew that the only thing I could do was to move forward. But it's hard to do that without anyone understanding what I've been through. Even as I try to justify it to myself, it sounds absurd, but I feel like I share some kind of morbid connection with The Coastline Killer's latest victim, like I managed to escape what she couldn't, like I owe it to her to pay my respects.

Logically, I can accept that my reasoning is flawed. Ricky was not The Coastline Killer. I did not escape the clutches of a homicidal maniac. But for the hours I was trapped down there with him, I believed that he was the serial killer who was, at the exact same time, torturing Lucy.

She deserved better. She deserved a second chance, like the one I've been given. I glance around at the people gathered to celebrate Lucy's life, to grieve her death.

I'm reminded of Mel's funeral, a day so heartbreaking for me that I've tried my best to forget it. It was a day for us to gather, to remember, to grieve. Not a day for strangers to make themselves feel better, or to seek closure. I shouldn't be here. I don't belong.

I slowly turn away from the huddle of mourners. The woman by the tree watches me, a strange smile playing on her lips.

The walk back to the car is excruciating. It's only a few hundred yards, but my leg is aching and my chest feels like it's on fire, despite the chill in the air.

When I get back to the silver Mazda, Celia's already waiting inside, playing with her phone. I collapse into the passenger seat, wrangling my walking stick through the gap between the two of us.

'So?' Celia asks expectantly.

I pause. 'So now I know,' I say, 'that you were right. This was pointless.'

'I never said it was pointless,' she says gently.

'You didn't need to. I don't know what I thought this would fix, but whatever it is, it hasn't worked.'

'But at least you know. At least you won't be wondering.'

I nod, unsure what to say next.

Celia doesn't push any further. She starts the car, and I pull on my seatbelt, thankful that I don't need to explain myself. I don't think I would know how.

'So while you were at the funeral—'

'Memorial,' I correct her.

'Memorial,' she concedes. 'I did some googling. And we have to make a quick pit stop on the way home.'

I glance at her, suspicious. She looks back, a mischievous smile on her face.

'Where?'

'Voodoo Donuts,' she says, her eyes wide. 'They do a maple bacon flavour.'

I laugh, relieved.

'That's disgusting,' I say. 'But fine. You can get your weird-flavoured doughnuts. As long as we can stop in Seattle on the way home for chowder.'

'Deal,' she laughs. 'Now let's get some road trip tunes going.'

As we speed towards downtown Portland, the stereo blasting nineties hits, I open my window just a sliver and let the air rush at my face and through my hair. I let myself absorb the fact that I'm alive. That I'm with my best friend, that the world is still in front of me.

And for the smallest of moments – maybe just a split second – my mind isn't focused on The Coastline Killer, on

Ricky, on the basement that held me under the earth for those terrifying hours.

For the first time since I was rescued – since well before that, truthfully – I'm free.

Epilogue

THE SCULPTOR

I wouldn't usually visit a Muse's funeral – memorial, whatever this is. Too risky. I've seen enough cop shows to know that murderers are expected to turn up at their victim's funeral, so the police will lurk at the back, guns and radios ready for when the perpetrator makes his entrance.

I don't like to think of myself as a murderer. And I don't like to think of my Muses as victims. But I know the law would disagree with me on those points, so generally I stay away, although it's always been a temptation. The lure of discovering how the world saw someone I'd spent so many hours with, so many days and weeks observing, has always been tantalising.

Never more so than now.

Lucy was different. For many reasons.

For starters, she's the first one who's really known me, who's really understood who I am. She saw my studio, she crept through my cabin, she put all of the pieces of the puzzle together, and she saw a glimpse of her fate. At least, what her fate would have been if the earthquake hadn't shaken my life apart.

I was in downtown Seattle when it hit, with my next Muse, a personal assistant called Susie. She was a bit of a loner, didn't have any close family, lived alone with her two cats. Lovely hands, which worked perfectly for the sculpture I had in mind. I'd planned to take her on the Friday, so that it would be Monday by the time anyone actually reported her missing. I'd have had a two-day head start on the authorities, at least.

The plan was pretty simple, really. I'd wait inside her office building, near the reception desk, where I could see her. I'd call, posing as a neighbour of hers. I'd tell her that I'd just seen a cat being hit by a car. I'd then describe one of her beloved felines in great detail, and she'd rush out of the office to get home, not stopping to question how I got her number, or who I actually was. Not only would her colleagues understand if she didn't reply to their messages, but this plan also had the added bonus of breaking her routine.

Routine is necessary for planning, for getting to know a Muse. But people who are in their usual routine will notice the tiniest ripple in their day-to-day world. It's best to break that, so they're vulnerable; easier to manipulate.

So I was in her building's reception, about to make the call that would lead her, defences down, panicked and disoriented, right to me. All I'd have had to do was bump into her – literally – notice her distress, offer to help. Your cat's hurt? I'd have asked. And then I'd have told her that I'm a vet, that I could come with her, that I'd be happy to, of course it was no trouble. She'd have stepped into my car without a moment's hesitation.

That's the thing about being a woman. We're not threatening. As long as we're invisible.

Over the years I've posed as a slightly hapless and utterly off-trend yoga student, a nurse, an Uber driver, a dowdy receptionist, and a stay-at-home mom with oatmeal stains down my front. It's amazing how many of my Muses came with me so willingly. A stranger. A stranger who was going to kill them.

I used to wonder how Ted Bundy got away with it. I mean, a plaster cast and a dog leash? Please. But actually, I understand it now. Take away the element of threat, and people will follow you down a dark alley at night.

I didn't need a dark alley though. If the earthquake hadn't hit, everything would have gone according to plan, like it always does.

My hours in that building with Susie and her colleagues were unbearable. I was injured, although nothing too lasting, thank goodness. Susie didn't make it, in the end. I'd tried to help, despite that going against my very nature. I'd done what I could.

But it was getting out, and checking in on Lucy, that had mattered more to me. Susie wasn't a risk, even if she'd survived. I hadn't made my move. She'd never have known who I am or what I do. So as soon as I got out, I'd swiped a bike from one of the rescue teams – not my finest moment, even I can admit – and had cycled furiously, swaying wildly, thanks to my concussion, collarbone screaming from the pain, for over fifty miles to reach my hideaway in the mountains.

It was the most excruciating journey I've ever taken, and yet my mind wasn't on the pain, or the concern that I should have been seeking medical treatment. It was on Lucy. On the threat she could pose to me, could have already posed. When I was able to tear my mind from the fact that the police could already be hot on my trail, the only other thing I could think of was that I'd have to rethink my Erato collection entirely, perhaps shelve it for a few years until I could work out the logistics of obtaining two Muses without leaving one unattended.

By the time I reached my home – destroyed by a fallen tree, I discovered – I was utterly spent. But I didn't have the luxury of collapsing. I had to check on my Muse. At first, I thought everything was fine, that I'd panicked for no reason. The garage door was open a foot or so, but I couldn't remember if that had been me – surely I wasn't so careless? – Or perhaps the earth's shuddering that had caused it to move.

When I opened the cupboard door that leads to my studio, though, I knew. The trapdoor, the square portal that's hidden behind the clock, was gaping wide open. The rope ladder was not in its usual bundle on the floor beside the door. I checked, just in case, but as I feared, Lucy was gone.

At that point, I'd panicked. The earthquake had been a terrifying ordeal to live through, but this was a hundred times worse. I didn't know where she was, but she knew everything she needed to know to bring me down: who I am, where I live, what I look like.

And then my fear had turned to anger. How dare she bring me down? She, of all people, should have understood. She'd seen my art, knew what I offered to the world. If she couldn't appreciate that, then she needed to be stopped. It was dark by then, and cold, but I didn't care. On aching, fatigued legs, I ran through the forest with nothing but a flashlight to help me see and fury to fuel me, tripping and falling and smacking into tree trunks as I went.

I found her, though. Eventually. She was weak, almost hypothermic. She'd been relieved to see me at first, relieved just to see another human. She thought I was there to help. Then she caught a glimpse of my face and she collapsed. She knew.

It was hard work, dragging her back to the cabin. I was frail as it was, but trying to haul a hundred-and-fifty-pound unconscious lump of flesh a couple miles uphill almost killed me. Once again, though, there was no time to luxuriate in my pain, to wallow in my exhaustion. I had work to do.

I'm not sure why I cut her arm away, when I was never going to use it. At first I tried to tell myself that I wanted The Coastline Killer to get the credit for her, when her body washed up. I've come to enjoy those headlines, after all. And there's some truth in that. But I'm starting to admit to myself that I did it because I wanted to.

Just like I killed her because I wanted to. And this time, I enjoyed it. I enjoyed her fear, and I enjoyed dumping her corpse in the water under the cover of night.

The limb I took ended up not in a sculpture, but in my kiln, the rich, meaty smoke curling around my swimming head, filling my tender lungs, until I passed out, the exhaustion taking over once my task was complete.

I spent a week in a catatonic state, Lucy's face and voice coming to me in snatches, nightmares of being found, of my collection being melted and poured into the ocean remembered in feverish snatches. I woke up, curled around a half-finished clay tiger sculpture I'd been working on for some months, just for fun.

I had to abandon my Erato collection. It was too risky, and I had a lot of work to do on my cabin, on the white room. I needed to make it extra secure.

Except now they're on to me. Some rich kid discovered human bones inside one of my pieces, and so my career is effectively over. I can no longer operate as The Sculptor.

And now I've found myself at my final Muse's memorial service, standing on the fringes of the huddle of her parents, siblings, colleagues, friends and boyfriend. I'm doing my best to look sympathetic, but it's hard, because they're all being so self-indulgent, going on about what she would have wanted. I have to physically bite my lip to resist telling them that she's dead, that what she wanted is completely irrelevant right now. What she would have wanted was to be alive, for this event not to be happening.

I manage to stay silent.

After all, *I'm* here, aren't I? Even I couldn't resist the lure of promised closure. Now that I'm here, though, I'm wondering why I came. What did I hope to achieve? What kind of closure did I expect to find? As a woman in a billowing blue dress steps onto the makeshift stage, I turn to leave.

But then I see her, and something makes me stop, pull back, take to the shadows.

She limps along the path, pain written plainly across her pretty face. But it's not her face that captivates me. My eyes trail down the tailored black dress and cornflower-blue woollen coat to her legs, covered in black opaque tights, the curves of them still visible in the soft winter light. She's gripping a wooden walking stick, her knuckles white with the effort. Her shoes are incongruously plain, orthopaedic-looking things that jar with the rest of her impeccable outfit.

Her legs are slim and long, but I imagine, beneath the nylon of her tights and the smoothness of her skin, broken strands of muscle knitting themselves to damaged bones, repairing, restoring themselves, coming back to life, growing and developing and transforming. I'm transfixed.

I'm addicted.

The last time I felt this way, a hiker had stumbled upon my cottage in the mountain, lost and dehydrated, just looking for a glass of water and some kindness. This time there's no message from a higher power, no bolt from above.

This pull comes from within.

The woman lingers at the edge of the memorial for a few

minutes and as she leans, panting, on her walking stick, I fix my eyes on her legs.

I've been so obsessed with perfection, with portraying muscles and skin and tendons and veins of the finest specimens. But the earthquake changed me. It destroyed more than just the earth and the cities it ravaged. It shook my own assumptions, the way I see the world. It showed me my own fallibility, my weakness. It revealed parts of myself I've tried to hide, tried to explain away.

Suddenly, she moves, and I look up in surprise. She's hobbling away, leaving the memorial, as though she just stumbled upon it and then realised that she was in the wrong place. I follow her, keeping a safe distance behind. It's slow going as she staggers down the path, but I'm mesmerised by the movement of her muscles, of the strength it must be taking for her to walk when she's in such obvious pain.

I'm ashamed. Embarrassed that I haven't thought of this sooner. After all, I am a student of Rodin's work. I've wanted to emulate his vision through my own creations. Only, I clearly hadn't been paying attention. Some of the Master's most inspired pieces: *Man with the Broken Nose, She Who Was the Helmet Maker's Once-Beautiful Wife*, and even *The Muse*, the piece that so moved me when I saw it all those years ago in a gallery in London... they weren't based on perfection. They were inspired by brokenness, and the beauty that exists within it.

And now, so am I.

She's going to set me free, I understand.

No longer will I need to create in the name of perfection and beauty and immortal Muses. No longer will I pretend that I have no control over it, that I'm above the basest parts of my nature.

I don't know how I will take her, now that I'm on the run,

now that my white room has been breached, now that my home is destroyed. It doesn't matter. Things will be different now, anyway. They have to be. I want them to be.

All I know is that when I do this – when I kill her – I'll finally allow myself to savour every moment of my victim's pain.

I'll be free.

Acknowledgements

It was March 13, 2020 when I first sent *Buried* to my editor, with the briefest acknowledgement of 'everything going on at the moment.' Just weeks later, the concepts of both an event that could shake up everything I knew, and of being trapped (albeit with food, the company of someone I love, and windows), suddenly felt far less like fiction than they did when I sat down to write the book.

One of the things the last year or so has taught me is that, even on the bleakest of days, the simplest things can make the world of difference: the sun shining, a woodpecker on the tree outside, a text from a friend...

Writing is a bit like that. The worst days are made infinitely better by a small word of encouragement, a sentence that flows with ease, or remembering that there's a team of people behind me, without whom my words would just be abandoned in random files on my laptop.

That team is led by my husband Brendan, to whom I owe my biggest thanks. Not only do you believe in me and my abilities far more than I believe in myself, but you also provided me with laughter and cocktails and baked goods and endless positivity in lockdown, and for those things (and many more) I'll always be grateful. There is no-one else in the world I'd have survived being stuck in a one-bedroom apartment with for a full year.

I'd probably have given up long ago without my writer

333

friends. Niki, thank you for the many phone calls, for telling me what I need to hear, for believing in me, and for inspiring me with your incredible books. To Victoria and the Criminal Minds, thank you for all of the laugh out loud funny messages, fox videos, and jellyfish of encouragement.

Thank you to Ariella Feiner for being a constant champion of my work. To know that you always have my back makes even the hardest writing days feel so much easier. Thank you for your constant belief in me, for brainstorming with me when I'm completely stuck and for your brilliant ideas. I'm so grateful to have an agent as dedicated and passionate as you are.

A book takes an entire team to publish – as you can see from the credits over the page – so to the talented team at Orion, especially my editor, Francesca Pathak: thank you for all you've done to bring *Buried* to life.

To my friends and family – you know who you are – I love you and miss you and can't wait until we can hang out and hug and eat without shivering outside.

And finally, to every single person who has picked up one of my books, who's bought it or borrowed it from the library, who's told a friend about it, or left a review or tagged me in a social media post: thank you!

Credits

Elle Croft and Orion Fiction would like to thank everyone at Orion who worked on the publication of *Buried* in the UK.

Editorial
Francesca Pathak
Lucy Frederick

Copy editor
Marian Reid

Proof reader
Laetitia Grant

Audio
Paul Stark
Amber Bates

Contracts
Anne Goddard
Jake Alderson

Design
Debbie Holmes
Joanna Ridley
Nick May

Production
Ruth Sharvell

Editorial Management
Charlie Panayiotou
Jane Hughes

Finance
Jasdip Nandra
Afeera Ahmed
Elizabeth Beaumont
Sue Baker

Marketing
Folayemi Adebayo

Sales
Jen Wilson
Esther Waters
Victoria Laws
Frances Doyle
Georgina Cutler

Rights

Susan Howe

Krystyna Kujawinska

Jessica Purdue

Louise Henderson

Operations

Jo Jacobs

Sharon Willis

Lisa Pryde

Lucy Brem

Publicity

Alainna Hadjigeorgiou

Don't miss Elle Croft's thrilling debut psychological suspense novel...

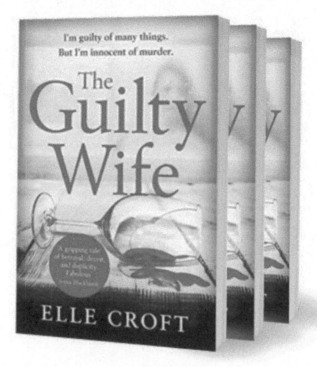

WIFE. MISTRESS. MURDERER.
If you were being framed for murder, how far would you go to clear your name?

'An accomplished debut with a relentless and intense pace that kept me completely rapt and eager to find out answers. I loved the final twist'

K.L. Slater, international bestselling author of *Safe With Me, Blink* **and** *Liar*

Or *The Other Sister*: a gripping, twisty novel of psychological suspense with an ending you won't see coming!

How far would you go to uncover your family's deadly secret?

'The Other Sister *is an original and thrilling page-turner with an end I didn't see coming'*

Victoria Selman, author of *Blood for Blood*

And finish with *Like Mother, Like Daughter*: a compelling and shocking thriller exploring who your family really are...

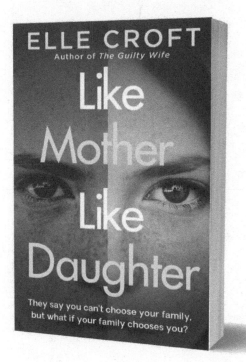

They say you can't choose your family.

But what if your family chooses you...?

'Excellent writing with intriguing characters and a dark, original premise that kept me turning the pages...'

Jenny Quintana, author of *The Missing Girl*